PRESENT DANGER

Also by Stella Rimington

*Open Secret: The Autobiography of
the Former Director-General of MI5*

THE LIZ CARLYLE SERIES

At Risk

Secret Asset

Illegal Action

Dead Line

STELLA RIMINGTON

Present Danger

Quercus

First published in Great Britain in 2009 by

Quercus
21 Bloomsbury Square
London
WC1A 2NS

A CIP catalogue record for this book is available
from the British Library

ISBN 978 1 84724 994 4 (HB)
ISBN 978 1 84724 995 1 (TPB)

10 9 8 7 6 5 4 3 2 1

Typeset by Ellipsis Books Limited, Glasgow

Printed and bound in Great Britain by Clays Ltd, St Ives plc

To my granddaughter, Meena

PRESENT DANGER

1

Aidan Murphy was woken by a loud knocking on the door. He lay still, trying to decide whether he had a hangover or was just tired. There was another, louder knock. He rolled over and looked at the clock radio. *10:31*. Why didn't his mother answer the door? The knocking turned into a hammering and someone was yelling his name.

He climbed out of bed, grabbed a T-shirt and underpants off the floor and went slowly downstairs. Two men were outside. The older one was Malone. The other he didn't know. Heavy-set, with dark stubble and swarthy skin, he looked Spanish.

'Boss wants to see you,' said Malone flatly.

'What, now?' Aidan was confused. He was due at work at three –couldn't it wait until then?

'Yeah, now,' Malone growled. The dark man said nothing.

Aidan shrugged. 'I'll get dressed,' he said, and went back upstairs to his bedroom. The second man stayed by the open door while Malone stood at the foot of the stairs, positioned where he could keep an eye on the door to Aidan's bedroom.

What's this about then? Aidan wondered, catching sight of his scrawny chest in the mirror. He felt a flicker of alarm. Stay calm, he told himself; you've done nothing wrong.

He threw on a shirt, a fresh one from the drawer, neatly ironed by his mother. There were benefits to living at home, even when you were twenty-three years old. He finished dressing, ran a comb through his hair, then grabbed a jacket and went downstairs.

He followed the stranger to a red Vauxhall Vectra with racing tyres, parked in front of the house. He didn't like the way Malone walked close behind him. It reminded him too much of the time when as a kid he was arrested by the police for shoplifting. The two men got into the front seats, Malone driving. Aidan relaxed – if he was in trouble one of them would have sat in the back with him.

Malone pulled out sharply and they sped down the monotonous terrace of red brick houses, heading towards the city centre. Neither man spoke, and to break the silence, Aidan asked, 'Did you see Celtic on the box?' Malone shook his head, and the other man didn't even do that. Sod them, thought Aidan, and he sat back silently with folded arms and looked out of the window.

They turned into Divis Street, past the flats where his father had died, shot in a stairwell by British soldiers. He'd been an IRA sniper, and he'd died doing his job. Aidan had wanted to follow his father into the Provos, to avenge his death by killing British soldiers, but they were on ceasefire now, so instead he'd found The Fraternity. Or they'd found him.

Dermot O'Reilly had recommended him – old Dermot, who had been interned in the Maze with Aidan's father; Dermot, who had been tried twice on arms charges yet somehow had avoided another stretch in prison. There was no questioning *his* nationalist credentials, and when he'd said that The Fraternity wasn't what it said it was, giving Aidan a wink, Aidan understood his meaning at once.

2

The Fraternity purported to be a 'political consultancy', which Aidan took as code for carrying on the fight. It put up a good enough phoney front, with smart new offices in the centre of town, and an Irish-American who called himself Piggott at its head, a strange man who had more degrees than you could shake a stick at.

Aidan soon learned that The Fraternity's money-making business had nothing to do with consultancy, but everything to do with supplying: drugs, guns, even women. However much he tried to gild it, his own job was courier: he delivered packages to pubs, restaurants, bookmakers and sometimes private homes. From the bits and pieces he'd overheard from other members of The Fraternity, Aidan knew that he carried cocaine, ecstasy, methamphetamine, crystal meth and occasionally a gun, and on his return journeys, lots of cash in large, sealed, padded book bags, which he never, ever looked inside.

None of this had bothered him at first, since O'Reilly assured him these commercial transactions were funding other business – carrying on the war against Ireland's enemies. But Aidan never got near to the real business, and he knew that his father, who like all good IRA men passionately disapproved of drugs, would have skinned him alive if he'd known what Aidan was up to. It must have been a great thing to have had a cause to die for.

They approached the usual turn to the office off Castle Street, but Malone drove straight on. 'What's going on?' asked Aidan, unable to disguise the fear in his voice.

'Relax kid,' said Malone with a glance in his rear-view mirror. 'We've got a bit of a drive. Sit back and enjoy it. They say the sun will be out soon.'

Some hope. It stayed grey and gloomy as they headed south on the dual carriageway. Where were they going? Aidan decided not to ask – he was pretty sure Malone would only tell him 'wait and see' – and then he remembered two of his colleagues mentioning that Piggott had a place down on the coast in County Down. One had been there to collect a shipment of 'stuff'. It was an odd place for a Republican activist, if that's what he was, for it was Protestant country; but perhaps chosen just because of that. It would be the last place the security people would expect to find him.

Aidan wasn't scared. Why should he be? He'd done nothing wrong. Helping with the distribution of the goods, he had no responsibility other than to follow orders. Which he had been doing faithfully and without complaint. Well, almost. It was true he'd made it clear to some of his friends and associates that he wasn't happy with The Fraternity. He'd told them it was all money-making and no action as far as he could see. But he'd been careful to whom he complained, just a few close mates in the back room of Paddy O'Brien's pub. Dermot O'Reilly was sometimes there, but he could be trusted. O'Reilly couldn't believe the war was over either. No, Aidan told himself now, even if he had opened his mouth, he'd been talking to friends who thought like he did.

Suddenly in the distance ahead he saw the Irish Sea, rocky outcrops and slits of sandy beach, the Mourne Mountains miles to their right, heavy and dark. They drove along the coast for several miles, through a grey stone village on a wide bay, its long street practically deserted, its ice-cream hut shut up for the winter.

At the end of the village the car slowed and turned sharply down a narrow track that skirted the bay. The tide was out, revealing a vast expanse of sand dune pockmarked by marram grass, the wet sand gleaming in the grey light. They crossed a narrow bridge and came up to a closed five-bar gate. Malone pressed a button on an electronic device he held in his hand and the gate creaked open, allowing them in to pass directly in front of a small, high-gabled Victorian house, the gatehouse to an estate that ran up the gentle slope of land away from the sea. Past the house, the road turned into a track and Malone drove slowly, his eyes intent on his rear-view mirror. Instinctively, Aidan looked behind him. There was no one following.

A quarter of a mile further on, through another gate and a small copse of trees, the track ended in front of a large stone house. The car stopped with a sudden crunch of tyres against gravel. Malone led the way to the front door. An elderly woman wearing an apron tied around her waist let them in, keeping her head down and her eyes averted as they walked into a large hall.

Malone said, 'Wait here,' and Aidan stood with the Spaniard while Malone went through a doorway to one side. When he returned a minute later he gestured towards the back of the house.

'Come on,' he said, leading them down a hall, through a large kitchen with a massive Aga at one end. In the short hall behind the kitchen, he flicked a light switch and they followed him down a steep flight of stairs.

They were in a cellar, a damp empty room with exposed brick walls and a rough concrete floor. It was dark, almost dungeon-like, and Aidan began to feel apprehensive again. Fastened to one wall was a metal cabinet, which Malone opened with a key. He pulled down a switch and immediately with a high-pitched whirring noise the far wall of the cellar slowly moved to one side, revealing a room behind it.

This room was furnished comfortably, almost lavishly. The floor was carpeted in sisal, topped by a few small oriental rugs, and at the far end sat a mahogany partner's desk, with a green-shaded desk lamp on one corner. Ceiling-to-floor bookcases held old leather-bound volumes and on the other walls hung landscape paintings.

The room could be the study of a wealthy, bookish man, but if that's what it was, thought Aidan, why go to such effort to hide its existence?

'Sit down,' said Malone, pointing to a wooden chair that faced the partner's desk. He sounded tense.

As Aidan sat down he heard steps on the stairs from the kitchen, then on the hard floor of the cellar behind him. Someone came into the room, and Aidan watched as the tall, thin figure of Seamus Piggott walked around the desk and sat down in the leather chair behind it.

'Hello, Mr Piggott,' said Aidan, managing a weak smile. He had spoken to the man only once, when he had first been taken on by The Fraternity, but he'd seen him several times when he'd been in the Belfast office on errands – to collect what he'd been told to call 'materials', or to return the padded envelopes of cash.

Piggott, with his rimless glasses and short cropped hair, looked like a professor and Aidan knew he was meant to be a brain box, a brilliant scientist, an aerospace engineer who when he was young back in the States had designed hand-held rockets, which the IRA had used to try to bring down British Army helicopters. But they said he was weird, too clever to be normal, and the way he was staring now – coldly, almost analytically, with an air of complete detachment – made Aidan understand why.

'Are you happy in your work, Aidan?' he said, his voice soft and almost toneless.

What was this about? Aidan didn't believe that Piggott was interested in his job satisfaction. But he nodded vigorously nonetheless. 'Yes. I am, Mr Piggott.'

Piggott continued to stare at him, and for a moment Aidan wondered if his answer had been heard. Then Piggott said, 'Because as CEO of this organisation I need to feel my staff is fully on board.'

'I am on board, Mr Piggott. I'm treated very well.' Aidan was scared now and his mouth was dry.

Piggott nodded. 'That's what I'd have thought. Yet you've been heard complaining.'

'Me?' asked Aidan. Oh Christ, he thought, thinking of his indiscretions in Paddy O'Brien's. Who on earth could have shopped him?

'I won't waste a lot of time on you, Aidan. You are a very small part of my operation, but even from you I require complete unquestioning loyalty and I haven't had it. You've been complaining,' he repeated. Piggott leaned forward in his chair, flipping a pencil onto the desk. 'Why?'

Why what? Aidan almost asked, though he knew full well. And rather than trying to explain or deny it, he found himself saying, 'I'm sorry, Mr Piggott.'

'Sorry,' said Piggott, his lips pursed as he nodded his head. There was something in this display of understanding Aidan didn't trust. 'Sorry's a good place to start,' Piggott added mildly, then his voice grew cold. 'But it's not where things end.' And for the first time he took his eyes off Aidan and nodded sharply at the two other men.

As Aidan turned his head towards the Spaniard next to him, he felt Malone's hand suddenly grip his arm. 'Don't—' he started to protest, but now his other arm was gripped as well. The dark man grunted, looming over him.

'What?' Aidan asked, unable to keep the fear from his voice.

'Give him your hand,' said Malone.

And as Aidan raised his left hand from the arm of the chair, he found it gripped by the Spaniard's hand. It felt as if his fingers were in a vice that was starting to turn. As the pressure grew Aidan gasped. 'Stop—'

But the grip kept tightening. Aidan tried to pull his hand away but he couldn't. As the pressure on his fingers increased, Aidan gave a cry, and then he felt and heard his third finger crunch as one of the bones broke.

Agonising pain filled his hand. The Spaniard let go at last, and the hand flopped like a rag onto the chair arm.

Tears welled up in Aidan's eyes and he could barely breathe. He looked down at his fingers, red and compressed from the strength of the Spaniard's grip. He tried to move them one by one. His third finger wouldn't move.

Aidan leaned back in his chair, trying not to be sick. For a moment, the room was completely silent, then he heard the noise of a child, sniffling and sobbing. He realised he was making the sounds. Lifting his head up, he blinked to clear his eyes of tears, and found Piggott staring at him from across the desk. The man nodded, as if in a lab, satisfied that his experiment had proved successful.

Piggott stood up, brushing the sleeve of his jacket, as if to rid it of an unwanted piece of fluff. Without looking again at Aidan he came out from behind the desk and walked towards the open wall into the cellar. As his footsteps rang out on the concrete floor, he called back to Malone and the Spaniard, 'Before you take him back to Belfast, break another one. We don't want him to think that was just an accident.'

2

Liz Carlyle was surprised to find the church full. It sat in what had once been a proper village, but now formed one link in the chain of affluent suburbs that stretched south and west from London along the river Thames.

She guessed the church must be Norman in origin, judging by its fine square tower, though the prodigious size of the nave suggested a later expansion – the sheer number of pews reminded Liz of the wool churches of East Anglia, massive edifices created when there wasn't much else to spend the sheep money on. Now it would normally be three-quarters empty, reduced to a tiny congregation of old faithfuls on most Sundays.

There was nothing reduced about this congregation, though. She reckoned from a quick count of the rows that there must be three or four hundred people present. She'd known there would be many colleagues from Thames House at this memorial service, for Joanne Wetherby had been with MI5 over ten years, and had never lost touch with the friends she'd made then (and of course her husband had continued with the service). The director general was here, along with director B, Beth Davis, responsible for all personnel and security matters. Virtually every other senior member of MI5 was present and a number from MI6. She noticed Geoffrey Fane, his tall, heron-like figure towering over his row. But what Liz hadn't realised was how many friends, neighbours and family would also be here today.

Ahead of her she could just see Charles Wetherby in the front row, flanked by his two sons and others, presumably relations. There was a woman in the row behind them, smartly dressed in a dark-blue suit with an elegant black hat, who was leaning forward whispering to Charles's younger son, Sam. She must be another relation, thought Liz.

She hadn't seen Charles since Joanne's death and she felt a sudden pang seeing him now, so obviously bereft. She had of course written to him, but she wished she could have done more than just send a few lines.

He'd written back, thanking her. The boys, he'd said, had been pillars of strength, though naturally he worried about them, and he'd be keeping a particularly keen eye on Sam, the younger of the two, still more boy than man. Charles ended by saying how much he was looking forward to returning to work.

Liz hoped that meant he was looking forward to seeing her as well. She had missed him at work, both as a boss (the best she'd ever had) and as . . . what exactly? She had only recently acknowledged to herself how strong her feelings were for Charles, yet they had never exchanged so much as a kiss. She wondered if that would change now, then immediately felt guilty about envisaging a future with Charles that Joanne Wetherby would never now have.

Next to Liz, her mother's friend Edward Treglown put the order of service paper neatly folded on his knee, and whispered something to Liz's mother on his other side. Liz had been astonished by the coincidence that Edward, who had known her mother for only a couple of years, was a childhood friend of Joanne Wetherby. It turned out that they had grown up together in the same town in Kent. As adults they had lost touch, but came back into contact – because of Liz, curiously enough.

After Liz had been badly hurt several months before, during an investigation into a plot to derail a Middle East peace conference, she had gone to her mother's to convalesce. Concerned about her safety there, Charles Wetherby had contacted Edward; meeting in London, the two had immediately taken to each other, even before discovering Edward's earlier friendship with Joanne. By this time Joanne was already very ill, but Liz gathered that Edward and her mother had been to see both Wetherbys on more than one occasion. If either Susan Carlyle or Edward had any inkling of Liz's own feelings for Charles, they kept it to themselves.

The Bach Prelude ended, and there was a chilly silence in the church, the only noise that of light rain thrown by the wind against the stained glass windows. Then the vicar stood before the congregation and the service began. It was traditional, with old standbys for the hymns, and a short appreciation by an old friend of Joanne's. There were two readings, given by the sons; Sam's voice quavered as he reached the end of Keats's 'Ode to Autumn', a favourite of his mother's as he'd told the crowded church. There were tears in many eyes as resolutely he gathered himself together and finished with a strong, resonant voice:

> *The red-breast whistles from a garden-croft,*
> *And gathering swallows twitter in the sky.*

A final hymn and the service concluded. As the haunting sound of the organ playing Purcell filled the nave, the congregation rose and began slowly to file out. The thin drizzle had ended, and the sky had lightened slightly to a chalky mix of greys as Charles stood outside the church with the boys next to him. Liz let Edward and her mother go first to offer condolences. Then it was her turn.

'Liz,' said Charles, gripping her hand firmly. 'It's lovely to see you. Thank you so much for coming. How have you been?'

'I'm fine, Charles,' she said as brightly as she could. It was characteristic of him to ask how *she* was.

'You've met Sam before,' he said, turning slightly to include his son. The boy smiled shyly and shook her hand. The woman in the black hat Liz had noticed in church came up to the other son, laying a comforting hand on his arm. Was she an aunt? Charles said, 'Liz, I want you to meet Alison.'

The woman looked up and smiled. She had a striking but friendly face, with high cheekbones, a sharp nose, and unusual violet eyes. 'Liz,' she said. 'I've heard so much about you.'

Really? thought Liz with surprise. From Charles? Or from Joanne?

Charles explained, 'Alison lives next door to us. We've been neighbours for years.'

'Yes. Joanne brought me a cake on the day we moved in.' She looked fondly at Sam. 'You weren't even born then, young man.'

Other people were waiting to speak to Charles, so Liz moved on. She had been invited with others for refreshments at the Wetherby house several miles away, but she couldn't face a large gathering just now – she wanted to see Charles, but she wanted to see him alone. Her presence or absence would be neither here nor there among the dozens of people certain to be found at the Wetherbys.

Saying goodbye to her mother and Edward, she left, having decided to drive straight back to Thames House and get on with her work. She'd see Charles there soon enough. If he needed someone to talk to today, Liz sensed that his neighbour Alison would be happy to stand in.

3

Something was holding them up. Their driver tapped his fingers impatiently on the wheel and Beth Davis looked out of the window at the patchy woods that lined the A307 south of Richmond. She had two meetings planned for that afternoon and was wondering if she'd be back in time for either of them.

She glanced at DG sitting next to her. He looked the soul of patience. Typical of him, thought Beth. God knows how many meetings he must have scheduled, yet at the gathering after the service at Charles's house, he had been a model of tact: solicitous of Charles, polite to the array of friends and relatives he'd been introduced to, never giving any indication that he had pressing business elsewhere.

The car inched forward, tyres churning the slushy piles of leaves in the gutter of the road. 'Lovely service,' DG said with a small sigh.

'The boys read beautifully,' said Beth, and DG nodded. She went on, 'It must be awfully hard on them, especially now that they're boarding.'

'I think only the eldest is boarding yet. And boarding may be a good thing. They're kept busy, lots of distractions, all their friends around them. Being at home might be much harder. Too many ghosts; too many reminders.'

'I suppose you're right. Still, it will make it more difficult for Charles when they're both away. Wandering around that house all alone.'

DG gave a small grunt. After a moment he said, 'Our lot made a good show of it, I thought.'

'Yes. Thames House must have been seriously undermanned for a few hours.'

'I didn't see anyone leaving the service, so let's hope there were no crises.' DG smiled, then grew serious. 'I didn't see Liz Carlyle.'

'I did; she was at the church, with her mother. She didn't go on to the house though. She must have had to get straight back.'

DG nodded and looked thoughtful. Beth sensed what he was thinking – it was no secret that Liz and Charles were close, though no doubt the two of them believed no one else had noticed. But how could you fail to observe their obvious mutual attraction? The way Charles's face would light up when Liz joined a meeting he was chairing. The rapt look on Liz's face when Charles was speaking. You would have been blind to miss it.

The couple's feelings for each other would not have been a problem if Liz had worked for anyone else. But now she was reporting to Charles again, since he had taken over the counter espionage branch, and that's where matters grew complicated.

It was not an unknown, or even uncommon situation. It was understood within the service that the secrecy of the job made it hard to forge relationships with anyone 'outside', and that therefore office romances were inevitable. Joanne Wetherby herself had worked for Charles, Beth remembered, though once Joanne and Charles had started seeing each other she'd been posted – to work for DG in fact, when he had still been a director.

What was expected, however, was that the participants in office romances declare themselves at once, and understand that one of the pair would have to be moved. The power of love might be accepted, but its inevitable impact on working relations couldn't be.

As far as Beth knew, Liz and Charles had nothing to declare. If anyone had told her that the pair of them sloped off quietly at lunchtime to the City Inn Hotel on John Islip Street, or rendezvoused at the weekend in a West Country B&B, she would not have believed them. Charles was far too upright, too devoted to his wife to do anything like that. And Beth simply couldn't see Liz in the role of mistress, waiting restlessly by the phone for a call from her married lover. Beth was sure that with these two, there had been no illicit affair. And that was the problem: everything was bubbling beneath the surface.

DG sighed again, this time more loudly, usually a sign that his thoughts were about to find vocal expression. They were in Putney now, about to cross the river. DG said, 'I think we've got a bit of a problem on our hands.'

Beth nodded; there was no need for him to say what the problem was. She waited patiently and at last he added, 'It could be very difficult for them both.' He threw up a hand to indicate his own ambivalence. 'I mean, there's nothing stopping them now, is there?'

'I suppose not,' said Beth.

'Though my father used to say "forbidden fruit looks less attractive once it's off the tree."'

Beth gave a small snort. 'With all respect to your father, I don't think the mutual attraction's going to diminish. It's other things that will get in the way.'

DG fingered his tie soberly. 'Like what?'

'Like guilt, unjustified though it might be. And I suppose

the fear that what you've wanted so long could finally be yours.'

'Fear?'

'Yes. Not that it won't turn out to be what you wanted, but that somehow you don't deserve it. They say long-term prisoners are often terrified when their release date approaches. It's just too much – the prospect of having what you've desired for so long is too daunting.'

'You think it could be that bad for those two?'

Beth shrugged. She was paid to understand people, but had long learned that such understanding was precarious, and never to be assumed. She said, 'I'd like to think not.'

'But you're not sure,' said DG, and it wasn't posed as a question. 'In which case their work will almost certainly be affected. So I think they might profit from a break.'

Beth must have looked horrified, as if he had suggested ordering the two to go off together for a week's leave in Paris, for he added hastily, 'I mean a break from each other.'

'Oh,' said Beth with relief.

'Yes,' said DG.

What now? she thought warily. Personnel and postings were her responsibility, and he rarely interfered directly. But now she could see he had made his mind up. She didn't want an argument, so she hoped she'd be able to go along with whatever he'd decided.

He said emphatically, 'I think Liz should be posted – at least temporarily, while Charles settles back in at work. There's a lot for him to do, you know,' he said, almost accusingly, as if he thought she might think he was being unnecessarily harsh.

'Where do you want to put her?' she asked. Counter terrorism, she imagined. That's where Liz had been before. Working for Charles when he had been director there.

16

'We'll have to work that out,' he said, rather to her surprise. If he'd already decided, as she suspected he had, he clearly wasn't ready to say. 'It's got to be something challenging. I don't want her to think it's in any way a demotion. That wouldn't be fair on Liz.'

'No, though—' and Beth hesitated. When DG looked at her questioningly, she sighed. 'She's going to see it that way, I fear.'

'Probably.' DG shrugged lightly. 'But that can't be helped. And so long as we make sure her new posting is tough enough, she'll soon get stuck in. She's too good an officer not to.'

4

The call came out of the blue and Dave didn't recognise the name.

'Phil Robinson,' the man on the end of the phone repeated, with an English-sounding voice. 'I'm a warden with the National Trust. I was in contact with the RUC Special Branch in the past. I was told to ring you.'

Dave Armstrong had been in Northern Ireland for a couple of months. He was part of the team that was gradually filling up the smart new MI5 offices in Palace Barracks, the army HQ a few miles north of Belfast city centre. With power-sharing in Northern Ireland taking its first staggering steps, the new Police Service of Northern Ireland that had replaced the Royal Ulster Constabulary had handed over intelligence work in the province to MI5.

With that transfer of power went all the records of the large stable of agents – the human sources that had fed the RUC with information from inside the Republican and the Loyalist armed groups during the Troubles. It was information far too sensitive to retain in a police service that might find itself answering to government ministers or members of a police board who were once themselves part of the armed groups. The last thing the new police service wanted was a spate of revenge killings or score settling.

So Dave and a couple of colleagues in the agent-running section of the MI5 team had the job of sorting through the list of sources they'd inherited, closing down the many who were of no future use and getting to know the few who might continue to be of value. For although the so-called 'peace process' was well established and the security threat in Northern Ireland had changed, it hadn't gone away. The Provisional IRA might have disbanded its armed groups and decommissioned its weapons but there were still those among its former ranks – and Loyalists on the other side of the divide – who did not support the peace process. For them the war was not over, which meant Dave and his colleagues were monitoring several renegade groups determined to do all they could to keep the war very much alive.

Phil Robinson. The name now rang a bell. It had stuck out of the list of old sources because of the National Trust link. It had seemed an unlikely connection, but Dave knew that National Trust properties had been the target of IRA attacks in the past. In 1973 two young IRA volunteers had blown themselves up in the Castle Ward estate with a bomb they were trying to plant. After that, the security forces had paid more attention to the Trust's properties in Northern Ireland, and Robinson had been one of the people who'd been recruited to advise them.

'How can I help?' asked Dave now.

'Something's come up. I wonder if we could meet.'

'Of course,' said Dave, thankful to have something active to do. He was finding the routine job of reviewing old files and standing down old cases tedious. Maybe this would turn out to be nothing, but Robinson sounded sensible. So Dave said, 'How about this afternoon?'

*

They had arranged to meet in the middle of the city. Dave took one of the operational cars from the garage and drove, working his way through the traffic into the heart of Belfast, busy even in mid-afternoon. When he'd first arrived, it had been a pleasant surprise to find the middle of the city lively, vibrant, humming with activity. The images Dave had grown up with – soldiers with automatic weapons, barricades and barbed wire, the apprehensive looks on people's faces – had been replaced by teeming shops, pedestrian areas (from which cars were now banned for reasons that had nothing to do with security), and a buoyant nightlife. It was hard to believe that not so long ago the city had been to all intents and purposes a war zone. And although Dave's job gave him a healthy scepticism about the new-found peace, the citizens of Belfast seemed too intent on enjoying 'normal life' to let things be derailed by a few murderous malcontents.

He was living in one of the flats the service leased in the suburb of Holywood, just outside Palace Barracks. It was an area of the town that had been comfortably safe in the Troubles but now, for someone living on their own like Dave, it was rather dull and lonely. He had a girlfriend in London, Lucy. They'd been together for two years, which for him was a long time. But it was difficult keeping it going when they were so far apart. He was too busy to hop over to England every weekend and there wasn't much point in Lucy coming to see him if he had to work. But he was serious about her and that meant he wasn't looking to meet girls in the bars of Belfast's lively nightlife – he didn't join his younger colleagues when they went out partying.

But he'd just heard some news that had lifted his spirits. Michael Binding, the head of the MI5 office in Northern Ireland, had told them all that morning that Liz Carlyle was coming out to head the agent-running section. Dave knew that Binding didn't have much time for Liz, or she for him. But Dave had both affection and respect for her, though he wondered, now that she was going to be his boss, if their relationship would change. Not that they had been very close for the last couple of years. Liz had been transferred from counter terrorism, and it was only a fluke that they had recently worked together – in Scotland, at Gleneagles, on a plot to ruin a vital peace conference. It had been good working with her again; she was formidable without being aware of it, straightforward, clear, decisive.

That wasn't all, of course. For a time, five or six years ago, they had been not only good work colleagues but close friends as well. They might even have been more than that, but some mutual hesitation had held them back. More 'mutual' for her than me, Dave thought sadly, because he'd realised ever since that a part of him regretted that they hadn't got together. Well, that was out of the question, now. For one thing he was with Lucy and for another, you didn't get a second chance with someone like Liz. Anyway, he knew that her heartstrings were tied somewhere else – to Charles Wetherby. When Joanne had died two months ago, Dave's first thought had been that Liz and Charles would be together. So why on earth was Liz coming to Belfast?

Whatever the reason, he was delighted. And only partly because he was looking forward to seeing her dealing with Michael Binding.

Phil Robinson was a tall man with greying hair. He spoke without a hint of Ulster brogue in his voice, and with his tweed jacket and checked Viyella shirt looked completely English, a bit like a retired civil servant who'd spent the morning helping his wife tend the roses. He seemed out of place in Northern Ireland, thought Dave, and as if in answer to the thought, Robinson told him that he had come over to Northern Ireland from England for the National Trust on a temporary posting thirty years before – and stayed.

'I fell in love with the place despite myself,' he said with a small grin. 'Then I met my wife, and fell in love with her as well. Only please don't tell her it was in that order.'

They were sitting in a coffee shop in St George's Gardens, around the corner from the Europa Hotel, which after years of being the most bombed hotel in Europe now seemed to be flourishing. When Dave had walked past it, a long line of Japanese businessmen had been queuing outside for cabs, while foreign guests of every conceivable race and nationality – Indians, Arabs, Orientals – went in and out of the big revolving doors. Only the doorman, standing erect behind a rostrum just outside the entrance, had looked pale enough to be Irish.

Robinson explained that he now worked only part-time for the National Trust.

'Consulting?' asked Dave politely, since that was how everyone seemed to describe any work they did after retiring.

Phil Robinson gave a self-deprecating laugh. 'Hardly. I help with the migrant bird counts up in Antrim, and stand in when too many wardens go on holiday at the same time. But my grandest job is south of here in County Down. Near Newcastle.'

'Doing what?' asked Dave politely.

'My wife and I look after the holiday cottages on the Drigillon Estate – I was joking about the grand bit. They're let for a week or two at a time, or sometimes for short breaks of two or three nights. There are three of them on the estate – so it's a fair amount of work, particularly in the summer when they are occupied all the time.'

'So why did you want to see me?'

'I'll tell you what it is. One of the cottages – it's not really a cottage; it's a house, the old gatehouse to the estate – has a gate in front of it which is usually closed. It works electronically. If you have a remote control device it opens automatically and then closes behind you. Some local members of the National Trust who like to walk on the estate have remotes to open the gate and anyone staying in the cottages is given one. In the last six months or so, several people who've been staying at the gatehouse have complained that people were opening the gate at odd hours in the night – it makes rather a crash as it closes – and driving cars up past the house into the estate. Of course, our renters often complain about something or other – one even moaned about the quality of the soap – so I didn't take much notice at first. But when several tenants said the same thing – cars, coming by at three in the morning – I felt I had to take some notice.'

Dave nodded, but inwardly wondered why this necessitated a call to MI5. Surely the local police should have been the first port of call.

Robinson seemed to sense his scepticism. 'I know, it may be nothing at all,' he said modestly.

'But something tells you it's not?' Dave asked gently. There was no point writing off the man's story yet.

Robinson nodded, and said, 'Yes. My wife and I stayed in the gatehouse for a couple of nights, between lets. Val thought I was mad, but it seemed the best way to find out if anything was going on. And sure enough, one night the gate was opening and shutting and there were cars driving by at four o'clock in the morning. Then after breakfast, two of them came back down the track. I was out walking our terrier.'

Dave nodded. 'Are there any other houses on the estate where they might be going?'

'Just the old farmhouse. But that's not owned by the Trust. Whoever does own it had a lot of work done to it a year or so ago. There were builders' lorries going up and down the track then. But not in the middle of the night. I wondered at first whether this was young people having a rave or taking drugs, but I've seen no sign of damage on the estate or rubbish – empty bottles or syringes or that sort of stuff.'

Robinson continued, 'That's not all. You see, when the two cars came down the track after breakfast, I was just by the gate. They slowed down to wait for the gate to open, and I recognised one of the men in the cars. At least I think I did – I didn't get a very good a look at him. But I'm pretty sure it was Terry Malone, an old IRA hand. I doubt you've heard of him, but he used to be well known over here. He was fairly high up in the Provisionals, and he had a brother, Seamus Malone, who went with the other side when the IRA split in the seventies – he was Official IRA. When Seamus was murdered in Dublin, the crack was that his own brother – that's Terry – fingered him for the killers. Who knows? But I'm almost certain it was Terry Malone I saw in the car.'

While Robinson finished his coffee, Dave thought about this, then asked, 'What are you suggesting? Do you think there might be some renegade IRA outfit in this farmhouse?'

Robinson shrugged. 'All this coming and going could mean anything. An awful lot of former Provisionals are finding life pretty difficult – all the organisation's money goes on Sinn Fein election pamphlets these days, instead of Armalites. These guys are up to all sorts of stuff to try to raise money to keep the war going.'

'Is the gatehouse occupied at the moment?'

'Yes it is, until the middle of next week. But then we have a week when it's empty. We always keep a week in January for spring cleaning, but that will only take us a couple of days. I could let you have a key for the end of the week if you wanted to see for yourself.'

'Thanks,' said Dave. 'I think that could be very useful.'

5

When the tyre blew, Liz's car suddenly veered right at a forty-five-degree angle. She knew that at fifty miles an hour things could go either way – the car might go out of control and there would be nothing she could do but hope, or there was just a chance that she could manage the situation if she acted force-fully and immediately.

Instinctively Liz hooked both hands through the steering wheel and braced her forearms, struggling to hold the steering wheel as it fought her with enormous torque. The car slewed across the slow lane, cutting in front of a black van, which braked with a squeal, then honked furiously.

She used all her strength now, and the skidding car just missed the concrete barrier on the road's hard shoulder; then, as if it had a mind of its own, the vehicle moved right, back out into the road. Narrowly avoiding a sports car that swerved and accelerated past, it headed this time towards the central barrier, but just before hitting it at speed, the steering wheel slackened slightly. Liz managed to turn the car away sharply, then rode the resulting skid once, twice, then three times, weaving through the lanes as other cars swerved desperately to avoid her. At last the vehicle slowed down, like a runaway horse recognising it's been caught, and Liz brought it to a sudden stop back on the hard shoulder.

She sat for a moment, trembling violently, waiting for the drum roll in her heart to slow. Then she got out, and inspecting the damage she saw that one of the rear tyres had virtually disintegrated, its vulcanised rubber now hanging in shreds from a black lump around the metal wheel. She was quite capable of changing a tyre – her father had taught her as a teenage girl before he let her drive alone – but the warped mass around the wheel was going to require more than the jack stowed in the boot.

As her fear subsided, it was replaced with anger. The car had been left for her to pick up at the airport by her new colleagues in the Palace Barracks office. What the hell were they doing, leaving her a car with dodgy tyres? She grabbed her mobile phone and dialled Michael Binding's secretary. As she punched in the numbers she looked down the road and saw a sign facing the traffic. Its cheerful message read, *Welcome to Belfast.*

Seven days before, Liz had sat in Director B's office in Thames House. The low winter sun had glanced through the windows; she could see, half a mile down the river, the postmodernist headquarters of MI6 bathed in golden light.

Beth Davis had been friendly, praising her recent work, but then she had dropped her bombshell – Liz was being posted to the MI5 headquarters in Northern Ireland. 'We need you there to take charge of the agent-running section. You'll have much more responsibility, Liz. All the agent runners will be reporting to you. They have a big job to do – there's a lot still going on over there – and we need someone with your background to decide where the priorities lie. They're all enthusiastic, but some of them haven't been with the service very long; they do need guidance.'

She continued for a few minutes, couching her words carefully, but Liz found it hard to understand why she had been chosen. She knew that of all the service's new regional offices, Belfast was the most important, because it was going to act as a backup HQ in the event of a terrorist attack on Thames House in London. But even though she'd done short stints on the Northern Ireland desk when she'd first joined the service, she'd never actually been posted there, so she couldn't see why she had been chosen for this job.

'When do I start?' she asked, thinking of the arrangements she'd have to make. If she were going to be there any time, perhaps she should think about letting her flat.

'Michael Binding's expecting you next week.'

Oh God, thought Liz, trying not to react. She and Binding had crossed swords on more than one occasion; she imagined he would relish being in a position to tell her what to do.

Beth said, 'Call in on the postings team this afternoon, Liz; they'll sort out the details.'

Nice of Beth to take the time to build me up, Liz thought sourly as she left. Then she told herself to get a grip. There must be a reason for this posting, though for the life of her she couldn't see what it could be. And why so fast? This was the real sting in the tail, she knew – not because she had any major unfinished business at work, but because . . . Oh go on and admit it, she told herself. Because Charles was due back at work any day now, and she was longing to see him. And now it would be just her luck to leave Thames House only days before he returned. It was almost as if Beth Davis were keen to get her out of the way before Charles was back.

Don't be so silly, Liz told herself. They couldn't have any idea of her feelings. She'd never told anyone about them, and had made a point of always acting completely professionally with Charles. No, she was sure she had kept her secret well. Something else was going on to account for this posting.

While she was ruminating about this, a car drew up beside her on the hard shoulder and she recognised Maureen Hayes from A4 at the wheel, with a younger man sitting next to her.

'Hello, Liz. I got your message from Michael's secretary. That looks pretty nasty. Are you OK?'

'Well, I am now,' said Liz. 'It's good to see you. Have you got many cars over here with ropey tyres?'

'I'm amazed,' Maureen replied. 'This one was serviced last week and I drove it myself to the airport to leave for you. It seemed fine then. Get in and I'll take you to the office. Let's bring your luggage, and Tom here will wait for the pickup truck. It's on its way.'

'I thought you'd like to see your office first,' said Michael Binding's PA, a thin young woman with spiky ash-streaked hair. She led Liz down a corridor until she stopped at an open door. It was a good-sized room, but with its bare desk, tall steel cupboard, and two upright chairs it looked utterly cheerless.

'You're due a meeting table and chairs and a couple of armchairs. We've got some art as well,' she said. 'I'll have a few pictures brought round, if you like. You can pick a couple to make the place look a bit more homely.'

Liz nodded, and looked out of the window at the view of the half-empty barracks. In the distance she could see the A2, where the traffic was speeding along towards Belfast ten miles away.

'Michael wanted to be here when you arrived, but he's been called over to Stormont unexpectedly. I'll let you know as soon as he's back.'

29

'Dave Armstrong around?' Liz asked, suddenly keen for a familiar face.

The girl shook her head. 'I know he wants to say hello, but he's out meeting someone. He said to tell you he'd see you tomorrow. Some of the agent runners are in – their office is just along the corridor.'

An hour or so later Liz was feeling better. There were several familiar faces in the agent runners' room and the welcome had been warm, as had the coffee. Then the PA stuck her head round the door.

'Michael's back.'

Liz followed her along the corridor, past the centre lift shaft, until they came to a large office in the corner. The view here, Liz noted, was of farm fields stretching into the distance in rolling curves.

'Ah, Liz,' said the tall, wide-shouldered man as he got up from his desk, and shook her hand without a smile, 'I was sorry to hear about your car accident. Driving here is usually so safe.'

He looks different, thought Liz. Michael Binding had always favoured the country squire look – tweed sports jacket, checked shirt and highly polished brown brogues. But now he was wearing a long-sleeved khaki pullover, with leather patches on the sleeves, narrow corduroy trousers in a curious shade of faded pinkish-red, and brown suede shoes. His hair, previously short and neat, was now curling up off his collar. Liz realised that he had changed from squire to military officer. She sat down and waited to see what the new image portended.

She knew Binding as a clever but impatient man, whose impatience was at its worst when he had to work with female colleagues. More than impatience, in fact, since he patronised them in a manner so anachronistic and breathtakingly rude that he somehow got away with it. He had become famous for it throughout Thames House and, far from taking offence, most of the women he worked with put up with it and treated it as a joke, swapping stories of occasions when he had called them 'dear' or sighed loudly and raised his eyebrows when they disagreed with him. It was a matter of speculation among the women in Thames House what made him do it. Most thought that it was probably because his wife bossed him about at home.

Liz had never had to work for him before, but a few years previously she had had to interview Binding during an investigation – the same one that had unearthed a mole at a high level of MI5. Binding had been difficult, obstreperous, objecting to her questioning until Liz had warned him that she'd bring in DG if Binding did not cooperate, which reluctantly and sulkily he then had.

After that, she had kept as far away from him as she could, and when their paths had occasionally crossed he had treated her with cautious resentment. So she watched warily now to see how he would react to her joining his staff.

'I must say,' he opened, 'I was hoping to be sent someone with Northern Ireland experience. I understand you have very little.'

Liz gazed at him levelly while she decided how to respond. 'Not much,' she said eventually in a bright, cheerful voice. 'But as I'm sure you know, I have a lot of agent-running experience and I assume that's why I was chosen for this particular job.'

Binding said nothing for a moment. First blood to me, thought Liz to herself. Then, changing tack, he said, 'It's busier here than you may think.' He spoke defensively, as if he sensed scepticism. 'I know there isn't much coverage on the mainland of things over here, but the Troubles have far from gone away. Sometimes I think the media doesn't *want* to report any problems in the hopes they'll just disappear.'

'What exactly are the problems?'

'Well, with no Northern Irish background you may find your-self at a disadvantage in understanding the current situation.'

Liz forced herself not to respond and kept her face expres-sionless as he went on.

'The usual, just on a much reduced scale. Our estimate is that there are over one hundred paramilitaries still active on the Republican side. They are not particularly well-organised, thank God – they belong to almost as many splinter groups as there are members.'

'Still, a hundred individuals could do a lot of damage,' said Liz.

'Precisely,' he said in the pedantic tone Liz remembered, designed to make her feel like a pupil who was being marked on a test. 'Equally worrying, they can trigger a reaction on the other side. For now, the Loyalist groups have laid down their arms, but a few sectarian murders could change that overnight.'

'Where are these fringe people getting the resources to carry on? Is there still any foreign support?'

'Not that we know of. Al Qaeda aren't moving in, if that's what you're thinking,' he added with heavy sarcasm,

'I wasn't, actually,' said Liz dryly. 'I was thinking about funding and weaponry – from the States, the Basques, North Africa, South America, wherever.'

He looked a little surprised that she knew anything about the past sources of IRA arms. 'Their funding is local now as far as we know. But none of it's legitimate. Crime of all sorts – drugs, prostitution, robberies. God knows what else.'

'How's our coverage of their activities? Have we any decent sources?' asked Liz, moving the conversation on to her own area of responsibility.

'Reasonable. As always it could be better,' said Binding. 'I gather you've met some of the agent runners just now. I've had Dave Armstrong acting in charge of the team. But Dave is an action man. He prefers to be out running his own cases.'

What does he think I've done for most of my career? thought Liz. But he obviously thinks the light shines out of Dave's eyes. Not that she'd disagree with that. 'I've worked with Dave before,' she responded. 'He's good. I'll certainly need his input until I get up to speed.'

Binding looked at his watch with undisguised impatience. 'Well then, why don't you get your feet under the desk, get settled in at the flat, talk to Dave? Then in a day or two, we'll meet up again and you can give me your first impressions.'

And you'll let me know where they are wrong, thought Liz. Different posting, different place, different clothes. Same Michael Binding.

6

'I'm going out,' Dermot O'Reilly shouted as he left the house. This was as far as he kept his wife posted on his whereabouts, a habitual secrecy that had originated during the Troubles, when it was safer not to let her know what he was up to.

She'd had a good idea, nonetheless, and when the knock on the door had come that day in 1975 and five RUC men had taken him away, she wasn't very surprised. 'Cheer up,' she'd said on her first visit to the H-Blocks at The Maze. 'Think of it as a holiday from me.'

The 'holiday' had lasted two years and had been especially hard on Cath. He knew he was a gruff man to live with, and he had never liked to show emotion, but he was devoted to his wife in his way, and understood how long-suffering she was. Especially since after he'd been freed he'd waited less than forty-eight hours before resuming the activities that got him interned in the first place.

He'd been the munitions officer of Company B of the Belfast Brigade, with weaponry stored in half a dozen safe houses and hidden caches under the floor of barns and sheds. He remembered with a half-smile now the weird farrago of firearms they'd had to rely on in the early days of the conflict – before Colonel

Gaddafi of Libya had sent them ships full of the latest of everything and cash to go with them. The Irish Americans had been
a steady source of revenue too. Did all those drinkers in the
bars in Boston really believe that when they dropped their cash
into the collecting buckets, it was going to go to widows and
orphans of the struggle? Seamus Piggott would know all about
that, since the boss of The Fraternity was from Boston.

Dermot didn't like Piggott. He didn't trust him. What was
an American doing carrying on the struggle? What was he
hoping to get out of it? But Dermot had joined The Fraternity
when he was approached, because of all the breakaway groups
it seemed the best resourced, the most professional.

At first he had been chief targeting officer. The plan was to
kill a cop in the new PSNI – to show them that though they
might have renamed themselves, to true Republicans like him
they were still the enemy. Piggott had got hold of a list of
addresses and Dermot had spent some cold, damp days on surveillance, watching policemen and their families coming and going,
planning the best way to attack.

Wherever Piggott had got the list from, and he certainly
wasn't revealing that to Dermot, it seemed to be an old one.
Some of the houses Dermot had watched had no apparent
police connection, so he assumed that they'd changed hands.
In others the inhabitants were middle-aged or obviously retired.
He guessed that the list had come from the RUC, before it was
turned into the PSNI, and that what he was targeting was not
current front-line police. When he'd mentioned that to Piggott,
he didn't seem to care. 'They're all bastards, and bastards don't
retire in my book,' was his response.

Dermot was too old nowadays to lie up in ditches, with his
binoculars trained on houses and garages, so he was glad when
Piggott acquired a couple of surveillance vans in which he could

sit in comparative warmth, parked up, with his camera trained through a slit in the side. The vans were repainted frequently so they didn't get noticed.

He walked under the bypass and into Andersonstown. Ahead of him he saw Paddy O'Brien's bar on the corner. It had tried to tart itself up for a while, in recognition of the new affluence of the city, for a brief time even offering a gastro pub menu. But the overt hostility of its hardcore clientele had discouraged middle-class customers. Within six months the place had reverted to what its habitués insisted it should always be – a man's saloon.

The barman was already pulling a pint of Murphy's before Dermot was through the door. When the thick brown stout was halfway up the pint glass, the barman paused to let the foam settle, then filled it to the top. With a wooden paddle he cut off the towering creamy head and placed the pint on the bar.

Dermot grunted thanks and looked around the pub. He liked coming here, finding a comforting, almost nostalgic pleasure in the place. It was an informal meeting place for many of the former Provisional IRA volunteers he had served with, especially those who were down on their luck. A few were in here already, crouched over the paper and a pint they'd nurse through lunchtime. I'll be like that soon, he thought with an intense bitterness. He wasn't going to work today, not after his last conversation with Piggott.

Above the bar there was a framed black-and-white photograph of the hunger striker Bobby Sands, with a one-word caption underneath: *Loyalty*.

Loyalty: the word turned to ashes in Dermot's mouth. Once it had been the maxim of his professional life – loyalty to the cause, to the organisation, to his superiors in the hierarchy. It was a principle he'd carried over to The Fraternity, squashing his doubts about Piggott; helped, he had to admit, by the fact that the money was so good. A state pension didn't get you far – barely drinking money – and in their new roles as Establishment politicians, Gerry Adams and Martin McGuinness didn't seem interested in establishing a fund for the foot soldiers who had got them where they were.

Dermot had never had money before, and he realised how easily he had got used to a comfortable life: the satellite dish on the roof bringing him all the Sky sport anyone could watch, and Cath her beloved films; the holidays on the Costa Brava each February, getting away from the grey, dank cold. And the prospect of retirement to that small cottage in Donegal he and Cath had often dreamed about. Two more years with The Fraternity and he would have been free and clear. Only now he'd been pushed aside.

Piggott had been clinical. 'I need a younger man in charge of operations. You'll be running security from now on.'

Security in the old days was a big, important job, when British intelligence was everywhere and intense precautions had been necessary to keep the Provisional IRA from being totally infiltrated. Now it just seemed to mean making sure Piggott's car and driver showed up on time, or locking the office's desks so the cleaning ladies couldn't snoop around. It was a dogsbody job, and Dermot was sure it was going to involve dogsbody pay. He'd be as badly paid and treated as Malone, who was nothing but a thug.

Piggott hadn't even had the courtesy to tell him by whom he was being replaced. Or to cushion the blow by praising his work. There had been no feeling in Piggott's voice, no concern whether this change would sit well with Dermot.

The barman was suddenly there again, though Dermot had barely touched his pint. He looked up at him from his bar stool, his disgruntlement showing on his face.

'Sorry to hear about Aidan Murphy,' the barman said, polishing a glass with a tea towel.

'How do you mean?'

'Oh,' said the barman, putting the clean glass on a shelf above the bar. 'I thought you'd have known. Being as you work together and all.'

Dermot pushed his pint away, and it sloshed sloppily on the mahogany top of the bar. He said angrily, 'Why don't you spit it out, seeing as you know so much and I don't?'

The barman raised an apologetic hand. 'Sorry, Dermot. His hand got all smashed up. He said he'd had an accident . . .'

Dermot stared at the barman. 'What are you saying? If it wasn't an accident, what was it?'

The barman shrugged, as if to say 'you tell me'. 'All I know is that they—' he caught himself – 'is that his hand was broken half to smithereens. He won't ever have full use of it again.' The barman sighed loudly. 'And him so young.'

And he went down the bar to check on another customer, while Dermot took in what had been said. He reached for his pint glass, and drained half the contents, medicinally rather than for pleasure. Christ, he thought, what had they done to the kid? All right, he had a big mouth, and he should learn to keep it shut – but not this way. He didn't need teaching a lesson.

It's Piggott, he thought.

He doesn't give a shit, he realised, with an anger he hadn't felt for years. Well, we'll see about that, he told himself.

7

The flat was on the first floor of a red brick house just a quarter of a mile from the university, on a quiet side street which stopped in a dead end against the black iron fence of a small park.

On the ground floor a door led to another flat, but Liz went straight on up the stairs and let herself in through her own front door.

She put her bags down and did a quick recce of her new quarters. Two bedrooms – room for her mother to visit, she thought – a large living room, simply but comfortably furnished, with a kitchen and a small breakfast alcove. Perfect – nothing too large to keep tidy; nothing so small to feel cramped. Someone had even come in and put tea and coffee on the kitchen top, and fresh milk in the fridge.

The bigger bedroom had a pleasant view of the park, where children were playing on swings and slides. She started to unpack and was just finishing when she heard a faint creaking from the door to the flat. Then a step, and another step.

Liz tensed, listening. She must not have closed the door properly. Looking around, she saw there was no phone in the bedroom – that would have to change. She took a deep breath and went out of the room and into the hall, wondering whom she was going to encounter.

A little girl with a mop of brown curls and big brown eyes was standing there, staring at Liz. She wore pyjamas decorated with colourful lollipops.

'Hello,' said Liz with relief. 'Who are you?'

'I'm Daisy,' she said, and with great formality extended a hand.

Liz shook hands, suppressing a smile. 'Pleased to meet you, Daisy. I'm Liz.'

Daisy nodded sagely, then suddenly declared, 'I'm not precocious, you know.'

Liz regarded the girl with amusement. 'I'm sure you're not,' she said.

'One of my teachers at school told my mother I was. They didn't think I'd hear,' she said, a little guiltily.

'Never mind,' said Liz. 'It's not a bad thing. Do you live downstairs?' she asked, gesturing with her head towards the floor.

'Yes,' said Daisy. 'Are you going to live here now?'

'I am. We'll be neighbours.'

A woman appeared in the doorway, white-haired, too old to be this girl's mother. She looked at Liz with a worried frown. 'I'm sorry, miss,' the woman said, with an accent that marked her out as local. 'She was just being curious. Come along, Daisy. I've got your supper ready.'

But Daisy didn't move. Looking at Liz she said, 'Are you the lady Mummy knows?'

'I shouldn't think so,' said Liz, wondering who her mother was.

A voice came from the hallway. 'Don't be so sure about that.' It was a woman's voice, followed by a laugh that could only belong to one person.

'Judith,' cried Liz, as a tall, elegant woman came into the hall. 'I had no idea you were living here.'

Judith Spratt had worked with Liz in counter terrorism. She was a desk officer, widely respected within the service for her acumen and relentless pursuit of leads. She had always been admirably unflappable, and Liz and she had become good friends before losing track of each other – Liz had been moved to counter espionage, and Judith had gone on extended leave after marital problems. Liz had heard vaguely that Judith had come back, but she hadn't seen her in Thames House – and now she knew why.

'I've been here over a year,' said Judith, as if amazed herself. 'Time flies when . . .' she paused, then grinned. 'When you're as busy as I am.'

By now the white-haired woman had a firm grip on Daisy's hand, and with a nod to Judith marched the little girl out of the flat. Liz and Judith went into the kitchen, where Liz turned the kettle on.

'And of course that's Daisy,' said Liz, remembering the tiny child in London who would clamber out of bed to interrupt her mother's dinner parties. 'My she's grown,' she added. 'How old is she now? Five? Six?' Going on twenty, thought Liz.

'Almost six. I found her a good school.' Judith's expression darkened. 'I'm divorced from Ravi now, you know.'

Liz was not surprised. Judith's husband had been involved in a prominent City fraud case; cleared by the Fraud Squad, he had almost immediately found himself charged with a credit card scam. Charming but volatile, he had left Judith at the height of the scandal, which had added humiliation to her shame, and made her loyalty to her husband in his travails seem pointless.

'Where is Ravi now?' Liz asked gently.

Judith shrugged, in a display of indifference that Liz sensed was not altogether sincere. 'He got a suspended sentence, but after that he couldn't work in the City again. He went back to India for a while; God knows where he is now. The way he fought me for custody of Daisy you'd think he'd be in touch, but I haven't heard a monkey's.'

'I'm sorry.' She had always admired Judith's ability to juggle career, marriage, and a child. It had been a big shock when things had fallen apart for her friend, and Liz had been taken aback to find such a paragon of self-assurance so upset and unsure of herself. Yet from the look of her now, Judith had picked herself up and built a new life.

'Don't be sorry. I'm all right now, Liz, and so is Daisy. She's at a very good school here and doing well. Mrs Ryan collects her every day, and looks after her until I get home. Don't be fooled by the white hair – she's quite feisty. But I like that. And I've come to rely on her – it's busy at the office, believe it or not.'

'So Michael Binding was telling me.'

Judith gave a knowing smile. 'I know you've never been keen on him, Liz. Nor me. He hasn't changed much but at least he lets us get on with it – I think he's got enough on his plate with the politicians not to interfere too much. Have you seen Dave?'

'Not yet. They told me he was away on a case.'

Judith nodded. 'Yes, he seems to think he's onto something new.' Her handsome, composed face suddenly broke into an unrestrained grin. 'Dave's so glad you're here. And so am I. There really is a lot more going on than people in London realise. I don't know what you're feeling about this posting, but I promise you one thing. You won't be bored.'

8

'They could easily stop it doing that,' said Technical Ted Poyser to his two companions, as the gate closed behind them with a long drawn-out squeal, then crashed shut.

'Good job they didn't. Or we wouldn't know there was anything going on.'

'If there is,' said Ted sardonically.

Ted had decided they would go into the gatehouse in daylight, dressed to look like National Trust visitors, letting themselves in with the key Robinson had provided. So Maureen Hayes had dropped them off in the village and they had walked the mile or so to the house, carrying their equipment in large rucksacks.

In the office, Ted, the service's master of all things electronic, didn't look remotely like an average National Trust member. But now his long black dyed hair was tucked inside a woolly hat with a pom-pom on top, which also hid his gold earring; he had discarded his black leather jacket and biker's boots in favour of a green anorak; and his costume of walking trousers and knee socks was finished off with brown walking shoes. The whole ensemble looked OK at a distance.

'I wouldn't mind a few days here,' said John Forrest as he finished unpacking his drills and looked out of the dining room window at the wide bay. The tide was in now, and the little football-like heads of seals were popping up inquisitively from the ripples.

'Well we haven't got a few days,' replied Ted, 'so let's get on with it.'

A couple of hours later, after some muted drilling and hammering, Ted was on the phone to the office at Palace Barracks. 'There's a woman with a dog just coming up to the gate now. How's the focus?'

'Clear as a bell,' came back the answer. 'But hang on there till a car comes past – we need to check the angle.'

A minute or two later a small hatchback came out, driven by a woman with a small child in a car seat at the back. 'You need to adjust the angle. The number plates are out of the frame. Just a few degrees down and to the left.' Ted relayed the instruction to John Forrest in the loft, the adjustment was made and the OK given.

As the team started to pack up they heard the engine of another car coming down the track. Ted stood at the side of the dining room window, half-concealed by the curtain, and watched as a red Vauxhall Vectra with racing tyres slowed as it reached the gate. There were two men sitting in front, and another in the back seat, but from the house he couldn't see their faces. As the gate clanged shut and the car drove away he thumbed in a number on his phone. 'Did you get that?'

'Brilliant,' said the voice at the other end. 'Front seat, clear enough for *Hello* magazine. But we're not going to be able to get the rear seat passengers, I'm afraid.'

9

The camera at the gatehouse had been busy. There were photographs of walkers, and several of a black Toyota hybrid car which came and went and had been identified by Phil Robinson as belonging to the holiday tenants who had taken a fortnight's let. But Liz was staring at several pictures of a red Vauxhall.

'The owner is called Malone,' said Dave Armstrong, standing behind her and looking over her shoulder. 'That's him driving. He has form.'

'What kind of form?' asked Liz, still looking at the photographs of the car.

'Six years in the eighties for the attempted murder of an RUC officer. He left his fingerprints all over a bomb that didn't go off underneath the policeman's car. After that he was more careful. We couldn't get him on terrorism, but he's got a list of convictions for violence. A GBH charge when he worked as a doorman in a nightclub in Cookstown, a couple of domestics when his wife got fed up and rang the police. Lately he's calmed down. He's middle-aged, like we'll all be soon.'

'Speak for yourself,' said Liz.

She looked again at the photographs. She could see the two

45

figures in the front seat clearly but the back seat passenger was not identifiable.

'Who is the other guy in the front seat?'

'Don't know,' said Dave.

'What do you think's going on down there?' she asked.

Dave shrugged. 'Hard to say. But I doubt it's above board.'

'Do we know who really owns the farmhouse?' asked Liz.

'It's a company in Belfast. I've got the directors' names, but none of them has a trace in the files.' His face brightened. 'I was planning to go out there this morning to have a snoop around. Why don't you come too? It will give you a chance to see a bit of the country around Belfast and get yourself orientated.'

'Are you talking about trespassing on private property?'

'Of course not,' he said, though from the glint in his eyes Liz was sure that was exactly what he was proposing. 'There's a public track that runs from the gatehouse up to a small parking place, then a footpath leads round the headland. It's used quite a lot by dog walkers. We should be able to get a good look at the farmhouse from there.'

She was surprised how quickly they moved out of the city into countryside. A dreary grey sky hung like a lead lining above them. A gusty wind was throwing rain against the windscreen in short, erratic bursts and as Dave came up behind a slow agricultural truck, spray from its wheels engulfed them.

'Not a great day for a stroll in the country,' said Liz, ruefully contemplating her walking shoes and wondering if they really were waterproof.

Yet half an hour later when they had reached the Irish Sea and were driving along a shoreline that seemed entirely deserted, a watery sun had broken through and was sparkling on the waves. 'Pretty?' asked Dave mildly.

Liz nodded. 'I hadn't realised how beautiful the countryside round here is,' she said.

'Neither had I. I thought it would be all council estates with "Up the IRA" and "Brits Out" painted on the walls.'

Through the long thin village street, Dave turned sharp left round the bay, along the lane and over a narrow bridge from where they could see the closed gate into the National Trust estate.

'How are we going to get in?' said Liz. 'Don't we need a gadget to open the gate?'

'Got one,' said Dave, slowing down and fishing in his pocket. 'Ted made a copy of the one Phil Robinson lent us.'

They passed in front of the stone gatehouse, with its high pitched gable. The black car was parked outside, indicating that the paying visitors were at home.

'Do we know who lives in the farmhouse?' asked Liz.

'Phil Robinson thought an old lady leased it, presumably from the company in Belfast.' He paused. 'I wonder if anyone's there now.'

The wind had picked up and now that the rain had passed the temperature had fallen. Liz, shivering in her city raincoat, resolved to go shopping for some outdoor clothes as she followed Dave, warm in his fleece-lined parka. The footpath ran from the small car park through a stand of pine trees towards the sea. Seagulls were swooping over the water and a flock of small birds was picking something off the low bushes, keeping just ahead of Liz and Dave as they walked. The path led parallel to a dry-stone wall that had crumbled over the years. Beyond the wall Liz could see the foundations of what must have once been an enormous house, the centrepiece of the estate. The path stopped at the corner of the stone wall, but Dave kept walking on.

'Are we still on the public footpath?' queried Liz.

'As far as I know,' said Dave, as they crested a mound and suddenly faced a farmhouse, less than a hundred yards away. It was a long two storey-structure with neatly painted stucco sides. The roof tiles had been re-laid recently and had yet to lose their gloss. Behind the house at one side was an outbuilding, a squat windowless brick structure about the size of a double garage.

Dave took a small pair of binoculars from his pocket but suddenly swung round and faced the sea, still with his binoculars to his eyes. Then quickly dropping them back in his pocket he turned towards Liz, threw both arms around her and kissed her full on the lips. Before she could begin to object he kissed her again.

What the hell was Dave up to? Furious, Liz was about to dig an indignant fist into his ribs, then slap his face for good measure, when Dave disengaged just enough to whisper, 'Someone's coming.'

She understood, and hugged him back fiercely, feeling more than a little ridiculous.

Then a voice rang out. 'This isn't a Lover's Lane.'

Dave and Liz let go of each other and turned together to face a man in a long waxed coat. He was tall and lean, with short greying hair, square features and rimless glasses. Behind him stood a shorter, dark-skinned man in a black leather jacket. His hands were deep in his pockets, and he was looking at them with dull, expressionless eyes. Liz felt pretty sure she knew what was in the pockets, and her backbone crawled.

'Sorry,' said Dave, in an uncanny approximation of an Ulster accent. 'The footpath just seemed to disappear.'

The man looked at Dave, then moved onto Liz, giving her a probing stare, a soulless once-over that had nothing to do with her being a woman – she might as well have been a piece of machinery for all the emotion in the man's eyes.

The man pointed sharply in the direction from which they'd come. 'The footpath's there. This is private. Didn't you see the notice?' There was no trace of an Ulster or an Irish accent, but something flat about his pronunciation didn't sound English. The man looked back at Dave. 'You're on my land.'

'Not for long,' said Dave. 'Our apologies.' He took Liz's arm and started walking quickly back towards the corner of the wall.

They went along in silence until they were well down the path towards the beach. Then Dave stopped and looked behind them. 'That shorter, heavy-set guy followed us to make sure we left,' he said. 'Did you recognise him? He's the man in the front seat in a couple of those pictures.'

'Not exactly a pleasant encounter.'

'I'll say. But what does he expect? If there is a sign, I didn't see it.'

As they retraced their steps to the car park, Dave said, 'Still, it had its upside.'

'You mean we got a sight of the inhabitants?'

Dave shook his head, then gave a grin. 'No. I was thinking of our clinch. Wait till I tell them back in Thames House. My stock will go through the roof.'

'Don't you dare,' said Liz. She added with a smile, 'That was strictly business and don't you forget it, Dave Armstrong.'

10

It had been almost two weeks since her arrival, and Liz was finding a rhythm to life, driving to the office each morning and returning against the rush-hour traffic at six – if she was lucky – or at seven or even eight when there was lots to do.

She had settled in to her flat, unpacking the few belongings she had brought with her, which she had supplemented by the odd find at the Saturday flea market, so the place was beginning to look slightly more lived in. Not that she had done it single-handed – one afternoon, Mrs Ryan, Daisy's childminder, had bearded her in the hall. 'Would you be needing a cleaner, Miss Carlyle?'

'I hadn't really thought.'

Mrs Ryan said, 'I'd think about it if I were you, miss. You work hard – you're just as bad as Mrs Spratt. You need to take it easy when you've got a minute to relax, like. And not be worrying about washing your smalls and vacuuming your sitting room.'

Liz smiled, seeing the truth of this. 'Would you know of someone?'

'I'd do it myself, miss,' the woman said firmly. 'It won't take long at all, and I'll charge you just the same as I do Mrs Spratt.'

'Well, if you're sure you have time—'

Mrs Ryan waved this away with a hand. 'Time's the one thing I have got, miss. My poor husband's been with his maker these last five years, and I've only my son Danny to look after, and he's out at work all day. I've more than enough time.'

So now Liz was living in unaccustomed cleanliness and order, which she had to admit to herself was rather pleasant, though she did miss the homely untidiness of her Kentish Town flat. She hadn't done anything about letting it. She wasn't even sure she wanted to.

Judith had asked her down to supper, after Daisy was in bed, and the two women had stayed up late, catching up with each other. Liz had reciprocated Judith's hospitality by cooking a big Sunday lunch for her and Daisy. How eventful Judith's recent life had been, thought Liz, and how well she had picked herself up from her husband's disgrace and their failed marriage. What had Liz to report in return? Nothing really, in terms of change to her private life. There was still no one man in her life, no marriage, no children; only the solace of doing work she enjoyed and knew she was good at.

The sole news of Charles she had heard came in a letter from her mother and it was not what she wanted to hear. Her mother and Edward had been to have supper with him, and Charles seemed very well. Her mother went on that Charles was busy again with his garden, and that he had help from one of his neighbours – that nice woman Alison who'd been at the funeral. Alison had also been a big help with the boys, apparently, and Sam, who was not starting boarding until the following September, went every day after school to Alison's house for his tea and to do his homework until Charles came home from work. Such a good arrangement, wrote Susan Carlyle enthusiastically; it must make life so much easier for Charles. I bet, thought Liz grumpily. I wonder what this Alison woman is getting out of it. There was no mention in her mother's letter of whether Charles had asked after Liz, which made her not so much grumpy, as sad.

She had explored the city centre extensively, and found that she liked Belfast. There were still plenty of signs of the sectarian divide that had caused the Troubles in the first place – IRA graffiti splashed in paint across a building she drove by each morning, for example – but they seemed like memories of the past rather than evidence of imminent hostilities.

But she thought again about her surroundings after a meeting with Michael Binding. The chief constable was concerned about an increase in activity by breakaway Republican groups. There were signs that policemen, current and retired, were being targeted for assassination. And threats were being made against contractors working for the police, and even against social workers. Binding had said, 'Ministers are very concerned that all this activity might upset the political balance. It's been hard enough to get it all in place. If one of these groups succeeds in killing a target, it could endanger the entire peace process.'

He looked worried for the first time. 'We don't want to make too many waves, but potential targets are being advised to increase their personal security. And we all of us need to be careful too.' He looked out of the window as he went on: 'Make sure that if you take a car from the pool you keep it parked at the garage of your flat, or here in the car park – don't leave it on the street. The mechanics change the number plates regularly, but we can't take any chances. And if you detect any sign of surveillance, please report it to A4 and me immediately.'

He turned his head and looked again at Liz with a thin smile. 'But of course I don't need to tell you any of this, with all your counter terrorism experience.'

Then why did you? thought Liz, trying her best to smile back.

Binding seemed to remember something, for he said suddenly, 'By the way, I've heard from A4 about that car you drove in from the airport. The wheel was damaged, but they think that's because you drove on it – the tyre was completely shot.'

'But what caused the blowout?'

Binding raised both hands in a 'who knows?' gesture. 'It could have been anything. A nail on the road, broken glass, even the way you were driving, I suppose. There wasn't enough of the tyre left to tell.'

Liz bristled at the suggestion that her driving had caused the blowout. It seemed a gratuitous insult. And how could Binding sound so certain it had just been an accident? But she resisted the urge to challenge him, knowing it would just confirm his view that women were hysterical.

11

Dave poked his head round Liz's office door. 'I'm going to see an old RUC Special Branch contact this afternoon. Maybe he can cast some light on things. I'm taking the photographs from the camera to show him.'

'Where are you meeting him?'

'At his house. He didn't want to come here. I'm getting the feeling that this place is behind enemy lines, which is a bit spooky.'

'What's his name?'

'Jimmy Fergus. He's retired from full-time work, but he's still winding up some of the old RUC cases. He's supposed to be a mine of information.' Dave sounded sceptical.

'I know him. He was a big help when I was on that mole case a few years ago. I'd like to come, too.'

Fergus lived in a comfortable suburb on the north side of the city. As they drove there Dave asked, 'How's it going with Binding?'

Liz shot him a look, but Dave kept his eyes on the road straight ahead of him. Eventually she caught him looking sideways at her, and they both laughed.

Liz said, 'He seems to think I screwed up that pool car. Apparently my inferior driving skills caused a blowout.'

'That's ridiculous,' said Dave.

'He didn't think so. Then he gave me a lecture on security – he seemed obsessed with where I parked my car.'

'Well,' said Dave, 'Binding's got a point, even if it kills me to say it. Don't underestimate the danger. Oh I know, on the surface it's all sweetness and light, but just twenty years ago any IRA man in Ulster would have given their eye teeth to kill either of us.'

He turned now onto a quiet tree-lined road, with detached red brick houses set back behind high hedges and no parked cars by the kerb. Only a van delivering laundry disturbed the peace.

He's lost weight but he's hardly aged at all, thought Liz, as her old acquaintance opened the front door. She was surprised to find him still working for the police service. When they had last met he had talked happily about taking over his father's farm in Antrim. But since then he'd married again – wife number four if Liz remembered right – so maybe he needed the salary.

'Liz,' he said beaming, and gave her a big kiss on the cheek. She introduced Dave, who sat silently, shifting in his chair as they talked of old times. Eventually, bored with a conversation in which he had no part, Dave opened his briefcase and laid out the photographs on the coffee table.

'I know three of them,' said Jimmy Fergus, leaning back in his comfortable chair and surveying the enlarged prints now strewn on the table. He scratched a finger against his pock-marked cheek. He was a big man, whose suits never quite fitted his powerful frame, and whose tie always slid an informal inch down his shirt front. But the ruffled sloppiness of his appearance was misleading; Liz knew he was an excellent policeman, with an intuitive feel for a case and a nose for what people were really like. These qualities had seen him steadily promoted over the years. During the worst years of the Troubles, when dozens of policemen had been murdered, they had also helped keep him alive.

'This guy,' he said, pointing at the photograph of the driver of the car that had passed the gatehouse several times, 'is Terry Malone. Long-time Provo volunteer. Enforcer type. Nothing sophisticated.' Fergus gave a short laugh. 'Got a Vauxhall now, has he? He's come up in the world. He used to drive an old banger that was always breaking down on the Falls Road.'

He paused to contemplate the photographs again. 'These other two are called Mickey Kinsella and John O'Sullivan. Small-time villains basically, not as heavy as Malone. This fourth guy. Don't know him – looks Spanish? What do you think?'

'Maybe he's Black Irish,' said Dave facetiously.

Fergus ignored him. 'Come to think of it, we had a tip off that someone had come here from the Costa del Sol. A hit man named Gonzales. Terry Malone was never an angel, but this guy's reported to be seriously hard.'

'Who's he working for then?' asked Dave. He seemed a bit prickly with Jimmy Fergus, while Jimmy was as easygoing in his rumpled way as Liz remembered.

'That's what nobody seems to know. And we'd like to find out – you don't bring in somebody all the way from Spain unless he's got a role to play. Where were these pictures taken?'

Liz explained, telling him about the tip-off from Phil Robinson and their reconnaissance of the farmhouse.

Dave broke in, 'We've checked who owns the farmhouse. A company – Fraternal Holdings. It's a private enterprise, Belfast based, with offices just off Castle Street.'

'Never heard of it,' said Fergus. 'What's it do?'

Dave shrugged. 'Hard to say. They describe themselves as consultants.'

Fergus snorted. 'Who doesn't these days? Every retired copper I know says he's a "private security consultant". It usually means they work the door at the local disco.'

'This is different,' Dave said testily. 'I drove past the offices – they've got an entire floor in a new building. The rents are high in that area, so there has to be some kind of business going on.'

'Who runs the business?'

'The managing director is one Seamus Piggott.'

'Ring any bells?' asked Liz.

Fergus thought, then shook his head. 'Can't say it does. It sounds familiar, but I think that's just because my old man worshipped the jockey Lester Piggott.'

Liz reached for one of the photographs and pushed it towards Jimmy. It was of an Audi that had passed the gatehouse, with the man named Malone at the wheel. Sitting beside him was a thin man in a suit. Liz said, 'I'm pretty sure the man in the passenger seat is the same man who confronted us when we were looking at the farmhouse. He didn't act like a thug, more like an irate owner, with muscle behind him.'

Fergus peered carefully at the still. 'I don't recognise the guy. I don't know the name either.' He sounded puzzled, and when he looked at Liz, he seemed uncharacteristically unsettled.

'What is it, Jimmy?' she asked.

'How can I say this? I thought I knew all the players, but I don't know anything about this guy. And that worries me. If a foreign hit man's involved, there must be something going on, and normally I would expect to have picked up at least a hint of it. But I haven't.' He gave a modest smile. 'Sorry. Maybe I'm getting past my sell-by date.'

'Well, it's not your responsibility anymore,' said Liz. And it was true. Any case with even the faintest whiff of sectarian politics had been transferred to MI5.

'Do you mind that?' asked Dave.

'Good God no,' said Fergus. 'It would have been a nightmare. If the new justice minister turns out to be an ex-IRA man, how could you go to him and say you've learned an old comrade of his is planning to blow up a policeman? It would never have worked.' He shook his head at the thought. 'I'm happy for you guys to take charge of that; it makes life far simpler.'

'Fair enough,' said Liz, then turned back to the business in hand. 'What if this mystery man Piggott isn't local? If he's the same character we met, he didn't sound any sort of Irish.'

Fergus shrugged. 'Could be from the mainland. First or second generation Irish there.'

Dave said, 'We've done some basic checking. Couldn't find anyone of that name in our files, and Dublin hasn't got anybody either. They've got some Seamus Piggotts, but none of them fit.'

'What about the States?' Liz asked. 'That might account for his strange accent.'

'Wait a minute,' Dave protested. 'How do we know we're looking for Seamus Piggott anyway? Or that he's the guy in the picture, or the same guy we saw the other day?'

There was silence in the room, and Liz realised both men were looking at her.

She said, 'We don't know, Dave. But what else do we have? Three small-time crooks and a Spanish hood. That doesn't explain a swanky set of offices in downtown Belfast, or a suspiciously expensive-looking farmhouse whose owner is paranoid about outsiders. There's something going on, and I'll feel much better once we know who Seamus Piggott is.'

12

Antoine Milraud stepped out of the tall double doors of his apricot-pink villa set high up above the little Provençal town of Bandol. He stood at the point where the drive, having wound upwards through the garden from the security gates, ended on a tarmac apron broad enough for a car to turn round. He was waiting for his driver, who was late, and he was annoyed. Milraud liked to be in control but there were some things he couldn't do for himself. He needed the chauffeur; it wasn't only driving that he required from him.

From where he stood Milraud could see over the tops of the umbrella pines towards the harbour where large white motor launches and yachts were moored alongside the art deco casino. Everything was dead at this time of the year, no tourists and very few residents around, and he liked it that way. If he turned to his left, he could look across the pine-clad hills towards the naval base at Toulon, and on a very clear day he might see the tall superstructure of a large warship. But today he could see no further than the first headland, for the clouds sat low on the hills, threatening rain. The mimosa flowers that covered the trees along his drive were being tossed by a January mistral, and as Milraud looked down at the road snaking into the village from the Marseilles/Toulon motorway he felt the sharp edge to the air. His car and driver should have been visible but there was still no sign of them. Shivering a little, he turned and went back into the house, firmly closing the doors behind him.

Milraud did not often think about his past. There had been too many episodes he would prefer to forget. After eleven years in Paris with his former bosses, chronic mutual fatigue had set in. The salary had been negligible, the suburb that was all he had been able to afford had not matched his self-image, and when his employers had accused him of overreacting, of using hammers to crack nuts, it had become increasingly obvious that his prospects for promotion were nil. He had managed to extricate himself from his post most advantageously, and the eight years since he had left had been good ones for Milraud.

He had his shop in Toulon, another in London's Camden Market, and a third in Belfast. They did well: antique furniture had lost some of its cachet in the last few years, but the growing demand for antique weapons, swords, pistols, cannons, all Milraud's speciality, had more than compensated for that downturn. All his shops brought in good profits, enough to justify employing a manager for each one, and now there was a catalogue business as well, which had gone online two years before and was thriving. His profits would have satisfied any dealer in the antiques trade, but Milraud wanted more: to pay his chauffeur's salary and maintain the Mercedes limousine he was paid to drive; to keep up the villa in Bandol as well as to employ the staff who ran the place, and to pay for the designer clothes and jewellery that his wife (still asleep upstairs) loved to flaunt in the restaurants and clubs she patronised in Marseilles and Toulon, as well as on her trips to Paris and London.

So although his antique business was successful, his three shops and the catalogue did not underwrite his current lifestyle; nor were they the reason that his driver carried a 9 mm automatic pistol under his dark-blue uniform suit.

His second business, for which his antique shops provided cover, was not one in which you made many friends, so he took extensive precautions to protect himself – electric gates to his property, razor wire on top of its perimeter wall, a state-of-the art movement-sensor alarm and cameras, and a driver who doubled as a bodyguard. Yet to date the greatest danger he'd had to face had been flying through a sandstorm in a prop plane to the desert redoubt of a customer in the Emirates.

But he had recently begun to wonder whether someone was paying him unwanted attention. The telephone in his house had gone out of order and since the line had been restored, he seemed to hear a strange echo in the background whenever he used it; his banker, discreetly located in Lausanne, had told him of an inquiry from France that had been withdrawn when challenged; a *permis de construire* had been issued for a planned extension to his house but only after an inspection of the interior which seemed to be unnecessarily detailed.

Was someone probing his affairs? And if so, who? It might be anyone – including his former employers, of whom it had been said that though you could choose to leave them, you could not guarantee they would leave you.

Conceivably, all this suspect activity could be entirely innocent. When you are on the lookout, you see a lot of shadows. Milraud had been trained long ago to be suspicious of coincidences, but after all, he told himself, one must avoid paranoia. A life of fear was not a life.

The buzzer sounded in the hall. Milraud stepped outside again as the Mercedes rolled quietly to a halt on the apron. The driver got out to open the car's door.

'You're late.'

'I beg your pardon, monsieur. There was unexpected traffic coming out of town.'

'Leave earlier next time,' he said brusquely, and slid smoothly into the cream-coloured luxury of the rear seats for the short journey.

It was a drive of only fifteen minutes to Toulon, where Madame Dipeau would be opening up the shop at any moment. The route took them parallel to the coast for twelve kilometres, and then down into the town. Every few minutes, Milraud turned and glanced out of the back window. Once he saw a telephone company van which seemed to be following them, but it turned off before he could be sure. Shrugging his shoulders, as if to rid himself of unwelcome thoughts, he sat straight in his seat and looked out of the side window as the car swung past the long, arcaded Maison des Cordes, past the elegant pink and white naval headquarters building behind its massive security gates manned by tough-looking sailors, past the great pillared doors of the Musée de la Marine, and into the avenue de la République, where it drew up at the end of a small side street of eighteenth-century buildings, the rue d'Alger.

Here Milraud got out and leaned down to speak through the front window. 'Come back at twelve,' he ordered. 'I am having lunch in Marseilles.'

He walked halfway up the street, through a weathered stone doorway and into the shop where Madame Dipeau was bringing out a pair of fine silver duelling pistols from the vault. She was a widow of indeterminate years, perhaps sixty, possibly seventy-five, who had made herself expert in eighteenth-century weapons. Even more important from Milraud's point of view, she was careful and discreet.

'*Bonjour monsieur*,' she said quietly now, with the nasal twang of the south. 'There has been a telephone call for you. A Monsieur Donovan. He said he would call again.'

'*Merci madame*,' he said, and went to his office in the rear of the shop, closing the door behind him. He turned on the small laptop he had brought with him, for much of the detail of his non-antiques transactions was too sensitive to be arranged on the telephone. Sitting down at his desk with yesterday's local paper, he lit a Disque Bleu, and waited.

Twenty minutes later the phone on his desk trilled faintly. He picked it up at once. 'Oui,' he said.

'It's me,' said the man calling himself Donovan. Though the name was unfamiliar to Milraud, the flat accent was unmistakable. Milraud knew immediately who his caller was.

'*Bonjour*,' said Milraud. 'It's been a while.' They had met during a negotiation in Spain several years before, and since then they had kept in touch.

'Too long. It would be good to meet.'

'*Oui?*' said Milraud cautiously.

'Yes. Were you planning to be over here any time soon?'

'*Franchement non.*' He'd visited Northern Ireland before Christmas and his next trip was planned for June. Business there was at best intermittent. Certainly not what it had been.

'That's a pity.'

'I can always alter my plans,' said Milraud, reaching for his diary. He respected Piggott. Piggott didn't waste time. His own or other people's.

'It could be worth your while. I may have some business for you.'

'Would this be a distance requirement, or close by?' he said, carefully avoiding any word that might trigger a listening device. He knew the man would understand his meaning.

'Both, actually. Not a big deal but important to make it happen.'

The best, thought Milraud. He knew what 'making it happen' meant, and it would cost the other man. He looked at the open page of his diary. There was nothing he could not cancel or postpone. 'I can be there the day after tomorrow. How does that sound?'

'Good. Ring me when you've arrived.' And the other phone went dead.

The next morning Milraud flew business class from Marseilles to Paris, where he broke his journey to visit a small office on the avenue Foch. It was run by a veteran of the trade, a Dr Emil Picard, whose business ran from East Timor to Colombia. Milraud was confident he could fill 'Mr Donovan's' requirements from his own holdings, but some back up was always prudent.

After establishing the position with Dr Picard, Milraud checked into his hotel near the Place de la Concorde, had an excellent dinner in its restaurant, then entertained a visitor from an escort agency in the privacy of his room upstairs.

He continued his journey next day, catching an Aer Lingus flight that landed in Belfast in the early afternoon. He had reserved a car at the airport and he drove it to the Belfast Hilton, a concrete tower right on the River Lagan in the middle of the city, where he had booked a small suite. At precisely five o'clock he phoned a number he had memorised, and arranged a meeting at an office nearby for the following day at eleven o'clock. From his bedroom window, Milraud could just see the street where the meeting would take place. He ignored the magnificent view of the distant hills and drew the curtains. He had work to do.

It would not have been surprising to find an antiques dealer scrutinising the thick catalogue of a recent sale at Bonham's in London, but if anyone had looked closely, a few of the pages would have seemed at the least odd. The detailed specifications and prices listed there evidently referred to more sophisticated and up to date goods than those listed in the rest of the catalogue. Donovan must be planning something big, Milraud told himself. He mentally added a nought to his own prospective invoice.

13

'We've got an Audi saloon, black A6, slowing down. It's pulled into the car park.'

Standing in the Operations Room at Palace Barracks, the A4 controller Reggie Purvis was listening intently. When the speaker had finished, he said, 'Can you get the number plate?'

'Victor, Echo, Zulu Seven . . .' the voice continued.

Back in the Observation Post in the centre of Belfast, less than ten miles away from the Operations Room, Arthur Haverford listened as Jerry Rayman finished reciting the registration numbers, then gave a large yawn as he put down his binoculars and reached for the cup of tea he had just made.

He was four years past retirement age, and though he'd been delighted to be called back by the service, he was feeling all of his sixty-four years. Still, he told himself, mustn't grumble; far better to be sitting here than pretending to be enjoying some Golden Age of retirement with Moira, his wife of forty-one years, with his days spent walking the dog in Tulse Hill.

There was a shortage of trained surveillance officers, they'd explained – with the terrorist threat increasing every day, A4 simply didn't have enough good men to go round. Or women, Arthur told himself, since Maureen Hayes, who was sitting in

66

a car not sixty yards away, could be sensitive about that sort of thing.

He knew they didn't want him for mobile surveillance; he was too old for that game now. He'd thought he'd just be helping out part-time in London, providing back up when Thames House found itself short of people to man the observation posts. But it had turned out to be more than that – here he was in Northern Ireland of all places, working full-time too until the powers that be could find enough permanent bodies for posting here.

Jerry Rayman was another old lag brought in to help, which suited Arthur as they had worked together in A4 for years. Jerry read a lot and had a quirky sense of humour that helped pass the time. And who knew how long it would last? Enjoy it while you may my son, he told himself, thinking again with relief of those dog walks he was missing.

The two men sat in a room on the second floor of a Victorian brick office building in the middle of Belfast. It had been refurbished and newly leased to a software group that had not yet moved in – and were therefore happy to rent out a single office at the front for the temporary use of a company (Dodd's Ultra Logistics) that had offered two months' rent up front.

Directly opposite, across the street, was another, much more modern office building, all glass and steel. Its first floor was let to Fraternal Holdings, the object of Arthur Haverford and Jerry Rayman's scrutiny. This was only the third day of surveillance from this temporary observation post, and so far it had been quiet. Quiet? thought Arthur. More like stone dead. From this vantage point they had a good view of the parking lot, which had four spaces; until this morning not one of these spaces had been occupied. Maybe now it would pick up, thought Arthur, as through his headphones he heard Maureen Hayes announce, 'The Audi's parking now. In the managing director's space.'

Below on the street, sitting for the last half hour in a Peugeot 405 directly across from the parking lot, Maureen Hayes was apparently reading a book, as if waiting for someone. She lifted the paperback slightly as she turned a page, which allowed her to point the slim camera inside in the direction of the Audi, where a man in a leather jacket was getting out of the driving seat. Someone in the back was also getting out – a thin, greying man dressed in a suit and tie. Must be the MD, she thought, as the shutter automatically clicked open and shut repeatedly while the men walked towards the entrance to the building. 'Two in,' announced Maureen to the microphone in her lap.

The reception area of the company was at the front of the building opposite, behind the huge plate glass window, and from his chair set back behind a partially drawn blind, Arthur had a clear view of it. He put down his tea and took up the binoculars, focusing on the reception desk. Twenty seconds later the lift must have opened (he could not quite see it), as the same two men entered the reception area. Neither stopped at the desk, but simply walked on, disappearing into the back of the building.

Arthur spoke into his microphone. 'The targets have entered Fraternal's offices.'

After this brief excitement, nothing happened for another hour. Inactivity was a watcher's enemy, but Arthur and Jerry were old hands, and knew how to make the time pass – usually by recounting stories that, though told many times before, had managed not to go stale – without ever losing focus on the parking lot and building across the street.

Suddenly Jerry started speaking into the microphone of his headset. 'We have another car pulling into the car park.' He read out the registration numbers for a blue Astra. An older man got out and walked into the building. He wore a parka and faded khaki trousers, and again Maureen raised her paperback.

A minute later Arthur, watching through his binoculars, saw the man wave at the receptionist and walk past her into the offices. Arthur reported that as soon as the man had passed her, the girl at the desk picked up the phone and spoke urgently into it.

On a hunch he kept the binoculars trained on the reception area, and sure enough, just a few moments later the older man reappeared. A heavy-set man was with him, whom Arthur recognised as the driver of the black Audi. He had a hand on the shoulder of the older man – it wasn't clear if he was consoling him, or strong-arming him out of the office, and then they disappeared in the direction of the lift.

Arthur swung the glasses down to the side entrance of the building. When the older man emerged he was talking to himself, looking agitated and angry. He got into his car and started the ignition right away, then accelerated with a squeal of tyres out of the car park.

'Something's got his back up,' said Arthur to Jerry.

They heard in their headphones Maureen's announcement from her car down in the street that the subject had left. Then to Arthur's surprise, only half a minute later she broke in again:

'Subject's pulled over down the street. He's parked and he's sitting in the car. He's got a bird's-eye view of the exit to the car park. Shall I recce?' she asked. This would involve her walking past the parked Astra, and surreptitiously photographing its occupant to get a close-up shot.

'Negative,' said Reggie Purvis back in the Ops room. 'Sit tight.'

Five minutes later another car arrived and parked. Its driver emerged, a stocky, square-shouldered man with a round bullet head and dark hair cut short. He was nattily dressed in a blazer, cream silk roll-necked shirt and wool trousers, and this slight flamboyance and the black leather purse he carried in one hand made Arthur wonder if he was gay. Though there was also a faint echo of the military in his upright bearing.

Jerry called out the numbers of his registration, and sixty seconds later Arthur confirmed that the man had stopped at Fraternal Holdings reception, then been sent through.

'What do you make of him then?' asked Jerry Rayman.

'Fancy dresser. Got to be gay,' said Arthur.

'I think he's foreign.'

'Yeah. That's it, probably a Frog.'

'Do you think the old boy in the Astra was waiting for him?'

'Could be.'

'Whatever he was doing inside,' Jerry declared, 'he didn't look happy when he came out.'

Forty minutes later the 'old boy' was still there when the foreign-looking visitor came out of the building. He drove away, heading west, and Maureen reported the blue Astra starting up and following him.

'Ah,' said Arthur triumphantly, when he heard Maureen's report. 'So he *was* waiting for him.'

14

Dave was walking carefully to his desk in the agent-runners' room, balancing a sheaf of surveillance photographs on top of a mug of coffee, when the phone on his desk began to ring. The flashing red light indicated that the call was coming in on one of his agent lines. In his haste to get to it before it stopped ringing, he banged into the corner of his desk and lurched forward, dropping the photographs all over the floor and spilling hot coffee on his hand. Cursing under his breath, he grabbed the handset and said, '7827.'

'I've got something for you,' said a hoarse, Ulster voice that he didn't recognise. It sounded middle aged, certainly not young.

'Who's this?' asked Dave, his pulse quickening.

'You don't know me, but I've got something for you.'

'What sort of thing?' Dave pressed the button that activated the recorder.

'Information. I'm not saying any more. I need to meet.'

'You'll have to tell me a bit more before I can do that. What's the information about?'

'It's about what's going on now.'

'What do you mean, going on? Going on where?'

'I'm not saying any more over the phone. I'll only talk if I can see you.'

'Just give me a steer. What are we talking about here?'

'I was a Provo volunteer. We're supposed to be on ceasefire. But there's things happening. I know what's going on and who's doing it.'

'You mean the breakaway groups? How do you know about them? Have you spoken to the police?' Dave was desperately trying to keep him on the line.

'It's just for you, not the police. You can't trust them. I'll ring again at twelve o'clock and you can give me the meeting place.'

The phone clicked and the light on Dave's handset went out.

Hooray, thought Dave, picking up the photographs from the floor and grabbing some tissues from his desk drawer to mop up the spilled coffee. This was what he liked. Action.

He turned on his computer screen and pulled up the list of available operational premises – safe houses suitable for meeting a source.

Liz Carlyle was examining the surveillance photographs taken by the A4 team outside Fraternal Holdings. It was a cold, sparkling morning and the sun was glancing through the window onto the prints on her desk. The new offices were well heated, almost overheated. She was feeling hot in the thick polo-neck sweater she had put on when she saw the frost glittering like snow in the children's playground outside her bedroom window. She was just contemplating removing the sweater, wondering whether the T-shirt she had on underneath was decent enough to reveal, when Dave walked into her office.

'You look very bushy tailed,' she said, observing his flushed cheeks. 'What were you up to last night? Do I detect the effect of lovely Lucy?'

'No, I haven't seen Lucy for weeks. It's strictly work,' Dave replied with a wide grin. 'I've had a phone call.'

'Lucky you! Sit down and tell me more. Who from?'

'That's the interesting part. I don't know. But I'm going to find out pretty soon.' And he gave Liz the gist of the message from the anonymous caller. 'Call came from a phone box, of course. He's calling back in . . .' Dave looked at his watch – 'two and a half hours.'

'What are you going to say to him?'

'I'm going to meet him in Blue Lagoon,' Dave replied, giving the code name of one of the safe houses.

'Which one's that? I haven't seen what we've got in the way of operational properties.'

As Dave described the location of Blue Lagoon, Liz's mind was turning over the situation. She was not used to being Dave's boss and she hesitated to start throwing her weight about at this early stage, but she felt uneasy at Dave's breezy approach.

'How did he get your number?'

'I don't know. I didn't ask him. But it's a number I've used for some time and it's known to the police. Frankly, he was pretty cagey over the phone. He said he'll only talk in person – he claims it isn't safe any other way.'

'He's probably right there,' said Liz. 'Though face to face isn't any guarantee of safety either – his or yours. I can't say I like the sound of this.'

Dave shrugged. 'Come on, Liz; we've got nothing to lose.'

'What back-up are you planning?'

'I don't need back-up for this. It sounds straightforward. There is a ceasefire on, you know.'

Liz hesitated for a moment. She was unwilling to have a confrontation with him. After all, she was a new arrival and Dave, who'd been here longer, must have a better feel for the situation. But, though she rated Dave very highly, she knew that he had one flaw as an agent runner – impetuosity. He was never reckless, but when action competed with caution, action would usually win. This didn't feel right to her; it could easily be a set up.

So she said, 'There may be an IRA ceasefire, but he's offering information on the breakaways. And they're certainly not on ceasefire. He's already said there's stuff going on. I think you should have full anti-surveillance back-up for this meeting and that means meeting him out in the open, outside the city, and definitely not in a safe house.'

'He'll be looking for surveillance. I don't want to scare him off.'

'You're not going to. You know how good A4 is. He'll never see them. You should meet him somewhere he's got to make a bit of a journey to get to, so we can watch him – make sure he hasn't got anybody else with him. If he's any good, it will reassure him that we're looking after him too.'

Dave looked at her unhappily. 'That will take a lot of resources, Liz. I'm not sure Binding will agree to it. I don't want to lose this guy because we're being over-cautious.'

'I don't want to lose you because we've been *under*-cautious, either. Leave Binding to me; I'll go and see him straight away. You line up A4 and I'll meet you in the Briefing Room in half an hour.'

'OK,' said Dave unhappily. 'You're the boss. But I hope we don't blow this.'

I hope not too, thought Liz. If this didn't go right, her reputation as head of the agent runners would be mud, and mud that would stick for a good long time.

15

Liz had not yet been to Bangor, up the coast of Northern Ireland from Belfast, but thanks to Google Maps she was beginning to feel she knew it pretty well, at least the layout of the streets in the centre of the town, which she and Dave had pored over with A4 the day before.

Now she was in the A4 Control Room, a smaller affair than its equivalent in Thames House, though the equipment was just as comprehensive. Unlike in Thames House though, the whole set-up was sparkling clean. It looked almost unused and Liz thought she could detect a faint smell of fresh paint still hanging around. There was only one blot on the newness and that was the old saggy-bottomed armchair that was parked by the door. Liz assumed this was the small brother of the ancient leather sofa in Thames House, kept for case officers to sit on when an operation was in progress.

The Control Room was the domain of Reggie Purvis, the operational controller. Liz was one of the few whom Reggie would allow near him when an operation was in progress. He liked Liz; she kept calm whatever happened and would only intervene when asked. Now she stood carefully positioned where she could see all the monitors, but well out of Reggie's way.

Michael Binding had proved surprisingly amenable when Liz had asked for approval for the resources for this operation. Indeed he'd been so interested in this new source and what he might have to say that for a moment Liz had worried he would insist on taking over the whole operation. Fortunately he'd been called to a meeting in Thames House, but as he'd left for the airport he'd told Liz to make sure to keep him closely informed.

Little squirms of tension were chasing each other in Liz's stomach. Reggie's jaws were moving rhythmically as he chomped on a wad of chewing gum. Each of the monitors in the bank in front of him was flickering like a television set tuned to a channel that has closed down for the night. Everything was ready for Operation Brown Fox to begin.

Suddenly a voice said, 'The eleven thirteen has arrived at platform three.' It was Mike Callaghan, sitting at a cafe table on the concourse of Bangor Railway Station, with a copy of the *Belfast Telegraph* and a large cappuccino.

Reggie Purvis spoke into his mouthpiece. 'Brown Fox should be wearing a green anorak and carrying a Marks & Spencer carrier bag.'

There was silence for a minute. Then: 'Got him. He's heading towards the main exit.'

Suddenly on one of the monitors Liz could make out the figure of a man, walking rapidly past the concourse cafe. The image was transmitted by Callaghan, using a miniature device that looked like a standard mobile phone, but which sent at high bandwidth and resolution. The image was slightly blurred, nonetheless, and the man passed by Callaghan too quickly for Liz to see much detail. But she knew the pictures would come up nicely when Technical Ted worked his magic on them later.

'Okay. Bravo, he's yours now. You'll see him in ten seconds.'

Maureen Hayes was parked in one of the short-stay bays,

engine idling, as if she was waiting for an arriving passenger. 'I have him. He's walking up towards the roundabout.' And then, after a short pause, 'Brown Fox has turned left on Dufferin Avenue. He's clean.'

'As instructed,' Purvis said, turning his head towards Liz. 'So far so good.'

Liz looked down at Reggie's desk where a laptop showed the satellite map of this small area of Bangor. They'd chosen it because it was outside Belfast, yet easily accessible by train and by car. As she stared down at Dufferin Avenue on the laptop screen, ten miles away Terry Fleming walked slowly down that road in the direction of the railway station. When he saw the man across the street walking in the other direction, he said in a voice barely louder than a whisper, 'Brown Fox moving north. There's no one behind him.' The miniature microphone under the lapel of his overcoat relayed this instantly to the Control Room.

At the corner of a small residential road called Primrose Street, the target turned right. A couple sitting parked in a Mini two hundred yards down the street stopped squabbling and reported that Brown Fox had stopped at a public phone box.

Liz thought how lucky they had been to find a call box in a convenient place. Probably one of only half a dozen left in the whole of Bangor, she had remarked to Dave, wondering what on earth they were going to do for this kind of an operation when there were none left at all.

The phone on the desk in front of Reggie Purvis gave a long, low buzz. He parked his chewing gum in his cheek as he pressed the button and spoke at once in low, controlled tones. 'Listen carefully. Walk back down Primrose Street, then continue right on Dufferin Avenue. Turn right onto Gray's Hill and walk towards Queen's parade and the harbour – you'll see it ahead of you.

There's a large car park right next to it – go in from your end, and walk towards the fountain in the middle. You'll be contacted.'

The caller said nothing and hung up. Seconds later, Maureen Hayes reported, 'All clear on Dufferin Avenue. We're across from the harbour now.' She had collected Terry Fleming and driven on another street to the car park.

'Okay,' said Purvis. He spoke over his shoulder to Liz. 'It all looks quite clean, but let's get an overview, shall we?'

He flicked a switch on the console and suddenly a *phut phut phut* came over the speakers. 'Air Three, can you hear me?'

'Loud and clear. We've circled the harbour and are just coming inland to turn round.'

The helicopter appeared to be searching for something off the coast, just coming slightly inland to turn around. The manoeuvre gave the pilot and his A4 passengers an unrivalled view of the network of streets that lay between the flotilla of yachts in the basin and the railway station less than half a mile away.

In the Control Room the camera positioned on the helicopter's front right strut began transmitting to the second monitor. It was like a moving version of the satellite map, but infinitely sharper – Liz could see individuals walking on the streets below. Including a lone figure approaching the car park.

A minute later, a voice spoke over the chopper's dense fluttering. 'All clear on Queen's Parade and back up Gray's Hill Road. No sign of hostile activity.'

By then another parked car had reported that Brown Fox had entered the car park. Suddenly on the third monitor a misty view of the car park appeared, shot through the windscreen of Maureen Hayes's vehicle. Liz watched the street-level view of a man in a green anorak walking towards the little fountain that sat in a kind of miniature garden in the middle of the car park.

Maureen zoomed her lens and the image grew sharper and closer – the target, an oldish man, in his late sixties at least, with a pinched face and grey hair cut short on the sides. Liz craned forward; he looked familiar.

The watchers in the Control Room heard the sound of a car starting up and a metallic grey saloon appeared beside Brown Fox. He must have heard it coming, as he turned and stepped to one side to allow it to pass. But as it drew alongside it slowed down sharply and stopped. Brown Fox stood still, looking startled as the passenger door opened. Then Liz heard Dave's voice on the audio say, 'Good morning. I'm your contact. Climb in.'

16

Dave had re-parked his car in an uncrowded corner of the car park. It gave him a clear view in all directions; equally, it allowed the two A4 cars discreetly stationed to cover the exits a clear view of him and his passenger. Further up on Gray's Hill Road another car sat, watching for new arrivals, whether on foot or by car. Above them all, the small unmarked helicopter moved at an altitude of a few hundred feet. Apparently focused on the harbour and the sea, it flitted in and out of the area quite unobtrusively.

'I'm Simon Willis,' said Dave, offering his hand, which his passenger slowly shook.

'Patrick.'

'Patrick? That's a fine Irish name. Have you got another one to go with it?'

'Not one you need to know.'

'Okay.' Dave sounded confident, thought Liz in the Control Room. 'You said you needed to talk to me.'

'No – you need me to talk to you.'

'Well,' said Dave, 'I'm certainly interested in hearing what you have to say. And why you want to say it to me.'

'That's my affair,' said 'Patrick'. He sounded surly, and Liz wondered just what his motivation was. He clearly wasn't acting out of any affection for the security services.

This was confirmed a second later, when Patrick announced, 'I am not here to betray the cause I served for twenty-five years. I'm here because someone else is doing the betraying, and I want it stopped. All that's different now is that you people and I have the same interests – *temporarily*.'

'I'm listening,' said Dave. Then he added, 'Do you mind if I take notes?'

'I certainly do,' said Patrick sharply.

Liz smiled at the classic ruse for distracting the agent from wondering whether he was being recorded.

'That's fine. I have a good memory,' said Dave easily. 'Ready when you are.'

Patrick sighed and took a deep breath. 'When the Provisional Army Council decided to sign the Belfast Agreement and go along the political route, not all of their followers went with them. Some wanted to continue the struggle just as before. You will be familiar with the groups I'm talking about. The splinter groups.'

'Continuity IRA. The Real IRA,' said Dave.

Patrick must have nodded, and he went on: 'For others the problem isn't that simple. The fact is, things have changed – to pretend they haven't is just plain daft. Now the leaders are wearing suits and taking jobs as government ministers and drinking coffee out of china cups in Stormont, we can't carry on the war like we did.' He added venomously, 'Not that most of us don't want to. But we've sworn loyalty to the leadership. And whatever we think, we're loyal buggers, and the leadership's come down hard on splinter groups. So we've had to find something else to do.' He added with a suggestion of embarrassment, 'There was also the problem of earning a crust.'

Dave said, 'I've often wondered how people have managed.'

'It's been bloody hard,' said Patrick harshly. 'While the bigwigs ponce about in Downing Street and Stormont, the rest of us poor sods have been left out in the cold. You've heard the expression 'jobs for the boys'? Well there have only been jobs for the top boys. It's a disgrace.'

Dave stayed silent, and Patrick continued. 'As I said, when Adams and McGuinness got into bed with you lot, the problem was how to stay loyal to the Movement while not getting left out. There weren't many options, and when you saw an opportunity you had to grab it quickly.' Suddenly he dropped the third person. 'So I did.'

'Tell me about the opportunity.'

'A new company in Belfast needed some technical assistance. It was a consultancy,' he added, 'and I guess you'd say I became their consultant.'

'Consultant in what?' asked Dave slowly.

'Technical aspects of security,' said Patrick a little grandly. Listening in the Control Room, Liz reckoned he'd prepared this answer before. 'Several of the employees of the firm were old colleagues of mine.'

'Where is this company?'

'Right in the centre of Belfast– just off Castle Street.'

That's about the first concrete information he's offered, thought Liz, wondering again why she found him familiar. And Castle Street also rang a bell. You had to admire Dave's handling of this man: the good agent runner never hurried the agent and took care never to prick the balloon of his ego. Dave was doing well on both counts.

Just then another audio channel broke in. 'Control, this is Air Three. We have a white builder's van just off Queen's Parade on Southwell Road. It's double-parked and been there for some time. But on our last pass a guy was unloading bags from the back.'

'These bags – can you describe them, Air Three?' asked Purvis tensely.

'Look to be canvas, long – probably three or four feet. Something like sports bags for cricket kit.'

Cricket kit in January? wondered Liz. It didn't seem likely. She studied her laptop – the van was only a few hundred feet from Dave's car. 'I don't like the sound of this,' said Liz softly, and Purvis nodded.

'Do you want us to take another look?' asked Air Three.

Purvis turned his head, and Liz shook hers. It was too risky; even in Northern Ireland people noticed a helicopter if it hovered too obviously.

'Negative,' said Purvis. 'We'll deal with it.'

Purvis switched to another channel, while Liz tried to focus again on Dave's conversation. He was saying to Patrick, 'And are you happy working there?'

'I was at first, especially as I was told that the firm's profits were going to help the Cause. It was a legit business but also a holding action, if you see what I mean, until the time came when the peace process fell apart and the struggle began again.'

His agenda's clear at any rate, thought Liz, wondering how many former Provos shared his views. One hundred, as Binding had suggested? Maybe more? The thought was depressing, and frightening – former terrorists waiting like crows for the fragile peace to crack so they could come in and finish the job, starting the whole futile spiral of violence all over again. Was the man unloading a van one of them?

She listened tensely as Purvis gave instructions: 'Corner of Southwell Road and Queen's Parade, a white van parked and unloading. Can you check what's being moved? Go easy; this might be hostile.'

On one of the monitors they had a distant overhead view from the helicopter of Southwell Road. It was clear enough for them to see two police cars shooting up it at speed, their lights flashing but no sirens audible over any of the channels. Good, thought Liz – Dave and the informant couldn't see the police cars from where they sat, and they wouldn't hear them either.

The two police cars stopped suddenly, one at each end of the double-parked van, so that it couldn't move. But then the picture disappeared, and Liz could no longer see either the van or the police cars. The helicopter must have turned away, and the monitor's screen showed only blue sky, then the dull pea-green expanse of the Lough.

Dave was asking, 'Can you tell me about your technical work?'

'No!' The man called Patrick was almost shouting. 'I'll tell you what you need to know.' There was an edge to his voice now.

'Fair enough,' said Dave steadily.

'The business turned out to have a retail side I hadn't been told about.'

'What are they selling?'

'What *aren't* they selling is more like it. They flog stolen lottery tickets, stolen booze, and foreign women.'

'Any guns?' asked Dave quietly.

There was silence in the car; for a moment, standing in the Control Room, Liz worried that the audio connection had been lost. She wondered what was happening with the builder's van.

Then Patrick said, not answering Dave's question, 'Worst of all, they sell drugs.' He snorted with contempt. 'We never touched drugs. It was a punishable offence to have anything to do with them. They could destroy our communities.'

'So this consultancy is really just a front for criminal activity of all kinds.'

'Looks like it.'

Suddenly there was the crackle of the police radio. 'Control, we've stopped and searched. Nothing to worry about. It's bags of curtain rods – the van driver owns a decorating shop down the road in Ballyholme.'

Whew, thought Liz, and noticed Purvis was smiling. He turned up the volume on Dave's conversation.

'Why are you talking to me?' asked Dave, sounding more assertive now. Liz reckoned he was probably thinking what she was – that this wasn't a matter for MI5, but for the new Northern Ireland Police Service. It sounded like a well-organised racket – a menace to be sure, but straightforwardly criminal, and no concern of theirs.

Patrick seemed to bristle. 'If you're not interested, just say so, and I'll be on my way.'

Dave ignored him. 'You know as well as I do that this sort of stuff is a matter for the police. So why did you want to tell me about it?'

Patrick must have decided he had been opaque for too long. He said, 'The company I'm talking about is called Fraternal Holdings.'

Bingo, thought Liz. Things were starting to fall into place – and now she knew why this man was familiar. He had been the old man in the Astra, the one who left the Fraternal offices in a rage. He was getting his own back now, it seemed.

'The boss isn't Irish, but he calls himself a Republican. He says we've all been let down by Adams and McGuinness. What he really wants to do is kill policemen – and he wants to kill one of your lot, too. He says that will demonstrate that the war goes on.'

'*What?*' exclaimed Dave, unable to contain his surprise.

'That's what I'm telling you,' said Patrick, and Liz could imagine him sitting there with his arms folded, smugly certain that he had justified this rendezvous.

'Let me get this straight,' said Dave. 'You're telling me you've gone to work for a boss who claims to share your nationalist ideals, only to discover he's running rackets of every conceivable sort all over Belfast. And now you're saying he wants to kill policemen and an MI5 officer. I don't get it.'

'What's there to get? If you don't believe me, say the word and I'll be off.' Liz heard him shake the door handle.

'Hold your horses. I'm just surprised. You would be too in my position.'

'Not very likely,' said the old man, giving a caustic laugh.

'I need to know more. You can appreciate that. This man isn't exactly the only guy in Northern Ireland who'd still like to kill a policeman, or shoot a British Intelligence officer. Wanting is one thing; doing it's another. Has he made any plans?

'If you're asking if this is just some fancy he's got, you're wrong. This guy is serious. He's got plans all right.'

'Do you know what they are?' asked Dave sharply.

'Not the detail. But I know he's called in external help for the job.'

'Where from?'

Liz recalled the man she'd seen at the farmhouse; Fergus had identified him as a Spanish hit man. But Patrick said emphatically, 'France – there's a Frenchman visiting while we're sitting here talking.'

'Have you got a name?'

There was a pause. Then, 'His name's Milraw or Milroe, something like that. He's supposed to be a dealer in old weapons –

antiques. He's got a shop here that's legit. But I think you'll find he sells modern weapons as well.'

'And he would supply weapons to your boss?'

'He's not here to sell him a blunderbuss.'

'Is there anything else you can tell me?'

'Isn't that enough?'

'It's a start, and I'm grateful. But there's something I still don't understand – why you are here. I know, I know, that's your affair. But at least tell me, is there something personal about your reasons?'

'Personal?'

'Well, I wouldn't have thought you'd give two hoots if a cop got shot or someone like me got topped. So what's this to you?'

And then for the first time Patrick let his taciturn front drop. 'What's it to me?' His voice rose. 'I'll tell you. I haven't given my life and worked my guts out for thirty years to have some little American prick come over and tell me what to do.'

'This guy's American?'

'Boston-Irish. University fella, clever, but just as bad as the rest of them. You know what I mean: all those brave guys sitting on barstools in Boston, throwing in a dollar or two when the NORAID bucket went round, acting tough but doing sweet F-all. Piggott's just as bad – only instead of getting sloshed in Jerry Kelly's Shamrock Saloon, or whatever phoney name they call it, he was sitting behind a computer in the university dreaming up the perfect missile. Only it never worked as far as I know. While we were literally *dying* over here.'

'Did you say Piggott?' Dave gave stress to the surname – for her benefit, Liz realised, in case the audio had not been clear enough.

'Why? Do you know the man?' asked Patrick suspiciously.

'Never heard of him. Is he related to the jockey?' He gave a small laugh.

Patrick didn't join him. He was quiet for a minute, possibly subdued; he must regret losing his cool like that, thought Liz. He had been so unwilling to talk about his reasons for contacting Dave, the representative of his arch-enemy, yet then he'd blown it. He was nursing a grudge. That was clear now. What Piggott had done to him was anyone's guess, but Liz didn't believe it was just his American citizenship that had provoked the Irishman's rage, and set him off on a quest for revenge.

Dave said, 'This is extremely helpful, Patrick. But it would be even more helpful if you could find out more and we could meet again. It wouldn't have to be so elaborate next time; we could meet in Belfast if that suited you.'

'No.' Patrick's voice was unequivocal. Liz heard him open the car door. 'If I need you again, I know how to get to you. You've had all you're going to get from me, and that should be enough for you to put Piggott away. No amnesty is going to save his arse. And if you can't catch him, and one of you gets blown away . . .' His voice suddenly assumed a gross caricature of an Irish voice. 'Well faith and goodness, wouldn't that be a terrible shame?'

17

Jimmy Fergus was an easy-going man, famously affable, a lover of women, pubs, and convivial company. His sunny front to the world masked his professional seriousness; it was his intense commitment to the RUC that had been responsible for the breakdown of his first three marriages. Determined not to let this happen to his fourth, he was now working only part-time for the newly formed Northern Ireland Police Service.

Fortunately Moira, his bride of just over a year, had understood from the beginning how attached he was to police work, and it was she who had encouraged him to defer retirement. Not for her a life in Ibiza or some other stultifying resort, where former policemen sat pickling themselves in sun and booze, stirring only to walk each day as far as the newsagent to pick up the *Daily Mail*. Jimmy had thought he might take over the family farm in Antrim, but when Moira asked him if he really wanted to spend his days milking cows, he realised that the prospect was more fantasy than ambition.

As it turned out, he had found that it was an exciting time to be in the police force, which made him even more pleased not to have hung up his boots. The new PSNI had swept away cobwebs that even the RUC's staunchest defenders acknowledged were there; it had also recruited more Catholic policemen than many old RUC hands would have dreamed possible – or, in some cases, thought desirable.

Jimmy welcomed the changes: he had no time for those who longed for the old set-up. He thought it right that as the country changed the police service should change too, and be much more representative of the community it was serving. He particularly welcomed the transfer of the intelligence work from the old RUC Special Branch to MI5, since it meant policemen could focus on fighting good, honest crime – there was plenty of that going on.

But though he was optimistic about Northern Ireland's future, he wasn't naive. He knew that in this bit of the island of Ireland, above all, the past never really died. Its tentacles went on twitching and could suddenly reach out and make trouble. Despite his big-shouldered *bonhomie*, the old policeman had a sceptical view of human nature, and he knew that for all the leopards who'd changed their spots, there were plenty who hadn't.

It was this knowledge, heightened by a well-honed instinct for self-preservation, that made him notice the laundry van the first time. It had been two weeks before, and the van was parked at the corner of the quiet side street where he and Moira had bought their house – a solid square brick residence with four bedrooms, ample space for visits by the children of their former marriages (now all grown up and with families of their own).

There had seemed nothing odd about the van's presence – its driver, wearing white overalls, was sitting behind the wheel ticking things off on a clipboard. And when Jimmy saw it again the following week, with the same driver (same clipboard too) he had reckoned it must now be making regular pick-ups from one of the houses down the street. It was only as he unlocked his front door, calling out a cheery 'I'm home,' to Moira, that he wondered why in that case the van was parked in a different place – much further along the street. By the time he went outside to have a look, the van had disappeared.

This morning he emerged from his house earlier than usual; he was due at Stormont by eight to discuss the details of transferring old RUC files. It promised to be the kind of meeting he hated (long, and full of bureaucratic detail) but it wouldn't do to be late.

He shouted goodbye to Moira and walked out of the front door, gripping a briefcase in one hand while he pushed up his hastily knotted tie with the other. His car, a reliable old Rover which he refused to trade in, was parked in his garage. No one in his profession ever left their car in the street or in their drive. There might be a ceasefire on, but too many colleagues had been killed or maimed by car bombs in the past to ignore that basic precaution. As he backed slowly down the gently sloping paved drive, thinking how pleasantly smooth it was since it had been re-laid, he saw over his shoulder that today the laundry van was parked right beside his gate. In fact it was partly blocking the road he was trying to back into. He was just starting to get out of the car and tell the driver to move out of the way, when he noticed that the driver was getting out. Then he saw there was another man getting out of the van as well.

Alarm bells were ringing loudly in his head. 'Excuse me,' the driver shouted out, walking towards Jimmy. He had a smile pasted on his face which the policeman distrusted at once.

'Would you happen to know,' the man began to ask, then he stopped, standing about fifteen feet away, and Jimmy saw that the other man, also dressed in white overalls, was coming into the drive. This man had his arms down by his sides, but Jimmy Fergus saw that he held something in one hand.

Reflexively, Jimmy reached for the Glock 9 mm pistol he always carried holstered under his jacket. As he grabbed its grip he saw that the man's arm was now extended. *Gun* thought Jimmy, just as the man pulled the trigger.

The bullet caught Jimmy Fergus high in the chest on his right side, next to his gun arm. He lost his balance and began to fall, knowing that he mustn't let go of his gun – *don't drop it*, he told himself, *or you've had it*.

He hit the drive heavily, landing on his side, and tried immediately to roll behind the open car door for protection. But waves of pain were seizing him just below the shoulder, and his legs would not respond to his mental command to move. His fingers still gripped the Glock, but when he tried to lift the pistol and fire, his arm did not obey.

The man with the gun was coming around the rear of the car now, and the van driver stood back to give him space. He turned to face Fergus, who was still lying sprawled on the drive. His gun was a semi-automatic, and as he raised his arm to fire, Jimmy could only think *this is it*.

But nothing happened. The man stared at his weapon with disbelief. It must have jammed, thought Fergus. He tried to roll underneath the car but he couldn't move, and he sensed his stay of execution would be short-lived.

Calmly clearing the jam, the man stepped forward, lowering the gun to shoot the policeman.

Suddenly a scream broke through the air, like the sound of shattering glass. Even through his pain, Jimmy Fergus realised it was Moira, coming out of the front door, still wearing the pink housecoat he had given her for Christmas.

The man with the gun jerked back, obviously startled.

'Get back,' Jimmy tried to shout. He saw the man turn to face Moira, who was running towards them down the path, still screaming. To his horror the man raised his weapon. And then Jimmy found his fingers could move after all, and he managed to lift the Glock an inch or two off the ground with his hand, and with more hope than expectation, pointed it and fired.

The gun kicked with enough force to fall from his hand. As its sharp crack echoed in the air, Jimmy heard a muffled shout – '*Agghh!*'

He saw his would-be executioner reaching down, to where a dark stain was seeping through one leg of his pristine white overalls.

In obvious agony, the man dropped his gun. The driver of the van ran forward and picked it up. Fergus prayed he would not finish the job. Instead the driver put a rough arm around his wounded accomplice, then half-ran with the hobbling, bleeding man to the cab of the laundry van. Seconds later the van's engine started up. With a long squeal of tyres, it turned a sharp one-eighty degrees and shot off down the road.

Then a hand was gently stroking his hair, and as he slumped down he heard Moira sobbing.

'Jimmy, Jimmy,' she was saying through her tears. 'Can you hear me? Are you all right? Oh God, please God, tell me he's alive.'

'Leave God out of it,' gasped Jimmy, 'and ring the ambulance.' Then he passed out.

18

'How is Mrs Ryan working out?' asked Judith Spratt. She was sitting in Liz's office, waiting for Dave to join them and review where they had got to in the Fraternal Holdings investigation.

'I haven't lived in such order since I left my mother's house. I hardly ever see her though, and when I do she's not exactly chatty. The strong, silent type, I'd say.'

In her first weeks working for Liz, Mrs Ryan had already reorganised almost everything in the flat, from the pan cupboard to Liz's underwear drawer. Liz was enjoying the unaccustomed luxury of being able to find things.

Judith took a last swallow of her coffee and put her mug down. 'Yes, I know. But thank goodness she and Daisy seem to get along OK. Daisy says she talks to her all the time; that's her excuse for not doing her homework. It's funny, because she never says much to me, either.'

'Perhaps she just likes children more than adults,' said Liz with a shrug.

Dave hurried into the office. It was clear from his face that something had happened. He looked at Liz grimly and didn't sit down. 'There's been an incident. One of the PSNI officers has been shot. I don't know who.'

'Oh my God,' exclaimed Liz. 'When?'

'An hour ago. The man's in surgery and they don't know if he's going to make it.'

'Does Michael Binding know?' she asked.

'He's at Stormont in a meeting. I'm sure they'll have heard.'

Liz exchanged a look with Dave. What had Brown Fox said? Had the threat been carried out, and so soon? She mentally shook herself. Until they knew more there was no point in jumping to conclusions.

'Okay, we'd better get on with things here. Judith, are there results from the number plate enquiries?'

'Yes,' said Judith, taking her cue from Liz and passing folders round. 'We've got an ID on the owner of the Astra that hung around outside the Fraternity offices.'

Liz looked at the first sheet in her folder, where she saw a photocopy of a driver's license. The mug shot was of a now-familiar face, and when she turned to Dave he looked up from his folder and nodded. 'Yes, it's him.'

Liz said to Judith, 'This is the walk-in Dave met yesterday, Brown Fox. What have you found out about him?'

Judith consulted her notes. 'He's Dermot O'Reilly, a long-time Provisional IRA volunteer. Interned in the Maze in the seventies, and believed to be the quartermaster for Belfast Brigade. After he was released he stayed involved, though he managed to escape prosecution for terrorist activity. But he's got convictions for two criminal offences: a drunk and disorderly outside a pub – got a fine for that, and a charge of receiving stolen goods – suspended sentence.'

'So what is he now, a crook or a terrorist?' mused Dave.

'It looks like a bit of both,' said Judith. 'He lives just off the Falls Road. When we checked his credit history it was terrible, not surprisingly – he's had cars repossessed for non-payment of loans, mortgage arrears, credit card debt – though God knows how he got a card in the first place.

'Here's the interesting thing, though: starting two years ago his situation improved dramatically – suspiciously so, I'd say. He wiped out the credit card debt, paid off half his mortgage, and now has over ten grand in the bank.'

Liz said, 'He said he's been working for Fraternal Holdings. Given the pictures we have of him at their offices, that's pretty clearly true. They must pay well.'

'I'd like to know exactly what for,' said Judith. 'He's certainly had a lot of cash for doing something in the last two years.'

'Do we know anything more about this man Piggott who runs the show?' asked Liz. 'According to Brown Fox – O'Reilly – he's the one we've got to worry about.'

'Not much,' said Judith, with a puzzled shake to her head. 'He owns a flat here in Belfast, and that farmhouse in County Down. He's got a local driver's licence he applied for three years ago. The Audi we've seen him in on the camera at the National Trust gatehouse is registered to Fraternal Holdings. That's it.'

'O'Reilly said he's a Yank, Boston Irish, a university type who designed missiles that didn't work,' Dave remarked. 'Though all that may be just sour grapes. O'Reilly's obviously got a big grudge against him.'

'I'd better start looking there then. Did he have any other information?'

'Not much. But it's all in my contact note. Our Mr Big seems to be a bit of an enigma.'

'I'll speak to Thames House and get Peggy to work her magic. She can see what's in the files and perhaps get onto the Americans. If all that stuff's true – about designing missiles for the IRA – then there's sure to be loads of stuff in the back files.'

Liz nodded. 'If there's anything to find, Peggy'll find it.'

A shadow fell across the open door. Liz looked up and saw Michael Binding standing there, his face pale and strained. He was still wearing his long overcoat.

'You've heard about the shooting?' he said.

Liz nodded and asked, 'Do we know who it was?'

'Yeah. Some chap who was supposed to be at my meeting in Stormont. He's an old RUC officer, semi-retired. His name's Fergus – Jimmy Fergus.'

'Oh no, not Jimmy,' said Liz. 'I know him. Dave and I went to see him last week – he's helped me before.'

'Do they know what happened?' asked Dave.

'He was just setting off for work, backing out of his gate when the gunmen attacked – two of them. A neighbour said they were in a laundry van. They must have had him under surveillance because the van's been seen before in the street. Fergus managed to fire back: he hit one of them – well, we think he did. There was blood where the van had been parked.'

'Is he very badly hurt?' Liz could hear her voice shaking as she asked the question.

'He took a bullet in the chest.' Binding's voice softened almost imperceptibly. 'That's all I know. I'll keep you posted.' He gave a little bow of the head and left.

'I wonder why they chose Fergus, if he's semi-retired?' asked Judith. She sounded shaken too. 'Do you think it's someone settling an old score?'

Dave stood up and walked to the window. 'God knows,' he said.

There was silence in the room. Dave went on standing by the window, shifting from foot to foot, looking agitated. Judith was obviously stunned. Liz stayed sitting at her desk. She felt as if all her energy had suddenly gone.

She found herself remembering when her first boyfriend,

Freddy Simmons, had been involved in a car crash, and the news had reached her at home. There had been several hours without even knowing how badly injured he was; there was nothing she could do to help, just sit and wait for news, all the time expecting the worst. As it turned out Freddy had been all right (a broken collarbone was the extent of the damage), but she remembered how her father had made her go out and help him with a bonfire in the garden to take her mind off it.

Judith broke the silence. 'I'll come back later, Liz, if you like.' She stood up and started to gather up papers. The movement triggered something in Liz and she felt a great surge of anger.

'No,' she said. 'Don't leave, Judith. We're going to find out who's behind this and what it's all about. So let's get on with what we were doing. This makes it all the more urgent.'

'I just thought you might want to be alone. I know you were close to Fergus.'

'No,' Liz corrected her. 'I wasn't close to him. But I was very fond of him.' Then she realised what she was saying. 'I *am* fond of him.' She took a deep breath. 'Look,' she said, 'there's nothing we can do to help Jimmy Fergus right now, so let's just try and stop thinking about it.'

She turned to Judith. 'We were talking about the number plate enquiries. You've mentioned O'Reilly. Now what about the other car? The one with the foreign-looking bloke?'

'We traced the car. It's rented from Davis Hire at City Airport.'

'When I first came here I picked up the keys to the pool car at their office.'

'Yes. The manager's a long-standing agent. He's been on the RUC's books for years and he's given us a lot of useful stuff too,' broke in Dave. 'I'll get onto him and see what he knows.'

'Is that the car that had the blowout?' asked Judith.

Liz nodded and Dermot O'Reilly's words came back to her:

What he really wants to do is kill policemen – and he wants to kill one of your lot, too. She shuddered.

Pulling herself together she said, 'What do we know about this guy? O'Reilly said he's French.'

'He is. Antoine Milraud. He flew in from Paris the day before yesterday. I checked with Interpol but they've got nothing on him. So to cover all the bases, I rang the DCRI. You know, it's the new French internal service. They've just had a reorganisation. I thought it might be difficult to find the right person to speak to so I wasn't expecting anything—'

'But?'

Judith pursed her lips, musing for a moment. 'Well, I got through to a senior officer called Florian. Her reaction was a bit strange, I must say. Her English was even worse than my French, but she managed to get across that they knew Milraud, or knew of him anyway. But she wouldn't tell me anything. When I pushed a bit she said they did have information about him, but someone would have to go and talk to them about it. I think what she was saying was that it was complicated and she wasn't going to tell us anything until she knew why we wanted to know. Shall I ask the MI6 station in Paris to go and talk to her?'

'Why the secrecy?' wondered Liz aloud.

'Do you know what that sounds like?' said Dave. 'It sounds as if he's a source of theirs. That's just how we'd respond if someone asked us about a source.'

'This is getting really complicated,' said Liz frowning. 'Who's at the MI6 Paris station, Judith? Do you know?'

'I don't know who the head of station is, but the deputy is Bruno Mackay.'

Dave looked at Liz.

'Oh no. Not him.'

'Your favourite old Harrovian, Liz,' said Dave with a grin. 'Speaks fluent French as well as Arabic, I'll be bound.'

'He may speak fluent French, but he's the last person to put into a delicate situation,' responded Liz crossly. 'I'll go myself.'

19

Danny Ryan wished Sean would shut up.

'Oh my God, oh my God,' Sean was saying, again and again, in between great shuddering racks of sobs. Danny couldn't concentrate. He was trying not to drive too fast, or do anything to call attention to the white laundry van he was driving.

More than one policeman was going to be looking for them soon enough. He needed to get off the road fast, before the call went out across the radio bands with a description of the van. The number plates were false, but that wouldn't help them if someone on that street had noted them down. And even though no one had been around, they must have been seen, especially after the gun had been fired.

Two guns in fact – and that was the problem. He looked sideways at Sean, sitting bent over in the passenger seat. Blood was dripping on the floor and had completely soaked the leg of his jeans. He had to get him to a doctor fast, or the poor bugger was going to bleed to death.

'Hang on,' he urged him, 'we're almost there.' But they weren't: he didn't dare run the risk of driving through the centre of Belfast – rush hour was just starting and he wasn't going to sit in traffic, waiting for the PSNI to pick them up.

So he took the Knock Road south through Castlereagh, almost to the countryside, until the road swung west and brought them to the beginning of Andersonstown. Here Danny drove fast, under the A1 and into the large industrial estate built on the edge of the Catholic neighbourhood. He turned the van into a small side street running around the back of Casement Park, the ageing football stadium that the city fathers kept talking about replacing.

Suddenly he braked sharply, and Sean groaned. There was a police car parked at the front of the stadium on Andersonstown Road.

Reversing would simply call attention to the van. There was nothing for it but to brazen it out. He slowed to a crawl as he neared the intersection. Would the van's description have been circulated? Would they notice the number plates?

As they passed, he sneaked a look. The patrol car was empty. He speeded up again. Two blocks away he pulled off St Agnes's Way, where a row of eight lock-up garages occupied one end of a small plot with a FOR SALE board stuck in the muddy grass.

'Hang on, Sean,' he ordered as he pulled up and the groaning started again. 'Help's on the way.'

Without looking around, Danny unlocked and lifted the steel shutter, then ran back to the van and drove it into the wide garage. Once he'd turned on the lights and pulled the door down again, he did his best to make Sean comfortable, lying him across both of the front seats. Blood was no longer spreading across his leg. Was that a good sign? Danny didn't know. He'd never seen anyone shot before.

He stood by the steel door to make sure the signal was strong, and dialled a number on his mobile.

'Hello.' The voice was terse, emotionless.

'Mr P, it's Danny.'

'Yeah.' His voice was terse.

'We've got a problem. It didn't go according to plan.'

'Why not?'

'It wasn't our fault, Mr P. We got the bastard, but he got Sean and—'

'Where are you?'

'At the lock-up. I'm sure we were spotted. But Sean's bad—'

'I told you not to go back to the lock-up.'

'We've got to get Sean help, Mr P.'

'Sean can wait. He's cocked it up.' There was cold fury in his voice. After a pause, he said, 'Now listen. Wait there till I send someone over. He'll take care of Sean. Then you get that van out of there. Drive it out, well out. Find a place, and torch it. Do you hear me? Torch it.'

'I hear you, Mr P.'

'Good. And don't call me again, understood? Just sit tight, then do it.'

Twenty minutes later, there was a sharp rap on the steel door of the garage. Danny peered through the window slit and saw the Spaniard, Gonzales, in his black leather jacket, standing to one side. He reached down and slowly pulled up the shutter.

Gonzales looked at him with cold eyes. '*Donde?*' he said.

'What?'

Gonzales pushed by him and walked to the van and looked in. He nodded, satisfied.

'He's hurt bad,' said Danny. 'He needs to see a doctor right away.'

Gonzales ignored him, and went out and got into his car. Starting it, he pulled quickly into the garage, forcing Danny to jump to one side. As he got out he opened the rear passenger door, then walked over to the van.

'We'll have to be careful with him,' said Danny. He peered in. Sean was slumped on his back across both seats; he was quiet now, breathing but barely conscious. The blood on his trouser leg had congealed into a black mess.

Without saying a word, Gonzales reached in and put his arms roughly under Sean's back, propping him up.

'Mind his leg!' Danny shouted. 'He's been wounded.'

The Spaniard ignored him, pulling Sean back out of the door until only his legs remained on the seat. He lowered his arms and wrapped them round the wounded man's waist, then with one movement he hoisted him out of the car, leaving his legs dangling on the floor. Sean screamed as the Spaniard lowered him onto the back seat of his car, where Sean fell, moaning continuously.

'Jesus, will you take care? He's been shot.'

Gonzales turned suddenly and stared at Danny. There was a cold menace in his look that frightened the younger man. In heavily accented English, Gonzales said, 'You know what to do with the van. Get going.'

An hour later Danny was driving through County Armagh. This was border country, traditionally sympathetic to the IRA. He took a spur, halfway between Portadown and Armagh, that led to the old Moy Road and stopped a mile short of a farm, where he'd been taught how to fire a pistol by three veteran Provos. That one didn't jam, he thought bitterly, wondering how Sean was getting on. If they'd been given a decent weapon, they'd have done the RUC bastard properly – he'd never have had the chance to fire himself.

He turned now onto an old cart track, half overgrown and muddy from the winter rains. It wound up a tree-lined hill, ending suddenly in a small sandy lay-by sheltered from the wind by the side of the hill; more importantly, it was sheltered from view by a small copse of young oaks.

Once it had been the site of a crofter's cottage, but the remaining structure was crumbling and decrepit now, more like a cairn of loosely piled stones than a cottage – only a few tiles and some bare timbers hinted that it had once had a roof. Behind it the ground tilted sharply downward. Locals had used the slope as a tip, dumping old refrigerators and broken bikes, even a sofa, its stuffing billowing out through a tear in the fabric. Wedged halfway down, against the trunk of an ancient tree were the charred, skeletal remains of a burned-out car.

Danny parked the van at the top of the slope. He was anxious to get the whole business over with, and to get away before anyone came. He checked the inside before getting out, to make sure he'd left nothing important in there. His fingerprints and Sean's would be all over it – as well as their DNA, which the forensic wizards would find, given half a chance.

But they wouldn't have that chance. He took a full can of petrol out of the van and sloshed half of it over the floor at the back, then over the cab, making sure the vinyl seats were soaked. Standing back he struck a match from a box of Swan Vestas, and tossed it onto the driver's seat. It went out as he threw it. Anxious now, he took a dirty handkerchief out of his trouser pocket and dangled the corner into a pool of petrol lying on the cab floor. Then, retreating a little, he lit the handkerchief and tossed it into the open window of the cab. Flames jumped up with a sudden *whoosh*, and he backed off a good twenty yards, and watched as the fire spread. Soon the whole van was ablaze.

He set off down the winding path, heading for the old Moy Road, where he'd hitch a lift into Moy itself. No fear of anyone who might pick him up in this area talking to the PSNI. From there a minicab could take him to Portadown, where he'd catch a train for Belfast and home. A long roundabout journey, but necessary if the evidence of the botched assassination was to disappear for good. Thank God he'd booked the whole day off; no one at work would be wondering where he was. His mother would be worried, but he didn't dare ring her. Not after that rocket from Piggott. She'd known he was up to confidential business anyway.

As he reached the road there was a loud boom. The van's petrol tank had just exploded. He gave a small, satisfied nod. That should take care of the evidence for good.

20

O'Reilly was restless. That bastard Piggott was always on his mind, and he was going to get him one way or another. But how? The meeting with the MI5 man had gone well. O'Reilly was pleased that he had stayed in control and the Englishman had got no more out of him than he'd wanted to give. But what would the Brits do with the information? Would they do anything? You couldn't rely on the spies any more than you could on Piggott.

He needed to be sure. He wanted to tie Piggott up in knots; to worry the cold American sod; have him looking over his shoulder, not knowing who he could trust. Then he'd start to make mistakes and that would be the end of him.

But Piggott was clever. And he wouldn't listen to anything O'Reilly said to him – especially not now that he'd as good as sacked him. He'd have to find another way to unsettle him and wipe that sneer off his Yankee face. But what way? An anonymous phone call had worked with 'Simon Willis' (or whatever his real name was). But Willis didn't know his voice; he'd never spoken to him before. If he tried an anonymous call with Piggott, he might recognise the voice. And there wasn't anyone else he trusted enough to make the call for him.

Then an idea came to him – an old-fashioned solution, the kind he liked best. No computers, nothing technical. And it should work.

His wife caught him by surprise. She was supposed to be out having her hair done, but there she was, standing in the kitchen doorway. 'What's going on?' she said, pointing to the mess on the table where in half an hour she'd be wanting to give him his dinner.

'Just give us a few minutes, will you? I'll clear it all up, but I need to be private now. It's work.'

'Work?' she asked with disbelief.

He put a warning hand up, and she knew better than to argue. She shut the kitchen door, and he could hear her go upstairs.

On the table he had a week's worth of newspapers, some scissors, a few sheets of A4 paper, and a glue stick. He examined his handiwork so far:

> You**R** Man Milr**aud** is a **toUt**. Seen with *Brit*ISH
> INTELLIGENCE **at** *rendez*vous IN LigonieL P**ARK**.
> W**at**ch youR B**ac** *k* . . .

Thanks to the *News of the World* and the *Irish News*, his message could hardly be more anonymous. With luck, Piggott should read it as it was intended – a warning from a Republican sympathiser that his new French 'mate' wasn't what he said he was. Piggott would certainly take it seriously: it was just too likely to O'Reilly's mind that Milraud, a foreigner, was a plant.

At the very least it would get Piggott thinking about the Frog. Which meant that sooner or later the two worlds would collide: with luck Simon Willis would be contacting the Frenchman before he left Northern Ireland, and when Piggott got the message he would be watching for him as well. The two strings O'Reilly had pulled would start winding round each other; if there was any justice in the world, they would leave Piggott trapped in the knot.

21

Two days later, Liz woke up in a small hotel in the boulevard Malesherbes, just round the corner from the British Embassy. She had arrived late the previous evening to a wet and windy Paris, having eaten nothing since breakfast but a stodgy sandwich, purchased on her 'no frills' flight from Belfast. She had slept uneasily in the hot, noisy bedroom, dreams of Jimmy Fergus lying wounded on his drive all mixed up in her mind with the recorded voice of Brown Fox warning Dave of plots to kill policemen and MI5 officers. Now, as she contemplated a day to be spent in the company of Bruno Mackay, a black cloud of gloom descended.

Liz had crossed swords with Bruno Mackay several times during her career. With his public-school manner, his perfectly cut suits and his permanent tan, she would have liked to be able to treat him as a bit of a joke. But she had to admit to herself that for some reason, a reason she was not prepared to examine, he got under her skin. Even now, just thinking about him, she felt her throat tightening with irritation.

Determined not to be outdone by Bruno or Mme Florian, Liz had brought her smartest outfit, a designer suit bought in the sale at Brown's in South Molton Street. The dark navy-blue put colour into her cool grey eyes and with its tight skirt and short jacket the suit emphasised her slim figure. To complete the picture she had a pair of black patent leather shoes with, for her, quite high heels. The whole outfit had actually been bought for Joanne's funeral; as Liz dressed, she found herself wondering how Charles was coping on his own, and wishing she could see him.

It was clear from the hissing of the car tyres on the busy street outside her window that the rain of the night before was still falling heavily. Thank goodness she had brought a mac, though she realised with dismay that she had forgotten her umbrella.

Half an hour later, as she walked the short distance to the embassy, the rain had turned to a light drizzle, just enough to plaster her hair damply to her head. Sitting in the embassy waiting room, she mopped drips from her forehead with a handkerchief.

The door opened and in sauntered the familiar tall, lean figure of Bruno Mackay, wearing an impeccably cut grey flannel suit, dark blue shirt and a tie covered with large blue and yellow flowers.

'Morning Liz,' he said breezily and before she could prevent him, leaned down to plant a kiss on her cheek. He stood back and casting an eye over her bedraggled hair remarked, 'Raining, I see. Never mind. We'll dry you out and I'm sure you'll come up a treat.'

Liz clamped her jaw shut. She wasn't going to let Bruno annoy her. After a moment, pointing to his tie she asked lightly, 'Are you moonlighting as a television newsreader?'

Bruno grinned, conceding a temporary draw.

He led her up the sweeping flight of stairs, then along a carpeted corridor lined with portraits of kings and statesmen.

He flung open an enormous mahogany door and showed her into a spacious, high-ceilinged room. Across from the door, a large antique desk faced inwards, centred between two wall-to-ceiling windows overlooking the back garden of the embassy, a sweep of lawn ending in a dense copse of trees. It was hard to believe they were a stone's throw from the Champs Elysées.

Bruno turned and smiled at Liz, as if to say 'not bad, eh?'

'Do sit down,' he said pointing to an Empire-style chair. 'What can I get you to drink? Coffee, tea, or something stronger perhaps?'

Tea and bone china cups and saucers bearing the royal crest came in on a tray, brought by a young woman who had eyes only for Bruno. When she'd left, Liz took a sip of her tea, then said, 'As you know Bruno, I have an appointment at the DCRI in an hour.'

'Ah, the new Direction Centrale du Renseignement Intérieur,' Bruno said rapidly, showing off his impeccable French accent. 'Excellent. When you've finished your tea, let's move into the station and we can talk about it.'

'Isn't this your office?'

'Come, come, Liz. You've been in an MI6 station before. This is the head of chancery's office. He's away at present. Our premises are much more workmanlike.' And getting up, he led her along the corridor to a blank door with a keypad beside it. Tapping in some numbers he pushed the door open and ushered her into a corridor, off which led a row of offices furnished with familiar grey steel desks and chairs and combination-locked cupboards. He ushered her into one of the offices, and they both sat down.

'You're seeing Isabelle Florian. She's very good. We'll go over in my car.'

'No need to bother you, Bruno. I'm sure you're very busy. I can take a cab.'

'I insist.' When she was about to object, he gave her his sweetest smile. 'Good French, have you, Liz?'

She hesitated. Six years at school, O-level, a reasonable reading ability, the usual difficulty with understanding the language when spoken at speed. 'Pretty rusty,' she admitted at last. 'But presumably they'll have an interpreter.'

He shook his head. 'They'll expect you to bring an interpreter. It's a courtesy.'

Liz ground her teeth. He was right, of course – and it was essential that she and Mme Florian understand each other. If Bruno was the only conduit for communication, then Bruno it must be. She would have to brief him about Milraud, though she decided to tell him only what he needed to know. Experience had taught her that Bruno was not only exceptionally annoying but also not entirely trustworthy. It did not seem to her that the MI6 station in Paris needed to be involved in the detail of the Piggott case; who knew what Bruno might do with any information she gave him? He had a habit of putting his fingers into every pie that came his way.

An hour later they both sat in an office high up in the head-quarters of the old Direction de la Surveillance du Territoire, the DST, the French counterpart of MI5, which had recently been merged with other intelligence departments to form the new DCRI. The building was a stone's throw from the Seine, and through the window the Eiffel Tower was just visible, emerging from behind some buildings. Isabelle Florian was not at all what Liz had expected. Far from the chic Parisienne in a sharp black suit of her imagination, Mme Florian turned out to be a businesslike woman in her forties, wearing jeans and a pullover, with a careworn face and her hair scraped back in a band. It was clear that both Liz and Bruno were definitely over-dressed for this visit.

Liz began by explaining the background to the enquiry about Milraud. Her French was good enough for her to understand that Bruno, to his credit, was assiduously translating exactly what she said. When she had finished, Isabelle Florian replied in a torrent of French lasting several minutes, hardly taking breath and not pausing for a moment for Bruno to translate.

When at last she slowed down and finally stopped, Bruno turned to Liz and said, 'Well, the gist of all that is that we are in the wrong place. She says that they do have a very considerable file on Milraud here. He was involved in some sort of operation involving her service, but the foreign service, the DGSE, were in the lead, and she is not at liberty to reveal any details to us without their agreement. She has spoken to the DGSE about our enquiry and they have agreed to talk to us. She says she also thinks he has been under some sort of investigation by that service recently.'

Liz sighed. She knew that the Headquarters of the Direction Générale de la Sécurité Extérieure were on the other side of Paris, far out near the north-eastern suburbs. 'Can you ask her who I should speak to there?' she asked, a little impatiently.

Mme Florian understood her, for she replied in English, looking directly at Liz. 'Monsieur Martin Seurat. He iz expectant of you.'

'*Bon*,' said Liz.

Florian smiled. She went on, '*Il parle anglais couramment. Vous n'aurez pas besoin d'un interprète.*'

'*Bon*,' replied Liz again.

They shook hands and thanked Florian as she showed them out of the building. 'Bit of a drive now, I'm afraid,' said Bruno as they stood outside the building. 'The DGSE's halfway to ruddy Charles de Gaulle.'

'Well really,' said Liz, now thoroughly annoyed. 'I can't think why she couldn't have said all that over the phone to Judith days ago and saved me the trouble of coming here.'

'Of course, she wanted to know why you were interested in him,' replied Bruno patronisingly. 'She wasn't born yesterday, you know.'

'Well, at least I won't need to trouble you anymore. I'll take the Metro from here.'

'But Liz,' he protested, and his surprise was a pleasure to watch. 'You'll need me. None of these buggers speaks English, and you don't understand French.'

'I understand enough to know I won't need an interpreter. Isabelle Florian said Seurat's English is fluent,' and she stalked off towards the Metro station, leaving Bruno standing on the pavement with his mouth open.

22

'*Enchanté*,' said the man, shaking Liz's hand. 'I am impressed you have found us all on your own. When I spoke with Isabelle Florian, she said you were accompanied by Monsieur Mackay.'

'I decided I could manage without an escort,' Liz said firmly. In fact it would have been much easier if she had allowed Bruno to drive her. The price of her irritation with him had been a rather complicated journey on the Metro involving two changes, and once she had had to use her fractured French to ask directions. But she had finally emerged successfully at Porte des Lilas to find the boulevard Mortier, a wide tree-lined avenue, bathed in sunshine.

The DGSE was an imposing compound of white stone buildings protected by a gatehouse manned by armed guards in military uniform, and by glittering razor wire running along the top of a high wall. A uniformed guard had led her to Seurat's office, a small corner room with half windows overlooking a wide gravelled courtyard that looked as though it had once been a parade ground. Seurat was a man in his mid-forties, five or six years older than Liz. With his greying hair cut very short and his dark check tweed jacket and grey turtleneck, he had an indefinably military appearance. The office was furnished with well-used dark wood furniture and comfortable-looking brown leather chairs. Though Liz had felt overdressed in Mme Florian's office, here she was glad she had taken trouble with her appearance.

'I will see Bruno some other time, I'm sure,' Seurat said now with a wide smile, motioning Liz to sit down. 'He is much in evidence in our circles over here.'

I bet he is, thought Liz.

'But Isabelle Florian tells me you are interested in Antoine Milraud. How can I help?'

'I gather he is known to you?'

Seurat pursed his lips. 'Yes. *Bien connu.* But what is your interest?'

'We have recently come across him in Northern Ireland – in Belfast, where I'm based at present. You may have read that all is now peaceful in Northern Ireland and that terrorism and armed groups are a thing of the past, but that's not entirely true. Though the IRA has declared a ceasefire, there are still some former members who want to continue the struggle. We call them breakaway groups and my service is responsible for intelligence work against these people. We're looking at what we think may be one such group, led by a man we believe to be an American calling himself Seamus Piggott. He's running a security business but we have recently been informed that it's a cover for one of these breakaway terrorist cells. The same informant also told us that Antoine Milraud is in some way involved in all this. We traced him with the DCRI and my visit to you is the result.'

Liz spoke without interruption from Seurat, who was leaning forward in his chair, watching her face with close concentration. When she stopped talking there was a momentary silence, then he said, 'Well, he's a businessman who lives near Toulon.

Not to be confused with Toulouse – it's a smaller town further west, along the coast towards Marseilles. He has an antiques business there, which is very successful; he also has a shop in London. And also, which of course is relevant to your story, one in Belfast.'

'That's an unusual trio of places. Are these businesses a front for something else?'

Seurat looked at her appraisingly. 'You are very direct for an Englishwoman, Miss Carlyle.'

She smiled. 'Not always. But I am finding this visit somewhat mysterious. When my colleague phoned, Isabelle Florian led her to believe this man Milraud was known to the DCRI, but she would only give us information face to face. When I arrived to talk to her, it turned out she had nothing to say, but she sent me to you. Now I'm here, but none the wiser. I cannot believe he is just an antique dealer.'

Seurat looked at his watch. 'I don't know about you, Miss Carlyle, but at this time of the day I am usually halfway through lunch. Why don't you join me? It's just around the corner.'

Her heart sank. She was getting nowhere. She was hungry, though. The breakfast in the hotel had been minimal – just a roll and coffee – and she'd had no dinner the night before. But she thought she could see what lay ahead – three courses, wine, a lot of small talk, and yet further run-around about the mysterious Milraud.

Seurat seemed to sense her frustration. 'It will be possible to talk freely at lunch. And I am not trying to avoid your questions – well,' he added with a grin, 'I would like to but I will not. And in case you are wondering why I know about an antiques dealer from Toulon, Antoine Milraud has not always worked in that trade.'

'No?'

'No, he had a long career doing something different alto-gether.'

'Is that how you know him?'

He seemed amused. 'The last time I saw him, he was sitting in the very chair you are occupying.'

'Oh, really?' She wished this man would stop playing games and get on with it.

'Yes, he used to come in for coffee and a chat almost every morning. You see, Antoine Milraud was once an officer of the DGSE. Perhaps now you can see why your enquiry is a little difficult for us. Shall we go to lunch?'

The Vieux Canard was a small bistro near the Metro, on rue Haxo. It had a front room, with several tables already occupied by locals, but Seurat led her into a small, dark room in the back which had one scrubbed wooden table and looked like the room where the family ate. The table was set for two. They were greeted by a petite black-haired woman in an apron, who kissed Seurat warmly on both cheeks before shaking Liz's hand.

As they sat down Seurat said, 'We all have our vices; mine is having a proper lunch. I eat here almost every day. Now, there is a *prix fixe* set lunch, or if you prefer, I can ask for a menu—'

'No, no. The set lunch is fine,' said Liz, hoping frog's legs were not the *plat du jour*.

'Ah, good choice. Believe me, if you leave yourself in the hands of Madame Bouffet you will eat well.'

They did, starting with a wedge of smooth pâté with brioche – simple but delicious – and while she ate Liz listened as Seurat told her about Antoine Milraud.

'Antoine was a good friend for many years, but he was also what I think you might call a troubled soul.'

Liz smiled at the phrase, and Seurat grinned back. And

suddenly, for the first time since she had landed in France, Liz felt relaxed. She had begun to enjoy the company of this man, so different from the arrogant Mackay. He seemed comfortable with himself, self-assured but without the need to dominate. Thank goodness she had left Mackay on the pavement outside the DCRI.

'As I say, Milraud was troubled, discontented, moody. So one day when he announced, quite matter of factly, 'I am not happy, Martin. I am not sure how much longer I can stay in this job,' – well, *franchement*, I thought nothing of it. I had heard the same before from him, though later, recollecting, I realised he had never said things so openly. I can see now that Milraud had perhaps grown fed up with his small salary, just enough to let him live in a suburb miles from the office. And his wife has always had expensive tastes. You know the type perhaps?'

Liz smiled as he filled her glass from the *pichet* of red wine. Seurat went on, 'Knowing her, I should say that she shared his discontent. Antoine was my friend, and I was loyal to him; at his best, he was a very good officer.' He gestured with his hand. 'Other times he was perhaps not so good. I think he was right to sense that his prospects for promotion were slight. He lacked balance . . . judgement perhaps is a better word.

'Then Milraud went on an operation and disappeared. It has taken me seven years to piece together what happened, but I think at last I know the full story.'

Liz waited while Madame Bouffet took away her plate, replacing it with a fresh one bearing a simple steak and *frites*. A bowl of béarnaise sauce and a green salad in a white crockery dish were placed between them.

'Milraud was assigned to an operation near the Spanish border, helping to infiltrate the Basque extremists who were operating with impunity on our side of the border. The Spanish government's protests about this had at last reached receptive ears, and both the DCRI and the DGSE were – in theory at any rate – working together to flush out these people who were using France as a sanctuary.

'Milraud was posing as an arms dealer, a middleman between the Basque extremists and some vendors from the Eastern bloc. This was after the end of the Cold War, of course, but before order had been restored in Russia. Milraud made the arrangements for an arms transaction, which would take place on neutral ground in Switzerland, near the French border.'

He sighed, cutting into his steak, then chewed thoughtfully. 'But then someone talked too freely: just as the deal was about to be done, thirty armed officers of the Swiss Federal Criminal Police, alerted by a phoned tip off, swooped in. You know the Swiss – quiet, cautious, but very efficient.

'Unfortunately the raid was premature – neither the guns nor the cash to be paid for them were discovered. The Swiss were livid, so much so that they deported both the Russians and the Basques summarily.

'In the aftermath, the Russians believed the Basques had taken possession of the weapons but not paid the cash; equally, the Basques were furious, thinking the Russians had taken their money without delivering the guns.'

He gave a wry smile at the thought of the two parties left fuming. 'Possibly because they were embarrassed at the hash they'd made of things, the Swiss authorities told us that they had managed to confiscate both arms and money. And I have to say that this is what many of my colleagues were happy to believe. Milraud disappeared and it has taken me quite a while to work out what he had done.'

A thin sliver of *tarte tatin* came next. Liz declined more wine and Seurat, pouring the remaining contents of the *pichet* into his own glass, went on, 'Milraud seems to have held on to the three hundred thousand euros he had been holding as the escrow agent, and the small arsenal of automatic weapons, which put him in an unparalleled position to become an arms dealer for real.'

He took a mouthful of tart, then put down his fork. 'And that is what he has been doing ever since. He is an international dealer in arms. With the exception of the Arctic, I doubt there is a continent where he has not done business. He has many enemies, not least the Russians and the Basques whom he cheated, but most of them are now either dead or in prison.'

'And you can't stop him?'

He gave a rueful smile, then said with sudden intensity, 'We are investigating his activities. We are working with the authorities in Spain; in Colombia we liaise with the Americans and in Africa we work on our own. Now he has crossed your sights in the UK, I hope we will be able to work with you too. One day we will have enough to arrest him. But he was always clever, and he has lost none of his cleverness in his new profession.'

Dessert was cleared, and Liz pondered all this over coffee. It was an intriguing story, and she had no reason to doubt any of it. She sensed in Seurat's account a feeling of betrayal, which she well understood.

'So tell me, are you very often in France?' he asked.

She shook her head. 'Sadly not. I like your country very much – and I love Paris. But . . .' and she waved a hand helplessly.

He laughed, a low chuckle she was coming to like. His looks would make him attractive to any woman, but it was his mix of the urbane and the unaffected that appealed to Liz. 'And your husband? He likes Paris as well?'

He knows full well I'm single, thought Liz. He had greeted her as Mlle Carlyle when she first arrived and in any case she wasn't wearing a wedding ring. But she was flattered more than annoyed by the unsubtle query. 'If I ever have a husband, he will be required to love Paris,' she declared firmly.

'Ha! That's excellent. My wife cannot stand the place.'

'Oh, really?' said Liz, disappointed in spite of herself.

'Yes, perhaps that is why she took herself off to her mother's house in Alsace. I believe she is living there still,' he said, flashing his infectious grin. Then he said more seriously, 'It is funny that you should be here asking about Antoine. I was thinking of him just the other day.'

'Why was that?'

He shrugged, nodding at Madame Bouffet as she plonked the bill down on the table. 'How long have you been with your service?'

'Long enough,' she said, ducking the question, but it was in fact almost fifteen years now.

'Then you'll understand me when I say that sometimes we all have our Antoine days. That's what I call them. The kind of day when everything seems . . . would the word be thankless? Yes. You work hard, the money seems very small, your personal life is *absolument zero, n'est-ce-pas*? Does that make sense?'

'Of course,' she said at once. She didn't have a name for what he was describing, but it was familiar enough. Her remedy was to take an hour off and walk along the Thames as far as the Tate Gallery. Sometimes she joined the tourists and went inside and stood in the Pre-Raphaelite room, contemplating one or other of the paintings – by which time her mood had lifted, and she was keen to get back to Thames House.

'It never lasts, and please do not misunderstand me – I like my work and there is not another job I would prefer.' He added jokingly, 'Not even selling arms. My point is, *au fond*, that in those moments I can see what came over Antoine, only for him it was a much more fundamental thing.'

'You can empathise then?'

'You mean "share" his feelings? *Non!*' He was suddenly emphatic. 'I can sympathise, perhaps, but that's all. And not for long. For his so-called freedom, Antoine has helped many people to be killed. None of them he knew; none of them he ever saw. But it is killing just the same.'

Again there was that bitterness, which suggested a personal as much as professional resentment. Liz said nothing as Seurat paid the bill, then they walked slowly towards the Metro.

When they reached the station, she held out her hand. 'That was a wonderful lunch. Thank you very much. And you have been extremely helpful.'

'Excellent.' He seemed genuinely pleased. 'Now perhaps you can help me with two requests. The first is to please keep in touch as you investigate what Milraud is up to in Belfast. It goes without saying that if we can be of any assistance, you must not hesitate to say so.'

'Of course,' Liz said simply, wondering what the second request would be.

Seurat looked hesitant and for the first time less than completely self-assured. 'The other is not perhaps not quite so professional. Would you have dinner with me this evening?'

'Oh Martin,' she said, suddenly realising they had slipped into first names during the course of their lunch, 'I would love to. But I have to get back.' An image of Jimmy Fergus flickered briefly in her mind.

'Another time then,' said Seurat mildly.

For all his good looks, there was something disappointed in this gallant acceptance of her rejection; it made Liz want to reassure him. She touched him lightly on the arm.

'There will be another time, I'm sure,' she said. 'I have a feeling Monsieur Milraud will see to that.'

23

He was suspicious of the letter from the start. Block capitals on the envelope – **SEAMUS PIGGOTT** – and the office address, then at the bottom: **PRIVATE**. His secretary had obeyed the instruction, and placed it unopened with the rest of the morning's post in his in-tray.

He slit the envelope cautiously. Letter bombs were bulkier than this, but it paid to be careful. A man with his background had many enemies, and he knew they were out there, just waiting for him to drop his guard and give them the opportunity to have a go. The Feds and their British stooges would love to be able to stick something on him, and there were others, people here in Northern Ireland, who resented the success of the Fraternity's activities. It was inevitable that a clever and determined man like him aroused the envy and resentment of weaker specimens.

There was no bomb inside the envelope, just a folded piece of A4 paper. He extracted it slowly and carefully, holding the corner with his fingertips and flicking it open with the point of a pencil. He was startled by the bizarre appearance of the message, and surprised by what it said.

Watch your back. Well, he'd spent thirty years doing that. Yes, he took risks, but only necessary ones; he had never been impetuous, and every step he took was carefully calculated beforehand. He cast his mind back with satisfaction to the boy Aidan, sitting trembling and terrified in his office in County Down. Before Malone had brought the boy in, he had already decided to have two of his fingers broken. That was the appropriate punishment for blabbing and complaining. Not three (that would have been excessive), but not just one either – that wouldn't have been enough. He was a fine judge of these things, he thought with pleasure.

He looked down again with disdain at the paper and its cutout letters. He didn't need some anonymous coward to instruct him to take care.

But the real thrust of the message – its warning about Milraud – was more puzzling. He didn't believe for a moment that Milraud was talking to British Intelligence. He and the Frenchman went back a long way. He knew something of Milraud's background; he knew what his previous profession had been and why he'd changed it. It was inconceivable that Milraud would betray him to MI5.

Still, never take anything for granted. He'd learned that long ago. Enduring loyalty was a contradiction in terms. Any allegiance was vulnerable; everyone could be seduced by something: money, women, power, fear or an ideology. There were many people in this little island whose lives were governed by ideology – be it Irish Republicanism or so-called Loyalism to the British crown. But of all people, Milraud was the least likely to have become attached to a political cause. He was far too cool-headed a businessman for that.

Piggott himself was happy to pay lip service to the ideology of Irish Republicanism. His credentials as a long-standing IRA supporter had helped to establish him in the Belfast under-

126

world almost overnight. But his only true ideology nowadays, the only thing he really cared about, was revenge. He'd made the money he had once craved, growing up poor in South Boston. Women had never mattered to him at all – it seemed inexplicable why so many men met their downfall chasing a skirt. And as for power, it was enough that people feared him; the people working for him did what he said, and everyone else gave him a wide berth.

So he had only one desire now: the burning urge, fuelled by anger, to get even with the people who had hurt him. To injure them as they'd injured him. That was what was driving him on.

He turned his attention back to the letter. *Watch your back.* He certainly would, as he always did. He picked up his mobile and thumbed the auto-dial.

After three rings a reedy, youthful voice answered. 'Hello,' it said shakily.

He knew Danny Ryan was terrified of him. Good – he was going to keep it that way. 'Danny, listen carefully. I've got a job for you.'

'Yes, Mr P,' he said, like a junior mobster speaking to *el capo*.

'Here's what I want you to do,' said Piggott with deceptive mildness. Then he added in a voice of steel, 'And this time you'd better not screw it up.'

24

'Where's Liz?'

Judith turned from her cupboard clutching a pile of papers to find Dave standing beside her.

'She's not back from Paris yet,' she said, dumping the papers on her desk and looking up at Dave. Judith had known Dave for years and they'd worked together often before they both came to Northern Ireland. His cheerful, breezy approach to life had buoyed her up through some difficult times at work and when her family life had fallen to pieces. But now she stared at him, shocked by his appearance. His round, boyish face looked thinner, drawn and tired. There was no sign of the ever-present smile.

'Dave. Are you OK?'

'Yes, I'm fine,' he replied flatly, sitting down suddenly in her visitors' chair.

'Well, you don't look it. What's happened?'

He rubbed a hand over his face, brushing back his hair. 'I expect you'll hear on the grapevine, so I might as well tell you. I've broken up with Lucy.'

Lucy was a second lieutenant in the Intelligence Corps stationed outside London. Judith knew that she and Dave had been an item for two years or so and Dave had even hinted that they might get married.

'It's not been easy being apart, but I thought everything was essentially fine, but then last night I phoned her and she suddenly said that she wasn't sure about us. She was thinking of leaving the army, she didn't want to be hitched to my job, she needed time to think and she didn't want to see me again until she knew her own mind.' He looked at Judith glumly. 'I think it's the end for us. She's probably met someone else and is trying to let me down lightly.'

'Oh Dave. I'm so sorry. I thought you were both so happy.'

'We were,' said Dave. 'But I think I'd better get used to the idea of life without her now. Anyway,' he said, shaking his head and standing up suddenly. 'I was looking for Liz to tell her that I'm seeing this bloke Milraud this afternoon.'

Judith's eyes widened. 'Where?'

'At his shop.' He looked at her. 'What's the problem?'

'Who's watching your back?'

'No one. It's just a social call,' he added. When she didn't smile, he said, 'It's not a big deal, Judith. I've told him I'm a collector of antique derringers wanting to look at what he's got. That's all. He has no reason to suspect anything else.'

'What on earth do you know about derringers?'

'I've got all the guff on them from the internet. I reckon I can pass as a collector.'

'Don't you think you should check with Liz first?'

'That's why I was looking for her, but I'll have to go ahead without her. Nothing's going to happen – it's a first meet. I'm just trying to get a handle on the guy and see if there's anything in it for us.'

'I think you should wait. Liz might have learned something useful about Milraud in Paris.'

'Yeah, but he's here now and he might not be for long. I don't want to miss him.'

Judith hesitated, looking at Dave's drawn face. She could see that he needed to be active to take his mind off his troubles, and active for Dave meant something that got the adrenalin flowing. But she felt uneasy. He was in the mood to take risks.

'Shouldn't you at least talk to Michael Binding?'

'Binding's virtually living at Stormont these days,' he replied impatiently. 'It'll be okay, Judith. Stop worrying.' And he walked off.

Later that day Dave drove into Belfast, parked in the car park at the Castlecourt shopping centre, then walked towards the University of Ulster. Milraud's shop was halfway down a narrow side street full of coffee shops and clothes boutiques.

The shop was on a terrace of two-storey Georgian buildings of yellowing stone, once houses, now all shops. Miraud's establishment was fronted by a long low window, in which a beautiful antique pistol was lying on a red velvet cushion, flanked by a pair of wooden-handled eighteenth-century derringers propped decoratively against each other. Looking through the window, Dave could see a large glass cabinet against a far wall, where more antique pistols hung from iron hooks.

Putting his hand on the highly polished brass handle, he took a deep breath and pushed. A bell rang, triggered by the opening of the door, and a woman looked up from behind a display counter at the far end of the shop. She smiled as she came out to meet him. This was obviously no ordinary shop and she no ordinary shop assistant. She was a slim middle-aged woman with beautifully cut grey hair, dressed in a plain black suit of some sort of rough silk, a thin gold necklace her only jewellery. Everything about the place murmured wealth and good taste.

Dave was glad he had dressed up a bit – no parka this morning, but a navy-blue blazer he had dusted off, a woollen v-necked jersey, an open-neck white shirt and sparklingly clean chinos. His shoes, a pair of black slip-ons, looked highly polished only because he so rarely wore them.

'Can I help you?' the elegant lady asked with a smile at once formal and genteel.

'Good afternoon. I'm Simon Willis. I have an appointment with Mr Milraud.'

'Good afternoon, Mr Willis. Please follow me,' the woman said, and led him through a door marked 'Private' into an office where a man sat at a small mahogany desk, leafing through a saleroom catalogue.

Milraud's face beneath his short hair was Gallic, with dark questioning eyes, and olive-tinted skin. He wore a maroon turtle-neck sweater under a grey plaid jacket. He could have been anything from a Foreign Legion officer to a lecturer in philosophy at the Sorbonne. When he rose to shake hands, though he was much shorter than Dave, his body was more muscular, and there was an icy element Dave sensed behind the facade.

'Would you like coffee, Mr Willis?' Milraud asked as they both sat down.

Dave shook his head. 'Thanks, but I'm fine. It's good of you to see me.'

Milraud shrugged, as if to say this was his business after all. 'You said on the telephone that you have an interest in antique arms.'

'Among other things,' said Dave. He wanted to put down a marker that Milraud could pick up at any time.

'What sort of arms are you looking for?'

'Derringers, at least to begin with. Eighteenth and nineteenth century. Continental ones especially.'

131

'Belfast is not perhaps the ideal place to look for French and German weapons,' Milraud said with a mild inquiring tone.

It was Dave's turn to shrug. 'You never know where things will turn up these days. Thanks to the internet.'

Milraud smiled in agreement, then said, 'Yes, but the internet cannot magically transport a piece that's residing in my warehouse to this shop. Not yet anyway.'

'True enough,' said Dave, then shifted in his chair to show he wanted to get to business. 'Have you anything at all of that sort here that you can show me?'

'Of course,' said Milraud, giving a faint smile. 'Even some continental items.'

He stood up and motioning for Dave to stay where he was, left the room, returning a minute later with a cherry wood box, which he put down on his desk. Lifting the lid, he exposed a small derringer sitting on a cushion of black velvet. He carefully took the gun out with both hands and handed it to Dave.

'It is made by Sabayone,' Milraud declared. Dave stared at the trigger intently and looked down the barrel, doing his best to act like a true aficionado.

Milraud chuckled lightly. 'Probably the only one to be found in this part of the United Kingdom. Are you an admirer of his pistols?'

'Absolutely,' said Dave. 'A master craftsman.' He handed back the pistol carefully. 'What would you ask for such a piece?' he said, hoping that was the right sort of thing to say.

A shadow of a frown flitted across Milraud's face, as if the intrusion of money into their conversation had a soiling effect. He said quietly without looking at Dave, 'Seventeen thousand pounds.'

'I see,' said Dave, his eyes widening with surprise.

'That is open to negotiation, of course,' Milraud conceded.

'Excellent,' said Dave, smiling inwardly at the thought of Michael Binding's face if he actually bought the gun.

'You're interested then?' asked Milraud, no longer quite so diffident.

'I might well be,' Dave said with conviction. 'It is certainly a lovely example. Do you guarantee its authenticity?'

'Of course,' said Milraud with a tolerant air, as if Dave's hesitation was of no real importance.

'I'd like to think about it. When could we meet again?' asked Dave.

'Well, tomorrow would be possible, I suppose. After that I will be back in France. Although Mrs Carson,' and he gestured towards the front room and the lady in the silk suit, 'can always negotiate on my behalf.'

Dave shook his head to show a surrogate wouldn't do. 'I'll come back in the morning if that's convenient.'

'*A demain*, then.' They both stood up and shook hands.

Dave said, 'And perhaps then we could talk about more modern armaments.'

Milraud raised his eyebrows a fraction. 'Why not?' he said with an almost imperceptible shrug. 'If you wish.'

That afternoon Milraud's mobile rang and he answered it cautiously. '*Oui?*'

'It's me.'

'James.' He continued to use Piggott's old names.

'Listen, my friend, I've had a communication.'

'Oh?'

'Yes.' Piggott gave a dry laugh. 'Someone's suggested you've been talking to my old British friends.'

'How interesting,' Milraud said non-committally. Milraud had done business with Piggott for many years, and they trusted each other – as much as anyone could in their kind of business. But Milraud was always cautious, and this was a lethal accusation if it were believed.

Piggott said, 'I was wondering whether anyone unusual had crossed your path lately. I mean, if I'm supposed to believe this message, someone should be making an appearance, if they haven't already.'

'Mmm. I think we should meet.'

Half an hour later the two men sat down at a table in a nearby cafe.

'I had a man in the shop just before you rang. He phoned me out of the blue, claiming to be interested in antique pistols. Derringers in particular. I didn't altogether like the look of him. I showed him a lovely example, and he made all the right noises, except for one.'

'What was that?'

'I told him the gun was made by someone called Sabayone. He agreed that Sabayone was a brilliant gunsmith.'

'And?'

'There wasn't a gunsmith called Sabayone. I made him up just to test him.'

Piggott gave a laugh that suddenly stopped – humour was like rationed food to him, allowed only in carefully measured portions. 'That sounds like our man.'

'It's possible.'

'What was he really after?'

'He dropped a heavy hint about modern weapons. I've arranged to see him again tomorrow morning and then I should find out. I'm sure he'll come.'

'Oh so am I,' said Piggott. 'You should see him, by all means. That'll give us a chance to see him too.'

Piggott walked away from the cafe, relieved. He hadn't ever really thought Milraud would double-cross him, but was glad to have that confirmed.

Yet he hadn't come entirely clean with his old associate, for he'd avoided telling Milraud that Danny Ryan had reported back to him an hour before.

'We did our best, Mr P.'

'Meaning?'

'We watched the shop, just like you said. There was only one customer this afternoon; he was inside for about twenty minutes. We got a good photo when he left. I followed him as best I could – you said it was better to lose him than get spotted.'

'So you lost him?'

'Not there. He was parked at the Castlecourt shopping centre. I picked him up as he left and trailed him as far as the harbour. He was heading towards the A2 when he got away from me.'

'M2 or A2?' The difference was important.

'A2, Mr P.'

And Piggott nodded to himself. The A2 went north. Towards Holywood and Palace Barracks, he thought. He'd have put money on it.

25

Bruno was waiting for Liz when she got back to the embassy. He made a show of looking at his watch. 'I was getting worried that you might have succumbed to Monsieur Seurat's charms. From the time you took, it would seem you did.'

She laughed. 'Bruno, I didn't know you cared.'

He was not amused. 'So how did you get on?'

'Very well. He was most helpful.'

He extended a fistful of paper. 'This came in while you were gone.'

She cast a quick eye at the pages. It was a long message from Peggy Kinsolving in London, marked *Strictly Confidential*. 'Anything urgent in this?' she asked dryly, as he had obviously read it.

'Not that I can tell. Though this chap Piggott sounds a handful. You'd better come into my office, Liz.'

Upstairs she went through the document carefully while Bruno pretended to attend to some paperwork. Peggy had been her usual thorough self, going through old files that were inaccessible to Judith Spratt in Belfast. She had unearthed a goldmine of information on Piggott. *Liz*, a prefatory note declared, *the following summary is based on our own files, which have drawn heavily on information from the FBI. Please also see the note I've attached at the end.*

PK.

Piggott born James Purnell in 1954 in Boston Massachusetts. Changed his name to Piggott by deed poll six months before moving to Ireland three years ago.

Purnell was the child of two first-generation Irish émigrés, and eldest of two sons. Grew up in the working-class neighbourhood of Dorchester – his father was a clerk in a law firm. Educated at the prestigious Boston Latin School after winning a scholarship. Attended MIT and took a Bachelor of Science in a combined mathematics and physics degree, followed in 1974 by a PhD. A brilliant student but references from teachers describe him as headstrong.

In 1972 a Purnell was recorded as a member of the extremist group the Weather Underground, but no firm connection between our subject, James Purnell, and the Weathermen was ever firmly established.

Purnell's advanced degree in mathematics and physics was of particular value in the military area of high grade missile technology. Purnell was offered a position with Arrow Systems, a Route 128 group specialising in missile control and retrieval software systems. Its contracts were predominantly with the US Defense Department. Accordingly Purnell was successfully positively vetted before being offered the post.

His name appears in lists compiled in the late 1980s by local fundraisers for the Northern Ireland Aid Committee (NORAID). Purnell visited England in June 1984 but he did not come to notice in contact with IRA sympathisers on the mainland.

In 1985 Purnell left Arrow Systems and established his own consultancy (The Purnell Group – or TPG), employing his younger brother Edwin as chief finance officer. Edwin was a trained *accountant, but also very active in IRA fundraising – his name appears in FBI files on NORAID activities, and he visited Northern Ireland on several occasions.*

Where Arrow Systems had specialised in anti-radar aspects of large-scale missile systems, TPG focused on hand-held projectile weaponry (RPG), and surface-to-air missiles (SAMs). Until the late 1990s revenues were almost exclusively derived from Department of Defense contracts, but cuts in procurement at the end of the Clinton administration forced TPG to look for other clients. These included US government-approved customers, Israel, South Africa, and Pakistan, but an FBI file suggests Purnell may also have been doing business with a range of illegal clients, including Somalian rebels and both sides of the Rwanda civil war – Hutus and Tutsi. It was believed that revenues from these sales were deposited in off-shore banks, first in the Seychelles, then in banks in those former Soviet countries that had refused to sign international disclosure agreements (Estonia and Moldova in particular).

In 1999 at the instigation of MI5, the FBI investigated a gun-running scheme to smuggle arms, including hand-held missile launchers, by ship from the coast of Maine into Northern Ireland. Three men were arrested, including Edwin Purnell. The trial of the Mattapan Three (named by the press after the South Boston neighbourhood where all three lived) took place in 2001, though coverage of the trial was overshadowed by the events of 9/11.

All three men were convicted, and Edwin Purnell was sentenced to six years for his part in the plot. He was due for parole in 2004 but died of kidney failure in a federal prison in Louisiana in 2003. Despite our suspicion that James Purnell was involved, the FBI was unable to link him to any part of the conspiracy.

After his brother's death, James Purnell closed down his company, changed his name, and moved to Northern Ireland.

When she had finished reading, Liz looked at the note Peggy had attached to the end of the document:

Liz,

The FBI special agent in charge of the Boston investigation of 1999/2000 was called Daryl T. Sulkey Jr and the same man is the new FBI legat in London. I phoned him and he could meet you first thing tomorrow – 8.15 a.m. at Grosvenor. Please let him know if you can't make it; otherwise he will be expecting you.

    PK

'Interesting,' said Bruno, when he saw that she had finished reading. 'But what's the connection with Milraud and this man Purnell? And why did Purnell move to Northern Ireland?'

Liz sighed. 'Ask me no questions, Bruno, and I'll tell you no lies.' Not that Liz knew the answers to his questions. She was hoping that the FBI man rejoicing in the name of Daryl T. Sulkey Jr might supply them.

26

Back at his desk, Dave was feeling uncomfortable. In the calm aftermath of the meeting with Milraud his depression over the break-up with Lucy had returned. Judith had looked in to see how the meeting had gone and he'd assured her that it was all just fine and he was writing it up before deciding what to do next.

But had it really gone fine? The more he thought about it, the more he wondered if Milraud had been playing him along. He was worried about Sabayone. He'd pretended to know all about him but he'd never heard of him and when he got back to the office he'd looked him up on the internet and found no trace of a gunsmith of that name. Whatever game Milraud had been playing, Dave was now convinced that he was not merely a prosperous dealer in antiques. There had been no puzzlement and equally no umbrage taken at Dave's clear desire to discuss more modern armaments.

He ought to talk to Liz about it before he went back for another interview. She would want to discuss with Michael Binding just how far out on a limb Dave the Derringer Collector should go. If there was information about Piggott and arms dealing to be got out of Milraud, how much were they prepared to pay? It was clear that at the next stage he would need to suggest that cash would be forthcoming in return for information.

But yet again Liz wasn't in her office. She was coming back via London, Judith told him, because of something she'd learned in Paris. He ought to wait. She might have found out something relevant. But it would be another day before she was back and with Milraud's departure imminent, there was no time to lose. The investigation of the attempt on Jimmy Fergus meant that there would be no spare A4 resources available at such short notice to provide adequate support for a meeting with Milraud the next morning. And if he requested it as a priority, and Michael Binding had to arbitrate, he would certainly give it to the Fergus investigation and order Dave not to go ahead without full back-up. By which time Milraud would be back in France, leaving the shop in the charge of the woman in the silk suit, who would profess to know nothing about anything except antique weapons.

And that would be that; all the hard work he'd done since the initial call from Brown Fox would go down the drain. No way, thought Dave. He couldn't bear the thought of his investigation joining his private life in ruins. Besides, Milraud had been receptive so far.

'The derringer is very appealing, but—'

'But?' asked Milraud with a knowing smile. 'I can move on the price to fifteen thousand, but no more, I am afraid. One reaches a point . . .' he gave a vague movement of his hands.

They were in the back office again, and small talk had been kept to a minimum. Milraud wore a tie today, and a suitcase in the corner suggested he would leave for the airport immediately after seeing Dave.

'I understand,' Dave said. 'The price is not the issue.'

'Ah. Then if I may ask, what is your position? Do you wish to buy?'

Dave hesitated. It crossed his mind that he should have found out more about the man before he embarked on a recruitment approach. But then 'nothing ventured, nothing gained', he said to himself. Milraud hadn't exactly thrown him out of the shop yesterday when he'd mentioned modern weapons. So he said, 'Perhaps other things might be included too.'

The Frenchman looked thoughtfully at him. He raised his eyebrows a fraction. 'Well, of course, Mr Willis, I deal in a wide range of weapons. But what have you in mind? I assume we are no longer talking about derringers?'

'No. Modern weapons as well.'

Milraud seemed to consider this, clasping both hands, elbows on the desk in front of him. 'It's conceivable. What kinds of weapons?'

'All kinds. Automatic weapons. Handguns and larger items. Possibly associated ordnance too. Grenades, mortars, RPGs.'

Milraud narrowed his eyes, and his hand wandered beneath the edge of the desk top; Dave tensed. Then it re-emerged, apparently from the upper drawer of the desk. Milraud popped something in his mouth.

'I assume, Mr Willis, that you are talking about legitimate weaponry? I don't have many enquiries from amateurs for the sort of things you mention. Of course, what my clients want, I try to find, that is true. But I would need to know more about who they are, and their reasons for making such enquiries. Particularly, if I may say so, in this town.'

Dave was beginning to feel uncomfortable. He had a suspicion that Milraud was playing with him. So he said, 'To be more precise, what I'm interested in is information. And we may well be talking about sums greater than fifteen thousand pounds.'

'I should think so, *mon ami*,' said Milraud, staring levelly at Dave. 'I should think so.'

There was a tap on the door. When it opened Mrs Carson stood there. 'Monsieur Milraud, I beg your pardon for interrupting. But could I see you for a moment please?' She threw a small smile in Dave's direction. 'I'm so sorry. A rather awkward customer in the shop.'

Dave waved an arm in understanding, relieved at the opportunity to gather his thoughts. As Milraud left the room, he wondered what to say next. Money seemed the object, pure and simple; he supposed in Milraud's world loyalty was always a function of the highest price. He was pondering his next move when he heard the door behind him open. 'Everything all right?' he asked.

'Could not be better, my friend,' said a foreign-sounding voice. It didn't belong to Milraud.

27

Liz opened the door of her basement flat in Kentish Town with a sinking feeling. After being away for several weeks she wondered what she would find. She remembered how she had left in a hurry without the rigorous clearing up and cleaning that she had intended to do. But apart from a musty smell, a layer of dust and a carton of milk in the fridge that had separated into curds and whey, all was well, though in contrast to the bright flat in Belfast, kept in sparkling order by Mrs Ryan, the place seemed dark and unwelcoming. With all its disadvantages, Liz loved this flat, the first property she had ever owned, but now she found herself wondering whether she would settle happily back here again.

It was late and she was tired after the day in Paris and the flight home, but her answer phone was flashing demandingly. When she pressed the button to listen to her messages, it informed her that it was full, so telling herself that all the messages would be out of date, she deleted everything without bothering to listen. Then she went to bed.

She slept uneasily and woke to a grey drizzle and nothing more than black instant coffee for breakfast. Something about being back in her home environment caused her to remember guiltily that she hadn't phoned her mother for days.

Susan Carlyle lived in Wiltshire in the gatehouse of a large estate, part of which was now a nursery garden which she managed. Liz's father had been the estate manager and Liz had been brought up in the beautiful surroundings of Bowerbridge. But her father had died shortly after Liz had come to work in London, and ever since then she had felt responsible for her mother. She had dutifully made the slow, awkward drive from London down to Bowerbridge on Friday evenings at least one weekend a month.

But in the last year her mother had acquired a boyfriend, or partner (Liz was never quite sure which was the correct term for their relationship), and in spite of Liz's fears that Edward Treglown would be a pipe-smoking, tweed-jacketed ex-military bore whom she would dislike on sight, he had turned out to be an excellent thing. Having been a Ghurkha officer for thirty years he was now director of a charity working to relieve blindness in developing countries – a charming and discreet man who seemed to be making her mother very happy. As well as liking him, Liz was grateful to him for that.

There was no answer from the phone at the house, but Liz knew that at Edward's insistence her mother had recently taken the (to her) daring step of acquiring a mobile phone, so she now dialled that.

Susan Carlyle answered on the third ring. 'Oh hello, dear. How is beautiful Belfast?'

'I hope it's a lot nicer than here. I'm in London.'

'London? So am I. We came up last night. How long are you here for?'

'I'll have to fly back later today. I was actually on business in Paris but I've had to stop off here on my way back.'

'What an exciting life you lead! Any chance of seeing you before you leave?'

Liz hadn't expected her mother to be in London. She thought about her day. 'Well, I might be able to do a quick lunch. My flight's not till six.'

'Lunch it is then. I'll bring Edward too, shall I?'

'Yes, of course,' said Liz. 'I'd love to see him,' she added truthfully.

At five foot eight inches Liz thought of herself as tall for a woman; even so she was used to having to look up at American men. But Daryl Sulkey was huge, probably a foot taller than Liz and far and away the tallest man she had ever encountered. She could see him waiting for her on the far side of the daunting security post at the American Embassy in Grosvenor Square. After her bag and jacket had gone through the X-ray machine and she had been patted down by an unsmiling uniformed female guard, she emerged on the other side to a warm welcome. Sulkey's arms matched the length of the rest of him and ended in enormous hands, on one finger of which he wore a heavy gold ring, set with an appropriately large blue stone. Liz was thankful that the power of his grip, as his right hand engulfed hers, did not match the size of his hands, and she managed to escape with her fingers uncrushed.

As she followed him to his office, she noticed that he moved his right leg awkwardly and that his right foot was crooked, and she wondered if his size and the length of his back and his legs had affected his movement. She was relieved when he finally sat down behind his desk and she was able to see his face on something like a level with hers for the first time. It was a thinner, more lined face than she had expected from his vast size and she wondered whether whatever caused his awkward walk also gave him pain.

Liz had been in a number of senior FBI agents' offices both in America and in London and she recognised the style. It was a very different feel from the set up in the CIA station, in another part of this massive embassy building, where the suspicious and distinctly unwelcoming Andy Bokus presided as head of station. Liz had recently encountered him in the course of another case and had got the impression that female MI5 officers were not his favourite form of life.

This office and its occupant had a much warmer feel. Behind the wooden desk crossed flags were draped and on the walls hung framed photographs of Sulkey with the director of the FBI, Sulkey shaking hands with a former president of the United States, and several of Sulkey sitting with a group of equally enormous men, obviously a basketball team.

'I used to play ball,' said Sulkey, seeing Liz eyeing the photographs, 'until I got my injury.'

Liz smiled sympathetically but thinking it more polite not to pursue the question of the injury, she broached the reason for her visit: Seamus Piggott, once known as James Purnell.

'Your colleague Miss Peggy Kinsolving told me on the phone that Purnell is now in Northern Ireland and causing you guys some concern. I've only been in London for a few months and I'm afraid I haven't got round to visiting Belfast yet. It seemed to me that with the peace process having removed the worst of the violence, it wasn't one of my priorities. But if James Purnell is causing trouble over there then maybe I was wrong.'

'Well,' said Liz, 'we're not entirely sure what he's up to yet. On the face of it he's running a perfectly legitimate business, but we've had some information from a source recently that Purnell is leading a breakaway group of ex-IRA people who are out to kill police and intelligence officers in Northern Ireland. Our files show that you were the special agent in charge of the investigation in Boston, and when I heard that you were here, it seemed a good opportunity to pick up some background on him – and to ask if you think that our source's information sounds likely to be true.'

Wrapping his long fingers around his coffee cup, Sulkey stared down thoughtfully at the dregs and said quietly, 'Nothing he'd do would surprise me. Let me tell you a bit about him.'

At first, there was little in what he said that Liz hadn't already read in Peggy's memo – the super-bright young Irish-American, specialising in academic subjects that ultimately made him an expert in missile technology. It was an expertise that for a long time was employed in the service of the US government.

'I gather you first came across him through investigating his brother,' Liz interjected, trying to move things on.

'That's right. And they couldn't have been more different.' Sulkey gave a wry smile. 'They say America is a melting pot, but sometimes people don't melt. As my colleague Tommy Birmingham likes to say, part of the Irish community in America has never really left Ireland. They call South Boston 'Southey'. It's New England's Dublin. If you go into some of the bars there – and with your accent I wouldn't advise it – you'd think the Easter Uprising of 1916 was still being fought.

'Edwin Purnell was James's younger brother by eight years. Their parents died when Edwin was still quite young and James looked after him. Edwin was an okay student but he dropped out of college and got in with the hard core of the Boston-Irish crowd. Only his brother's financial support kept his head above water and after a series of dead-end jobs he ended up working for James when James formed his own company.'

'Were they brought up to support the IRA?'

'Not really – that's the funny thing. Neither of their parents was political but the local Irish culture was political all right, and that's where Edwin seemed to pick it up. He grew more and more pro-IRA as the years went by.'

'But James was a bit of a firebrand too, I gather,' said Liz, recalling the file's account of his anti-Vietnam War activism.

'He was, when he was young,' said Sulkey, shifting uncomfortably in his seat and stretching out his long legs, 'but not especially about Ireland. He only got drawn in when Edwin was asked to help smuggle arms for the IRA. By then James's company was heavily into developing missiles – hand-held, surface-to-air. It was a legitimate business – but it was also just what the IRA was looking for in those days. I don't think James got involved out of nationalist conviction, so much as for the money and trying to keep his brother from getting caught. If James was the genius, Edwin was the dumbo. James clearly felt the need to look after him.'

'But they got caught.'

'They did, but not because of anything James did – or Edwin for that matter. Somebody in Northern Ireland talked to you guys in MI5. There was enough detail in the information that we knew what was going to be smuggled out – RPGs and SAM missiles – and where it was going from: Gloucester, a fishing town thirty miles north of Boston. We didn't know the exact timing, but we staked out the harbour and two months later we caught them red-handed.'

'But not James?'

'Nope,' he shook his head emphatically. 'He was the obvious source of the stuff, but we couldn't get evidence that would hold up in court. And in those days, long before 9/11, some of the judges were pretty sympathetic to that kind of activity. If you ask me, he would have taken the fall for his brother if he'd had to – he was that devoted to him – but it was too late: we had Edwin dead to rights. From James's point of view, there was no point going to prison if it wasn't going to keep his brother out.'

Liz said, 'And then Edwin didn't come out.'

'That's right.' He pursed his lips, musing. 'It was a freak thing. A kidney infection that was mistreated – I don't know about standards of medical care in Her Majesty's prisons, but in a Federal Penitentiary you're not usually looked after by Dr Kildare.'

'And James?'

'He was devastated. Well, as much as he was capable of feeling emotion. You see, this is a guy who was known as a loner, who has never married, and has no record of close relationships with anybody – male or female. Except his brother. Once his brother was gone, there was nothing to care about except avenging him.'

Liz said, 'It makes sense in a strange kind of way.'

Sulkey nodded and gave a small smile. 'Yeah. And whether it was in memory of his brother, or because it would give him a better chance to avenge him, James suddenly goes all Irish. He becomes Seamus, moves to Belfast, and from what you tell me, starts to act like a classic IRA hood. I've spoken to a lot of people about Purnell over the years and the words they've used to describe him were "single-minded", "ruthless" and "cold-hearted".'

Liz suddenly felt a chill run down her spine. 'So if he's decided to kill a police officer or one of us, he's going to keep going till he succeeds,' she said quietly. 'Or till we catch him,' she added, 'and you make that sound difficult.'

Sulkey gave a grim nod. 'Let's just say I never succeeded.'

Liz looked up at Sulkey's lined face. 'Thank you, I think I understand what's driving him much better now.'

They stood up together and as they shook hands again Liz said, 'There's just one more thing I was wondering about.'

'What's that?'

'Didn't Purnell also nurse a grudge against the FBI? After all, it's you who put his brother in the prison where he died. I'd have thought he'd have tried to get his revenge on you chaps first.'

Sulkey gave a short laugh. 'Funny you should ask. I think it's fair to say he had a try.'

'What did he do?'

'He tried to kill the officer in charge of the investigation.'

'Was that your colleague Birmingham?'

Sulkey looked at Liz. 'No, it was me. Someone tampered with the wheels of my car – I reckon it was Purnell, not that I can prove it. Two of my tyres blew out when I was doing seventy on Interstate Ninety-five.' He shook his head and looked down at his leg. 'I was lucky to survive. All I got left with was this limp.'

28

It was still raining when Liz came out of the embassy into Grosvenor Square, so she hailed a passing taxi and asked for Vauxhall Bridge. Nowadays pictures of Thames House, MI5's headquarters on Millbank, appeared on TV every time there was a terrorism story, so she never gave it as her destination. She felt it was uncomfortable if not downright insecure to link herself so closely to the intelligence world. It was a sensible precaution she liked to take.

As the taxi negotiated the morning traffic, she thought over what Daryl Sulkey had said about Piggott. It was a chilling story, and she decided to get Peggy Kinsolving to ring Judith and Dave to let them know that the threat was serious, and that the tip-off that Brown Fox had given them was likely to be true.

But when she walked into the open-plan office where Peggy had her desk there was no Peggy, just a note waiting for her.

Sorry to miss you. Got to go out. Hope Sulkey was helpful. Let me know if I can do any more. Lunch next time?

So Liz walked down the corridor to Charles Wetherby's room, with a mounting feeling of pleasurable anticipation. In the outer office Wetherby's secretary greeted her warmly. 'I didn't know you were in town.'

'I didn't know I was coming myself until yesterday. Is Charles in?'

'Yes, he is. Let me just check if he's free; I know he'd like to see you.'

She went into Charles's office, then a moment later came out, leaving the door open. 'Go on in.'

Liz went in eagerly but with slight apprehension, too. She hadn't seen him since Joanne's funeral. How would he be holding up?

'Liz. It's good to see you,' said Charles, coming out from behind his desk. He looked spruce in a dark suit and cheerful red tie. There was a bounce to his step, and his face had colour in it again.

He gave her a peck on both cheeks and motioned her to sit down. 'I didn't know you were coming over. What brings you here?'

'I had to see the FBI legat first thing. We've got an interesting case – an Irish-American who's moved to Belfast. He's set up a dodgy-looking business and surrounded himself with ex-IRA hardliners. At first we thought he was simply running a criminal racket but now it looks as though he's planning some serious attacks.'

'I hope you're being careful over there – I heard about Jimmy Fergus getting shot. Is there a link?'

'There could well be.' She was about to try and move the conversation onto a more personal level when there was a tap on the door and Wetherby's secretary poked her head in. 'Sorry to interrupt, Charles, but DG's just rung and asked if you could pop up to his office.'

'But the meeting with the Home Secretary's not for an hour,' he complained.

'I know, but he said he wants to go over a few things with you before it starts.'

Wetherby sighed, and looked at Liz with weary resignation. 'I'm so sorry.'

'It can't be helped,' she said with a brightness she didn't feel.

'Will you be over again soon?'

'I'm not sure. But I'll let you know in advance next time.'

'Yes. Do, and then we can have lunch.'

'How are the boys?' she asked, as he got up to go.

'Fine, thanks,' he replied with a smile. And then he was off, striding down the corridor to the lifts. As she watched him go, Liz realised how much she missed talking to him. On an operational level his advice was invaluable, but what she really wanted to know was how he was feeling now that he was on his own, and in particular what he was feeling. Did he miss her?

Through the window overlooking the Thames she could see the rain had stopped, and the cloud was slowly giving way to a watery sun. On the river one of the commuter boats that took people to work in the City was trudging slowly back upstream, almost empty. As she looked at her watch she wondered why she did this to herself.

Liz and her mother had agreed to meet at Tate Britain, on the Embankment, less than ten minutes' walk from work for Liz. She was early and she found Susan Carlyle and Edward in one of the galleries, staring at a stunning abstract by Howard Hodgkin. She watched them fondly for a moment – Edward, tall in a green tweed jacket, bending down to point something out to her mother; Susan, pretty in a camel coat with a fur collar, nodding vaguely in agreement. A tiny ripple of jealousy passed through her as she saw their warm companionship.

'I certainly don't know what it's supposed to be,' Edward was saying as Liz joined them and they all examined a crescent the colour of blood oranges painted on oatmeal canvas. 'But despite my old codger status, I *like* it.'

'Edward, I don't think you're as old as the painter is,' said Liz.

Susan Carlyle laughed. 'Well, I like it too, provided I don't have to see it every day.'

They went downstairs to the restaurant in the basement, a long handsome room with original Rex Whistler murals on the walls. Liz, sitting on a banquette with her back to the wall, looked around to see if she recognised any of her colleagues; it was a popular place for entertaining foreign visitors. But she saw no familiar faces.

'So how is Belfast, Liz?' asked her mother, after they'd talked about a play Susan and Edward were going on to see.

'It's full of life these days,' said Liz, as usual avoiding anything to do with work. She described her flat, making her mother laugh with an account of the redoubtable Mrs Ryan and her organisational skills. 'You must come over and stay, mother. You'd be amazed how well I'm looked after.'

'I'm sure I would. But I hope you're being looked after at work as well.'

Ever since the previous year, when Liz had been injured and had recuperated at Bowerbridge, it was obvious that both her mother and Edward had a clear sense of what Liz's job could involve. It was also clear that Edward knew a good deal about Northern Ireland; he'd had some kind of involvement when he was in the army, and he had strong views about the situation there.

He said, 'There are still two very different communities over there and I don't believe the root of the conflict has gone away.'

'You don't think the peace will hold?'

'I don't know enough to say,' he admitted. 'But what I do know is that given the past hatred, this is bound to be a fragile peace that needs careful nurturing. No one over here is paying much attention. We're treating it as yesterday's problem. While the violence stays at a lowish level, we're assuming everything will be all right.'

Liz nodded; as usual, she found herself sharing Edward's views. Having originally thought she was going to a backwater when she'd been posted to Belfast, she now knew how much was stirring underneath the surface calm. And in the case of Jimmy Fergus the surface had been broken.

Susan suddenly said, 'Oh, I know what I meant to tell you, Liz. We've been seeing that nice friend of yours from work.'

'Oh,' said Liz. She was curious, but felt no need to press, since Susan would tell her who the friend was whether she wanted to know or not.

'Charles Wetherby,' Susan declared, and Liz felt the blood rising in her cheeks. There was a momentary pause.

Then Liz said, 'Oh yes. Of course. You knew Joanne, didn't you Edward?'

'That's right,' said Edward, sounding less animated than Susan.

'We had dinner with him the other night,' said Susan chirpily. 'With his friend Alison.'

'His neighbour,' said Liz. 'I met her at the funeral.'

'Well yes, but she's clearly also his friend.'

Liz saw Edward's eyes on her. They looked understanding and a little regretful. In their unexpressed sympathy they confirmed her fears.

She made a show of looking at her watch. 'Golly, I'd better get a move on,' she said, and swallowed the last of her coffee. As she got up to put on her coat, she wondered whether, if Charles hadn't had to dash off, he would have said anything to her about Alison.

But later, as she stood in the crowded underground on her way to Heathrow, she found her thoughts drifting back to the bistro in Paris and pondering the tantalising question of what would have happened if she had stayed on for dinner.

29

'Liz. Thank God you're back,' said Judith, coming out from her flat into the hall as soon as Liz opened the front door. 'Have you heard from Dave?'

'No. Should I have? What's happened?'

'He's gone missing.'

'What do you mean, missing? Tell me. Let's go upstairs.'

'No, I can't leave Daisy. Mrs Ryan's gone home. Come in here.'

So dumping her bag in the hall, Liz went into Judith's sitting room. It looked unusually untidy. Daisy's toys were still spread out all over the floor and there were papers, an empty wine glass and a coffee mug on the table. Now that she could see Judith clearly in the light of the room, she saw that her eyes were two dark pools of worry and her hair, normally smoothly tied back, was flopping loosely in her eyes. This was not the fastidious, unflappable Judith Liz had always known.

'Tell me what's wrong while I put the kettle on,' said Liz, going into the kitchen.

Judith sighed, and her shoulders slumped. 'I can't reach Dave.'

'Since when?' Liz put tea bags in two mugs and poured out the boiling water. What she really needed was a strong drink, but tea might be better to calm Judith down.

'Since this afternoon. Yesterday, while you were in Paris, he had a meeting with Milraud. He went to his shop.'

'Really?' Liz looked at Judith sharply. She had assumed Dave would wait for her to come back and report what she'd found out before taking any action. 'I hope he had good back-up.'

Judith shook her head. 'No, he said he didn't need it. But that was okay; I mean to say, he just met Milraud in his shop and then came back. He was pretending to be a collector of some sort of gun. He'd researched it all on the internet. He was fine – but absolutely certain Milraud was dodgy.'

'He *is* dodgy. I found out a lot about him in Paris. I was going to tell Dave all about it and make sure he had plenty of cover before he met the man. Milraud is ex-DGSE and a gun runner. Dave's lucky he didn't see straight through him.'

'That's just it, Liz. I think he probably did. But Dave insisted on seeing him again. He was planning to proposition him. He said Milraud was going back to France later today and he couldn't afford to miss his chance.'

'Oh God. What happened? And where is he now? Surely he had police back up, A4 . . . ?'

She saw at once from Judith's face that he hadn't. 'Couldn't you stop him, Judith? That was crazy.'

'I know. He wouldn't listen to me. I'm not his boss,' she added.

'No, but Binding is. Why didn't you bring Michael in on this?'

'I tried. But he was tied up at Stormont. He'd left word with his secretary that he wasn't to be disturbed. By the time he was free, Dave had gone to his meet. I even tried reaching you over in London, but no one knew where you were.'

Of course Liz's mobile had been switched off in the US Embassy and in Thames House and at the restaurant, and she had never switched it on again.

Judith said quietly, 'I'm sorry.'

Liz sighed. 'It's not your fault, Judith. I just don't understand what's got into Dave. It was bad enough him seeing Milraud the first time without waiting to hear what I'd learned, but then to go back again? And without back-up.' She shook her head in exasperation. What had Dave been thinking of? He could be impetuous, but this went beyond that; this was mad.

'He wasn't thinking clearly. He was upset.'

'Why?'

'It's Lucy, I think. He rang her last night and she told him she was having doubts. She wasn't sure she fancied being an MI5 officer's wife. She said she wanted to think about their relationship and cool things down for a bit. He told me all this yesterday morning.'

'So his girlfriend has a wobble and he throws all caution out the window? That doesn't sound like Dave.'

'I think it was more than a wobble. He seemed to think she was telling him it was all over.'

'You mean that's it for them?' She looked at Judith with surprise. When Judith nodded, Liz said, 'I thought they were engaged to be married.'

'They practically were.'

'So Lucy broke it off?'

Judith nodded again and Liz groaned. She said, 'I know Dave – he wouldn't have said much, just plunged himself into work.' She thought for a second. 'Did he say he was coming back to the office after meeting Milraud?'

'Yes, he did. And I made him promise to ring me if for any reason he got delayed. I got that much out of him.'

'And you've tried ringing him?'

'Only about a hundred times,' Judith said. 'On his mobile, at his flat and I've got everyone alerted at the office to let me know if he shows up anywhere.'

'I'm going to phone Binding,' said Liz, putting down her mug. Now she was worried too.

Over the phone at Michael Binding's house, Liz could hear the clink of cutlery and glasses and the sound of conversation – he must be having a dinner party. He seemed reluctant to leave his guests and speak in private – Liz had to shout to make herself heard. 'Yes, he's missing,' she found herself saying for the third time. 'I'm going to alert the police.'

'Hang on a minute,' Binding said. She heard him talking in the background, then after a pause his voice came again more clearly and she heard a phone being put down. He must have moved into his study.

'Okay. Now tell me exactly what's happened.'

She gave him a quick summary of what she'd learned in Paris about Milraud, explaining that Dave had gone to see him for a second time, with the intention of propositioning him and without any back up. 'Milraud would have seen Dave coming a mile off. He's a trained intelligence officer. And now Dave's disappeared. We've got to do something, Michael. We can't just leave it.'

'Why wasn't A4 brought in on this meeting? Didn't you insist on that before you swanned off to France?' he said irritably, making it sound as if she'd been on holiday.

'We can deal with that later. Right now I want to find out where Dave is, and make sure he's okay.'

'Have you any reason to think this Milraud character would do Dave any harm, even if he did see him coming? He's not a terrorist, is he, or a murderer? Stop panicking, Liz. I expect you're just tired. Have a strong drink and go to bed. You may not have heard, but Dave's had a bit of a setback in his private life and he's probably just gone off to lick his wounds. Leave it now. And you do not have my authority to bring in the police. He'll turn up tomorrow right as rain, you mark my words.'

And before Liz could say any more, he rang off, leaving her angry and more worried than ever.

Later, back in her own flat, she toyed with the idea of ringing Martin Seurat in Paris to ask his advice. But it seemed so over the top to bring in the French, late at night, when her own boss had forbidden her to contact the police in Northern Ireland, that in the end she did nothing. But she was awake all night reproaching herself that she hadn't sent an immediate message from Paris or even from London, reporting what she had learned about Milraud and Piggott. Dave might not have walked into danger if she had.

30

Through the cloth bag over his head Dave couldn't see a thing. But he knew where he was, and that scared him.

During the drive from Milraud's shop, as he lay in the boot of the car, with his hands tied, he had concentrated hard on the sounds of the vehicle on the road. The journey took about an hour by his reckoning, first on fast roads, then for about twenty minutes on smaller ones, where the car stopped and started at junctions or traffic lights. Then they'd turned onto a rougher surface – some sort of track.

They could have been anywhere in the countryside of Northern Ireland. But then, just before the car stopped and he was bundled out, he heard a sound that he recognised – a noise he'd heard before when he was with Liz Carlyle. It was the squeak and bang of an electronic gate, the gate on the National Trust estate.

So he must be in Piggott's house in County Down – the house of the man who, as Brown Fox had told him, wanted to kill an MI5 officer. Until then Dave had thought he was either the victim of a kidnapping, or of a mistake. Now he realised he could be about to die.

He'd been lifted out of the boot of the car, put on his two feet and led into a house, bumping his shoulder against what felt like a door frame. Then he'd been walked down a flight of stairs and deposited unceremoniously on a hard chair. He'd been sitting there for a minute or two, not sure who was around him, trying to get his bearings and cope with the fear that was growing with each second he waited.

Suddenly, rough hands removed the bag from his head. He looked up into the dark face of the man who had walked into Milraud's shop and pulled a gun on him, the same man he had seen here, outside this house, when he and Liz had walked on the headland. Piggott's foreign-looking henchman.

Dave blinked in the sudden light and looked around the room, taking in the comfortable furnishings, the large desk, the leather-bound books in the bookcases and, incongruously, the camp bed in the corner. This must be Piggott's study, but why the bed?

Dave cursed himself for having gone to see Milraud without any back-up. Not just once, but twice. How could he have been so stupid, acting like a complete amateur? He should have listened to Judith and waited for Liz to get back. He had always known that danger was part of his job, and he liked to think that he conducted himself professionally, and without fear. No, that wasn't right – only a fool never felt fear. But he had learned to ignore the fear, and never to let it get in the way of doing his job. So it seemed a bitter irony that he had fallen into a trap he'd set for other people, as a result of his own foolishness.

But it was too late for regrets. They hadn't killed him yet – could they believe he was just a harmless collector? Maybe the dark-faced thug had not recognised him from their earlier encounter?

For a moment he nursed these seedlings of hope, but he was too much of a realist to let them take root. If they really did see him as harmless, then why had he been held at gunpoint, then taken forcibly from the shop? He thought gloomily about what they were going to do to him (just let it be quick, he prayed), when he suddenly felt agonising pain splay across his face – the foreign man had ripped the tape roughly from his mouth. Then, pulling a flick knife from his pocket, the man reached down and swiftly cut the cords binding Dave's arms.

The blood rushing back into Dave's joints hurt a lot, and his arms and muscles ached from his cramped position in the boot of the car. He gingerly moved his legs, but he stayed sitting in the chair while the dark face watched him expressionlessly, holding a gun pointed directly at his head.

He heard footsteps behind him and the tall, spare figure of Seamus Piggott appeared with another man. Dave recognised his face from the A4 surveillance – Malone. Malone was carrying an old-fashioned doctors' bag. Turning his head, Dave saw for the first time that Milraud was also in the room, standing in the corner, looking studiously detached, like a surgeon called in to witness a colleague's operation. Dave was tempted to ask the Frenchman what the price of a derringer was now, but realised sarcasm might simply accelerate whatever they planned to do to him. So he kept quiet.

Piggott said nothing, and didn't even look at Dave as he walked over to the desk. Malone put the bag down and Piggott rummaged in it for a moment, then his hands emerged holding a rubber tube in one hand and a syringe in the other. He handed the tube to Malone, who walked over and grabbed hold of Dave's right arm from the side – keeping out of the line of fire from the Spaniard's gun.

Now Dave panicked: this was how they were going to kill him. He hated needles, which made the prospect of a lethal injection even more terrifying. He shouted 'No!' and tried to wriggle free from the strong grip on his arms, but his legs felt like jelly and he hadn't the strength even to try and stand up. His shirt sleeve was swiftly forced up above his elbow and Malone tied the rubber tube tightly around his upper arm. Dave struggled frantically but Malone stood to one side and the Spaniard stepped forward, sticking the gun frighteningly close to Dave's face.

As Dave sank back in his chair, Piggott walked briskly from the desk and before Dave could move, plunged the syringe directly into the bulging vein of his bicep. Dave felt a cold sensation in his arm as the liquid moved into his bloodstream, followed almost immediately by a gentle lethargy that seemed to take him over. He was only partly aware of being stood up and frog-marched over to the bed, then put prone on the mattress, and strapped to the frame. He found himself incapable of resisting, and he didn't even want to.

A strong wind was gusting across the bay, whipping the sea into white-crested waves and blowing open Milraud's grey checked jacket. The fine cashmere sweater he wore underneath was not designed to cope with these temperatures, and he shivered as he walked down to the wooden jetty that jutted out into the small cove.

A substantial rigid inflatable dinghy was moored up firmly, rocking in the water's chop, its fenders rubbing against the wooden struts. Much further out, in the mouth of the bay, a large motor cruiser was anchored. At first sight, with its gleaming white paint and aluminium rails, it looked like the sort of rich man's toy that is ten a penny in the Mediterranean, but Milraud recognised the wide bow and strong lines of a boat designed for rougher seas and longer trips than cruising the usually calm waters of the Mediterranean. He knew that this boat made regular voyages to pick up the goods that James Purnell (or Piggott as he supposed he should call him here in Northern Ireland) imported and sold, under the cover of his consultancy company.

As he gazed out to sea, Milraud's mind was racing. He was used to dealing with the unexpected and turning it to his advantage, but the events of the last twenty-four hours had thrown him off balance. Ever since Gonzales had marched into the shop, he had been trying to keep things under control.

The Spaniard had been told to wait for Willis to leave, then follow him to try to find out who he was. But Gonzales had got his signals crossed, and had come into the back room where the Englishman had been sitting. At that point it would still have been possible to terminate the meeting and let him go – indeed, the man had actually started to make his excuses and leave. But Gonzales had pulled a gun. He'd said later that he could tell that the man recognised him, as if that somehow justified what he had done.

After that, there was no way they could let Simon Willis leave. If he was MI5, he would have been back five minutes later with a posse of armed policemen. Milraud had alerted Piggott, and the American had instructed Gonzales to bring the Englishman down here to the house in the bay. He was now lying, half-comatose and strapped to a bed in the basement room.

You had to admire his cool, thought Milraud, as he watched a cormorant swoop down and pluck a fish the size of a sardine from an oncoming wave. He thought about how Willis had sat in the back office guest chair in Belfast, seemingly unfazed by the 9 mm handgun Gonzales was waving in his face, sticking to his story – he was a collector of derringers. When it was suggested he had really come on behalf of the UK security services, Willis had looked at them all as if they were mad. It was almost a convincing performance.

They'd bundled him, hands tied, head enveloped by a sack, his mouth covered in thick strips of parcel tape, out of the back door of the shop and into the boot of the car brought round by one of Piggott's men. Milraud had followed with Piggott, and an hour later they had arrived here, and installed their unexpected visitor in the basement room. When Gonzales had untied him and taken off the tape, Willis had relaxed slightly.

He hadn't stayed relaxed for long, not after Malone had come in with his bag. At this point Milraud had left the room. He wished he had left earlier, though either way he was already implicated in everything that had gone on.

It was a fallacy that 'truth serum' could serve as a kind of cranial diuretic, flushing out of the brain all those things an undrugged person would never admit to. But what it did do, in the hands of an intelligent practitioner, could be just as revealing. Willis had apparently not told them *anything* directly, but nor had he shown the blanket ignorance he should have displayed if he had been the innocent collector he claimed to be. And he'd nodded drowsily at names he should not have found familiar. Any lingering doubt about Willis's true vocation had been dispelled.

But what was on Milraud's mind now was how to get out of this situation where he was party to the abduction of a British intelligence officer. And possibly to something worse than abduction, if he could not control Piggott/Purnell.

It was nearly dark now and getting colder. As Milraud turned to go back inside, he saw the American coming towards him from the direction of the house. His leather jacket could not have given him much protection from the wind but he walked upright, with his long strides, tall and lean, apparently impervious to the cold. It struck Milraud that the man seemed indifferent to so many things: clothes, food, women – all the aspects of life that Milraud enjoyed most. He knew there were things his associate cared about – there had to be, since nothing else could explain some of his actions. But the Frenchman did not know what those passions were, so buried were they beneath an almost perversely cold demeanour.

Nor did he think of trying to find out. Milraud was in a business where you did not enquire about your clients' motives or even their actions. You supplied them with the goods they requested and what they did with them was their own business. But now, through no fault of his, he found himself in a situation he had so far successfully avoided – involved in someone else's affairs.

Piggott said, 'There's a simple way of dealing with this, you know.'

Nothing was simple anymore, thought Milraud, but he made a show of being willing to consider this. 'What's that, James?'

'Let Gonzales take care of the problem. There's no danger then of Willis ever talking. And we don't have to worry about what to do with him.'

Milraud looked out to sea, rough enough that day to keep most craft firmly on shore. He thought he saw a tanker chugging south and east towards England, but in the evening light he could not be sure.

'Too late for that,' he said tersely, though just the idea of killing Willis made him feel sick. Milraud had a large, successful business which was now in peril; the last thing he needed was the prospect of a life sentence for murder. He said to Piggott, 'Listen James, it's bad enough as it is, thanks to Gonzales. Willis's people will soon find out that he came to see me, if they didn't know beforehand, which I expect they did. It won't take them long to get onto you too, once they start investigating, and then they'll be swarming over this place. Even as things stand I have to get out of here and I suggest you do too.'

He wondered how long he could count on Mrs Carson back at the shop to play dumb. Probably longer than he feared, but not long enough – for his business at any rate. He'd have to write off the shop and stay out of Northern Ireland. Otherwise, the authorities here would be all over him. Whereas if he could get back to France, slipping under their guard, it would be a while before they caught up with him. Eventually, the British would find him in Toulon and send someone over. But they had no evidence of anything substantial, certainly not enough even to try to extradite him.

He should be all right. Unless he listened to Piggott. The man had drawn him into some vendetta of his own, and Milraud resented that. Phoning him with that preposterous accusation that Milraud was working with MI5, and now suggesting a course of action that would have the British authorities down on them both like a ton of bricks. Because if the British could connect him with the murder of Willis they would never let the matter go: Milraud would be looking around corners for the rest of his life. The British were tenacious bastards. Especially if you hurt one of their own.

But recriminations had been pointless then and were point-less now, as well as potentially dangerous – Milraud sensed an only half-submerged menace in the American which he was wary of. If they were ever to cross swords, Milraud wanted it to be on his home ground. Another good reason for his plan.

'We should make Plymouth on the first day and I reckon we'll be through the Straits of Gibraltar in five days and in Toulon within a week. It gives us some breathing space.'

'But why take this extra baggage with us?' asked Piggott. 'Wouldn't it be simpler if we just left it behind? Especially since it couldn't tell any tales.' His voice was soft but insistent.

'Listen,' Milraud said sharply, realising he was betraying his own agitation. 'If we kill an MI5 man, we'll put everything at risk.' He looked at Piggott and what he saw chilled him. The man was completely unmoved, undeterred. Something was driving him that Milraud hadn't understood.

Piggott went on: 'What are we going to do with him in France, then? You can't exactly put him to work in your shop. And are we going to keep him drugged for six days on the boat?'

'We may not need to. We can lock him up. He can't go far at sea. Think of him as a commodity,' said Milraud, sticking to business. 'This particular commodity has considerable value.'

'To MI5? You think we can ransom him to his own people?'

'That's possible, but I wouldn't advise trying. Much better to sell him off to the highest bidder. Let someone else hold him. That will take the heat off us soon enough.' Milraud had contacts in several countries who might well be pleased to buy Willis. He'd make an attractive hostage. 'But meanwhile, we need to move our commodity to a safe place.'

'When do you want to leave?'

'We need to move fast. The next high tide is just after midnight. We should go then.'

Piggott thought about this, but his face showed no expression. Finally he gave a curt nod in agreement. 'I've some business to finish up before we leave. I'll go with Malone back into town to bring down another "commodity". But this one will be staying here. Permanently.'

And seeing the set expression on the other man's face, Milraud decided not to argue. At some point he would have to find a way of betraying Piggott to the authorities, or else Piggott would drag him down with him. But Milraud was going to pick the time and place for that. Meanwhile he was looking forward to being back in France.

31

Paddy O'Brien was pulling him a second pint of stout. Normally Dermot would have contented himself with a single glass, since there might have been more work to be done that evening. But now it wasn't clear there was any work to do at all, whatever the hour. He'd been by the office of Fraternal Holdings twice in the last three days, but there was no sign of Piggott, and no instructions left for Dermot either. He'd caught sight of Terry Malone, but when he'd asked where the boss was, Malone had shrugged and said he had no idea, though Dermot didn't believe him. There was something going on, he was sure of that, but whatever it was he, Dermot, wasn't part of it. At least there was no sign of that bloody Frenchman, Milrow or whatever his name was. Dermot hoped his letter had had its intended effect.

He looked around him at the half-dozen regulars in the pub, chatting quietly or reading the papers, and wondered if this was going to be his new office. He hoped not, but for the time being he had to sit tight, and if only to pass the hours a second pint had seemed advisable.

He'd had the first sip when 'Danny Boy' suddenly blared out from his trouser pocket. Paddy O'Brien looked startled, then chuckled as he realised the source of the sound. Dermot extracted his mobile and answered with a voice he hoped sounded stone cold sober.

'O'Reilly,' he announced carefully.

'Dermot, it's Piggott here. Where are you?'

O'Reilly looked around him guiltily – it seemed best not to say. 'I'm just off home, boss. I'll be there in five minutes.'

'No rush. But I'll need you about half past six. All right?'

'Of course,' said Dermot, breathing an inward sigh of relief. He could enjoy this glass then and be fine by six o'clock – he just had to make sure to call a halt at two pints. 'Shall I come to the office then?'

'No. I'll pick you up. Be at the memorial park on Falls Road.'

'Okay,' said Dermot, puzzled. It seemed a strange place and time to meet, but clearly something was up. He wondered if it had to do with his letter, though he couldn't see how Piggott could suspect that he had sent it. And he sounded friendly enough.

'Right then,' said Piggott, and Dermot waited for him to ring off. But Piggott added, his voice uncharacteristically soft, 'And Dermot, we'll need to talk about your new responsibilities. I know you were a bit upset by the change, but you shouldn't be. I've got great faith in your abilities, my friend, and important things for you to do. See you at six-thirty.' He rang off.

Dermot sat staring at the pint of stout, watching as the creamy head of foam settled, bubble by bubble, in his glass. He felt a growing satisfaction as he reviewed the phone call. Whatever Piggott had made of the letter, he clearly didn't think O'Reilly had sent it. He had work for Dermot to do, which was good news on two counts: Dermot would get paid, and as things played out (he thought briefly about the MI5 man he'd met in Bangor) he would have a ringside seat.

'Pint all right?' asked Paddy O'Brien, pointing to Dermot's full glass with concern.

'It's fine, Paddy. Just fine.' He pulled a fiver from his pocket. 'Why don't you have one on me?'

He had never liked the Remembrance Garden on the Falls Road. It was neat and well-tended – when flowers passed their best they were quickly removed and replaced with fresh ones – and he accepted that it was the right thing to do, honouring the dead of his cause by listing their names and regiments on large stone memorial plaques. But it was a gloomy little enclave, particularly in the early dark of a winter's evening, and it depressed him now as he sat on one of its low brick walls waiting for Piggott. The place had a sort of finality that suggested that the war was over and the glorious struggle past. Even the Republican flag hung limply, protected from the wind by the adjoining buildings.

A man came in off the street, bulky in a duffel coat, walking without hesitation straight towards Dermot. As he approached Dermot saw it was Terry Malone. 'Ready?' he said.

Dermot nodded and stood up; he had expected Piggott himself. 'I thought the boss—'

'He's waiting in the car,' said Malone, and turning round walked towards the street.

Piggott was in the back seat and motioned Dermot to join him. To Dermot's surprise, when Malone started the engine, he did a 180-degree turn and headed towards the outskirts of Belfast.

'We're not going to the office then?' Dermot ventured tentatively.

Piggott said, 'No. I need your help at the house. Something's come up.'

They drove in silence, punctuated by the frequent calls Piggott made on his mobile phone. He spoke elliptically, giving terse orders, and Dermot gathered he was going on a trip somewhere. But he knew better than to ask.

Once out of Belfast they made good time, and in less than an hour they were through the gate, passing the National Trust gate-house where the lights were on, and driving up the private lane. Instead of stopping on the gravel at the front of the house Malone drove into the low brick garage in the yard behind. When they'd all got out, Piggott carefully closed the double garage door. He doesn't want the car to be seen, thought Dermot. Why?

The mystery deepened when instead of all going downstairs to the private office, Piggott left them in the big sitting room on the ground floor and went downstairs by himself.

Dermot sat down in one of the soft chintz armchairs, and looked around at the plush curtains and antique furniture. He felt ill at ease, like a messenger treated by mistake as a guest. Malone had stayed standing near the door, as if he were guarding someone. Then it occurred to Dermot that Malone might be guarding *him*, and his nervousness increased.

Footsteps sounded from the back of the house, and Piggott reappeared, followed by another man. It was Milraud, and Dermot looked away.

'Here's my friend Antoine. Are you surprised to see him?' asked Piggott.

Dermot's heart begin to race. *Stay calm, boyo*, he told himself, but it was easier said than done, and he felt anxiety move through his limbs in waves. 'We've never met,' he said at last, and looked directly at the man. 'But I heard you were around.'

'Really,' said Piggott coldly. 'You know, I had a letter in the post a few days ago and I couldn't for the life of me figure out who'd sent it. It was warning me about Antoine here – said he might not be my friend after all. The odd thing was that the letter wasn't signed. I found that a bit cowardly. If someone has something to say, why not say it? I don't like poison pen letters. What do you think, Dermot?'

'I don't know anything about that, boss,' said Dermot, trying to look respectful and baffled at the same time.

'Fortunately, Antoine here and I go way back – we've done business together for over ten years, and in as many countries. If he was going to betray me, he would have done it long ago. God knows we've each had the chance. But even so, after a letter like that you can't help but feel a tiny bit of doubt.'

Piggott looked at the Frenchman, who was sitting calmly in a wing chair in the corner, and for a moment Dermot's hopes rose. But then Piggott turned his grey eyes back onto Dermot, and his icy gaze extinguished this brief flicker of optimism.

There was a noise from the back of the house, then more footsteps. The Spaniard, Gonzales, loomed in the doorway, and Dermot's agitation increased dramatically. He'd been set up, he could see that now. Piggott's cordial call had been a ruse to bring him down here. But how had Piggott discovered he'd sent the letter? He couldn't have any proof that it was him. There couldn't have been a leak from British intelligence, not that he'd put it past them to hang him out to dry if it suited their purposes. But he'd never told that MI5 man his name. Dermot was building a case in his head for his own survival, and persuading himself that he might after all see Belfast again. Then he saw the Spaniard nod quickly at Piggott.

'He's out then?' Piggott asked.

'Like a baby,' said Gonzales.

'Let's keep him that way,' said Piggott. He turned to Dermot, and said, 'We've had a visitor staying. Name of Simon Willis. Ring any bells?'

Dermot shook his head. Too fast, he told himself; he should have looked like he was thinking about it.

But Piggott didn't seem to notice, saying, 'Not very talkative at first, but it's remarkable what modern pharmaceuticals can do.'

While Dermot digested this, Piggott went on, 'He wasn't meant to be here – some signals got crossed – but he's already been useful. While I was figuring out what to do with him, we had a little chat. Funnily enough, your name came up in our conversation.'

Dermot tried not to show fear; he told himself again that MI5 didn't know his name. 'Why was that?' he managed to ask.

'Because I brought it up.' Piggott watched his reactions, then added, 'Along with a lot of others. I was trying to understand why this Willis guy had made an approach to Antoine just after someone had tried to stitch him up. Not a coincidence, I think you'll agree. So someone in the organisation must have talked to Willis.'

'I don't know the man, I'm telling you.' In spite of himself, his voice was rising in panic.

Piggott nodded, but it was not reassuring. 'It's only fair to say he didn't seem to react to your name – or anyone else's for that matter.'

Thank God, thought Dermot. Piggott added, 'Then we tried showing him some photographs. And I have to say, yours was the only one he reacted to. What do you make of that?'

Jolted, Dermot exclaimed, 'For the love of God, Mr Piggott, I don't know the man you're talking about, and I don't know anyone from MI5. You say someone's been trying to stitch up Milraud here. Well, it looks as though someone has stitched *me* up, good and proper.'

There was silence in the room. Dermot sensed Piggott was considering his appeal. After all, what evidence did he really have to go on? A drugged member of British intelligence nodding at a photograph? You couldn't kill a man for that. Could you?

Piggott suddenly said, 'How did you know Antoine was in Belfast?'

'The boys were talking about it.'

'I see,' said Piggott neutrally, and he sat down in another of the chintz chairs, directly across from Dermot. '*Loose talk risks lives*, they used to say. I would have thought you knew the truth of that expression.'

'I do, boss. It wasn't me who was doing the talking.' He felt his mouth drying, and he wanted to wet his lips with his tongue, only that would betray his nerves. It seemed important to look calm.

'I suppose it was "the boys" then. Which one in particular?' asked Piggott. He dipped his chin a notch, and Malone moved into the room.

'I think it was Sean McCarthy,' said Dermot carefully, picking the first name he could think of.

'You sure?'

He paused. He had nothing against young Sean: he was feckless, but then so were all these young kids Piggott had brought in. It didn't seem right to land McCarthy in it, but what else could he do? With luck, Sean would get away with a good kicking, he told himself.

He nodded emphatically. 'That's right, Mr Piggott. I remember it clear as a bell. It was the day before yesterday – I saw him at Paddy O'Brien's saloon. Why, he even bought me a drink – that's rare enough not to forget.' He tried to smile at his weak joke.

Piggott seemed to understand; you could tell the man's mind was churning over the news of who had been talking. He said, 'I tell you what, Dermot. Why don't you go with these two –' and he jabbed a long finger at Malone and Gonzales – 'and walk down to the cove. There are some cases on the speedboat that need unloading. Put them on the pier, and Antoine and I will bring the cars down in a little while so you can load them up. I've got some calls to make first.' And with a wave of his hand, he dismissed them.

Outside it was dark. In the cold, fresh air, Dermot breathed an enormous sigh of relief. He felt a little bad about Sean McCarthy, but his regret was dwarfed by his exhilaration at getting away with it himself.

'This way,' said Malone, and they crossed the small square of lawn that slanted downwards towards the beach. A line of low lights marked the narrow path to the cove. It led through a small copse of trees – alder, a few birches, some scrubby young oak that had managed to survive exposure to so much harsh salt air. Dermot found himself sandwiched between his companions. They were halfway through the copse when he saw the low mound at the edge of a tiny clearing on one side of the path. The earth had been freshly turned, piled not much more than twelve inches high, yellow from the sand in the soil. Malone just ahead of him stopped, and Dermot almost bumped into him.

'What's that?' Dermot asked, pointing to the low mound.

Malone turned around to face him, and his head was so close that Dermot could feel his breath when he spoke. 'You said back there that you'd been speaking to Sean McCarthy the day before yesterday. But you couldn't have been.'

'Perhaps I got that wrong,' he said, as weakness began to flow through his limbs. He sensed that behind him Gonzales had taken a step back.

'You did, Dermot. And it wasn't a wise mistake to make.'

Behind him Gonzales gave a harsh laugh. 'Cheer up, *señor*. Soon you can talk to Sean McCarthy for as long as you like.' Dermot looked again at the mound, and realised it was a grave.

His eyes turned to Malone beseechingly, but Malone wouldn't catch his eye.

There was a metallic noise behind him; Dermot knew it was Gonzales clearing the chamber of an automatic.

Malone said, 'Sorry, Dermot.'

32

By nine-thirty the next morning Binding had changed his tune. His dismissive cool of the night before had gone and he seemed to be operating in a kind of frenzied overdrive, constantly on the phone, making increasingly tense calls.

By eleven, when there was still no sign of Dave, he strode into Liz's office, his face a map of panic, his suit of thick grey pinstripes making him look heavy and sombre.

'I've spoken to DG. He's very concerned. As am I,' he added, conveniently wiping the slate clean of the previous evening's conversation. 'I'm going to ask DG to send an investigative team over asap,' he announced.

Liz nodded. She was glad to see that Binding was taking the situation seriously but was alarmed by how far he'd now swung the other way. What she would give for the calm command of Charles Wetherby . . .

'I wonder if it might be better to wait a little for that?' Liz kept her own voice mild, knowing how much Binding disliked dissent – he could go ballistic at the slightest demurral.

'Don't you realise time is of the essence? We need all the help we can get. DG will be informing the home secretary shortly.'

That was more than Liz could take. 'If you remember,' she replied icily, 'I wanted to inform the police last night. It was you who told me I was overreacting and should wait. In my opinion an investigative team getting involved now would just complicate things. There's nothing they can do at the moment that we can't – except get in our way. Even twenty-four hours should make things a bit clearer.'

Binding had gone red in the face, but Liz could see he was considering what she'd said. Whatever his faults – and to Liz they were legion – he was good at seeing where his best interests lay. He knew he needed to get this right. He said slowly, 'We can't be sure Dave's absence has anything to do with this Frenchman Milraud, can we?'

'Are you saying you think Dave's gone AWOL?' she asked, worried that he was going to flip-flop all over again.

'I don't know what to think. A4 went to his flat – no sign that he's been there since yesterday morning.'

'We should check at Milraud's shop,' said Liz, looking at her watch impatiently. 'Our source at the airport is looking to see if he caught his flight to France yesterday, but we need to confirm that Dave did actually meet the man.'

'The CCTV in the area will show if he went to the shop.'

'There's no camera on the street where Milraud has his place. We've got someone going through all the CCTV in the area, but that's going to take some time.' She stood up to go, already thinking of what she'd say at the Milraud shop.

But Binding had other ideas. 'Send someone else,' he said sharply. 'I need you close by. Things are getting tense.' You mean *you* are, thought Liz.

33

It was the smell that made him stop. Every three days or so, Constable Frederick Hughes drove along this lane as part of his shift. He was used to a variety of pungent odours as he passed the farms, from pigs' slurry to freshly cut hay and the woody smoke of smouldering piles of leaves. But not in midwinter. And anyway, this smoke was acrid. Whatever was being burned, it certainly wasn't leaves.

He pulled over just past Docherty's farm, once a notorious haven for IRA men on the run, heading for the border. A decade ago he would not have been patrolling here at all. What patrolling there was in South Armagh in those days was done by the military in helicopters or armoured cars.

But that was the past. Now he and his colleagues were far more likely to be hurt in a car accident than in an assassination attempt. Though maybe things were getting bad again – just days before, someone had tried to kill a half-retired officer outside his house in Belfast. No one knew yet who'd done it, or why. Perhaps it was some longstanding grudge, an ex-con avenging himself on the officer who'd brought him down. Hughes certainly hoped it was that. He liked the new comparative calm, the fact he didn't feel the need to keep his holster unbuttoned when he drove out on patrol.

He rolled his window down, and as cold air filled the inside of the car, he sat sniffing like a gun dog. There – he smelled it again. He got out of the car.

The smell was stronger still outside. Turning round, he felt the wind sting his cheeks and he shivered slightly. It was blowing from the north-east, across the unploughed dun-coloured fields. So he got back into his car and drove towards the source of the smell, taking the first right turn he came to, along an old track he didn't recognise. He drove slowly on, half-excited by the pursuit, half-scared of what might be around the next corner.

The track climbed gradually around Davitt's Hill, the highest point in this small stretch of valley. From here you could almost see the border with the Republic, the safety line for so many fleeing the law in the North. Once across the border the Provos had a habit of disappearing into thin air. It wasn't the Garda's fault. They'd never had any more use for the IRA than the RUC had. But unless you built an Irish equivalent of the Berlin Wall along every foot of the 220-mile border, you had a refuge route for terrorists that was virtually impossible to police.

The track suddenly stopped in a small lay-by in front of what had been a crofter's cottage. From behind the decayed ruins smoke rose in a twisty wisp, before dispersing in the wintry winds. It was only when he walked behind the cottage that he saw the remains of the white van. One of its tyres was still smouldering.

The forensic team moved fast – everyone did when a policeman had been shot. They checked for prints, but none had survived the fire, which was so hot that the steering wheel had been reduced to a metal spoke. A few fibres were found, miraculously untouched in a corner of the van's back compartment; they looked like wisps from a blanket.

Then one of the team discovered a big piece of metal about six inches long lying under the skeletal frame of the driver's seat. It retained enough of its original shape to be recognisable as a handgun.

'Old,' said the forensic team leader, when he was shown the find. 'Better get it to the lab right away. I doubt they'll be able to tell if it's been fired, but they might work out what make it is.'

And while the remains of the handgun were driven at speed to the PSNI laboratory, the team focused on the van itself. Over the course of the next two hours, they carefully extracted what remained of the engine from the vehicle's charred carcass. After applying acetic acid with a paintbrush they could make out enough of the chassis number to allow a technician at the lab to run a software programme used for identifying stolen vehicles. Its algorithm came up with four possibilities, of which only one was a vehicle large enough to be the burnt-out van found in South Armagh.

It had been a laundry van belonging to O'Neill's Laundry and Linen Service, a cleaning business run out of Sydenham in East Belfast by a family named – to no one's surprise – O'Neill. It had been reported stolen a couple of days ago. Twenty minutes later, two officers had driven to the home of the company's managing director, where they found Patrick O'Neill still irate at the theft of a van from his fleet of nine vehicles.

Did he have any idea who might have stolen the van? No, he replied; he'd assumed it was local villains who'd taken it out of the office yard. Had anyone recently left his employ? Well yes, a guy called Sean McCarthy had quit a few days before. He was a laundry collection and delivery driver, who'd never settled in the business. Was this before the van was stolen? Yes, come to think of it, it was just before the van was stolen ...

The PSNI had a suspect now, and they soon discovered from their own database that Sean McCarthy had a string of minor convictions as a juvenile, including illegal possession of a firearm. By now, too, the lab had come back and reported that the charred handgun found in the burnt-out van had been a .25 calibre pistol, probably more than twenty-five years old. Unfortunately, there was no description in the file of the kind of gun Sean McCarthy had been charged with possessing four years before.

McCarthy's file also showed that he had been an associate of several members of the Provisional IRA. There was no recent information about that strand of his life and one recent informant had opined 'the boy's gone straight', though his evidence for that appeared to be confined to McCarthy's being in full-time employment – at O'Neill's laundry service.

He was said to live in the house he'd been brought up in on the edge of Andersonstown – but a visit to his home found only his mother in residence. She seemed unconcerned about the absence of her son, and didn't seem to know anything about his friends or associates. The interviewing PC believed her – probably because he found her too drunk, at ten-thirty in the morning, to lie convincingly. This was her usual condition, according to a neighbour, who also had seen no sign of Sean McCarthy in the last few days.

34

Judith Spratt stopped for a coffee at a Starbucks two streets away from Milraud's shop. This was a part of the city she did not know well, a small oasis of galleries, restaurants and boutiques in what had once been a commercial area of small factories and warehouses.

She needed to collect her thoughts before she went into the shop. It had been decided that no publicity was to be given yet to Dave's disappearance, so Judith had to find some excuse for enquiring about him at the shop. She had been taken aback when Liz had asked her to do this job; she was not used to direct contact with the public and role playing was not her strength. Her job, at which she excelled, was the processing and analysis of information once it had been collected; when the pieces came streaming in she liked nothing better than to use her mind like a prospector's sieve, throwing out the dross and making sense of the few gold nuggets that remained.

Before she had joined the service she had been an analyst at an investment bank. That was where she had met her ex-husband Ravi. She had enjoyed the intellectual challenge of that job, but had found it ultimately unsatisfying; it had served no real purpose, other than to line the pockets of the firm's partners and sometimes to help a distant client somewhere to make a killing. With her husband's encouragement, and the knowledge that his fat salary made the reduction in her pay tolerable, she'd jumped at the chance of working in Thames House. Her subsequent divorce meant that money was now much more of an issue, but she never regretted her change of career. At MI5 the purpose of her work was always important, and sometimes frighteningly urgent.

She finished her coffee and walked down the narrow street to the door of Milraud's shop. She was wearing an ankle-length knitted coat with a fringed shawl draped round her shoulders, and flat shoes. The look she was aiming at was arty, bohemian, slightly ditzy but definitely genteel. As far away as could be imagined from an intelligence officer. She stood outside the shop for a moment and took a deep breath to calm her nerves, then she opened the door and went in. A bell tinkled discreetly.

'Good afternoon.' A woman stood up from a chair behind a low glass cabinet. She was middle-aged, smartly turned out, with elegantly coiffed grey hair and wearing a dark wool dress with a choker of pearls. She eyed Judith cautiously.

'Is Mr Milraud in?' Judith began, walking towards her and giving an eager, slightly goofy smile.

'Monsieur Milraud is not available, I am afraid. He is out of the country in fact.' Judith adopted a frown of disappointment. 'Did you have an appointment?'

'That's the thing. I don't know, and I'm not sure if I have the right day in any case. My cousin Simon asked me to join him here. He collects little guns, you see, and he said he was coming to see Mr Milraud about buying one. He asked me to meet him here this afternoon because we have to go down to the country after Simon has finished here. At least I think it was this after-noon, but if he's not here, perhaps I've got the wrong day – or the wrong time.' She gave a small sigh, and went on talking. 'But I know it was here we said we'd meet. He wants me to hold his hand while he negotiates with Mr Milraud. You know, to stop him spending too much money. Not that I'm an expert on guns . . .' Her voice trailed off.

The woman stared at her. 'As I said, Monsieur Milraud is not here.'

'Don't think I don't believe you. The only question then is what I've got wrong, not did I get it wrong – since we have established that.'

Judith saw the look of doubt in the woman's eyes and wondered if she was overplaying her role.

'Let me have a look at the diary, and perhaps I can see when your appointment might be.' The woman went through a door marked 'Private' at the back of the shop, returning a moment later with a leather-bound desk diary. 'Your name is?'

'Crosby. Heather Farlow Crosby.'

Judith watched as the woman consulted the pages of the diary. 'I see nothing here,' she said.

'Oh how silly of me,' said Judith, putting a hand to her cheek. 'It wouldn't be my name at all, would it? It would be my cousin Simon's.'

'Simon?' the woman said, her expression suggesting she was having to work hard to keep her patience.

'Willis. His mother was the Crosby, which is why my cousin and I have different surnames.' And she continued prattling while the woman ran her finger up and down the page, until she stopped at one line. When she looked up at Judith now her face was wary. 'A Mr Willis was here,' she said slowly. 'Yesterday in fact.'

'Ah,' said Judith with relief. 'So at least I was close.' Her smile went unreturned. 'And was I right about the time?'

'The time?' The woman was watching her carefully.

'Yes.' Judith glanced at her watch, a slim antique with a silver strap that, like most of the rest of her attire, she had borrowed from a colleague. 'Two o'clock?'

The woman made a show of looking at the diary. She seemed suddenly nervous. 'Yes, that is correct.'

'And could you tell me how long he was here? Did he make a purchase? I'm wondering if he went off to the country by himself. Do you remember when he left?'

'They left . . .' and the woman paused.

Judith pounced. '*They*?' There was nothing ditzy in her voice now. 'Did he and Monsieur Milraud leave together then?'

The woman said carefully, 'No. Your cousin left, then Monsieur Milraud left shortly afterwards. He had his plane to catch.'

'What time was that?'

'It must have been about two-forty-five that your cousin left. Monsieur Milraud left about three-fifteen to catch the plane.'

'And my cousin left alone? You're absolutely sure of that?'

'Quite sure, madam,' replied the woman tersely, dropping her mask of politeness.

'You see it's very important,' said Judith levelly, returning the woman's stare. There was little pretence left between them.

'I can assure you that he was on his own when he left.' The woman had regained her sangfroid and the shutters had come down with force. It was obvious that she knew more than she was letting on but Judith could see that she would get nothing else out of her now. 'I'm afraid I cannot help you further.' Judith was being ushered firmly towards the door.

Outside on the pavement Judith found that her nervousness

had been replaced with anger. It was obvious that something had happened to Dave and that this woman knew more about it than she was letting on. Now the woman also knew that someone was looking for Dave, and Judith doubted she believed for a moment that it was his cousin.

35

Liz stared out at the old barracks parade ground as the last flicker of sun gave way to the chill dusk of the February afternoon. Information was beginning to seep in but so far it was all negative. She still had no idea what had happened to Dave.

No results yet from the various CCTV cameras in the car park and the area around Milraud's shop, but at least she now knew, thanks to Judith's thespian efforts at the premises, that Dave had actually been there. If the shop assistant was to be believed, he had left safely and on his own at two forty-five. But that might not be true. Judith thought that at the very least the woman was not telling all she knew, and in spite of what she had said, Milraud had certainly not taken the flight to Paris on which he had a reservation. Nor had he been found on any airline manifest leaving Ireland in the last forty-eight hours. It was still possible that he had taken a private plane from one of Ireland's thirty-odd airports but nothing had been found to point to that, and if he had changed his plans, the question remained why had he done so. Preliminary checks with the ferry services in the North and in the Republic had come up with the same result: no sign of the man.

The main interest had come from analysis of the photographs

taken by the camera on the gate of the National Trust property in County Down. There had been an unusual amount of movement in and out since the previous afternoon. Timed at three-forty-four, the red Vauxhall Vectra had gone in, with the dark-faced thug and the man identified as Malone in the front seat. There seemed to be no one in the back, though the camera could not see the back seat clearly. At four Piggott had gone in driving his Audi, with an unidentifiable back-seat passenger. At five-thirty the Audi had gone out again, driven by the Spaniard, and had returned at seven-thirty, again driven by the Spaniard. Nothing more had happened until seven-thirty the following morning when the Audi had been driven out by Malone, possibly with a back-seat passenger who might or might not have been Piggott.

At the offices of Fraternal Holdings in Belfast, where A4 had been on watch since eight a.m., very little had happened. At nine a.m. the female receptionist had let herself into the offices with a key. She was now sitting in the reception area, clearly visible to Arthur Haverford and Jerry Rayman in their observation post across the street. She was painting her nails.

Two policemen had been to Piggott's house on the National Trust estate during the morning. The old housekeeper who had answered the door said that her employer had left the previous day and had not told her where he was going or when he would be back. The police officers had been told to do no more than enquire for Piggott and if he was there to ask him some question about an imaginary rave on the National Trust land. So they'd accepted what the housekeeper said and, after walking round the surrounding land and seeing nothing to arouse their suspicions, they had left.

As Liz was turning all this over in her mind, Michael Binding appeared in her office doorway, eyebrows raised in a questioning look. Liz shook her head. 'Nothing firm yet,' she said flatly. 'Still waiting for the CCTV.'

'I wish they'd get a move on,' he said, coming into the room and fiddling with his tie. He didn't sit down. 'I promised DG a progress report this evening. All I've got is a *lack* of progress report. It won't do.'

Liz didn't reply. It wasn't quite true. The threads of an investigation were beginning to emerge. The problem now was making sense of them and deciding what to do about it, without precipitating a situation that might put Dave in more danger than he was already in – that was if he were not dead already, something she did not wish to contemplate.

Binding wasn't finished. 'You were supposed to be in charge here, Liz. You go away for two days and your people end up all over the place. God knows what's happened to Dave, or why he felt he could just go charging off on his own.'

'He certainly didn't have my permission to do that.'

'So you say,' Binding replied infuriatingly. 'That Judith Spratt didn't tell me what was going on is something that I'll want to pursue.'

When Liz started to protest at the unfairness of this, Binding waved a dismissive hand. 'Later. There'll be plenty of time for post-mortems. Right now we need to do something. I want to talk to the police and put out an all-persons alert.'

'For Dave? Or for Milraud?'

He looked momentarily flustered. 'For Dave, of course.'

Liz turned away. What was he proposing to say? *Have You Seen This Man? He's an MI5 Officer and We Can't Find Him.* This was ludicrous. She decided to ignore it and said, 'I've been thinking over the leads we have.'

'None that I can see.'

'That's not entirely true. Remember, our informant Brown

Fox said Seamus Piggott wants to kill policemen and an MI5 officer. Jimmy Fergus got shot three days ago and now Dave's disappeared. We know he went to Milraud's shop and we're pretty sure from what Brown Fox told Dave that Milraud is working in some way with Piggott, probably supplying him with arms. It might all be coincidence, but that's what we've got to go on right now. If we can link the attack on Fergus to Piggott, that will let us grab Piggott, assuming we can find him, and that should lead us to Milraud. And with luck to Dave.'

He looked at her as he considered what she said. 'It's a tenuous chain you're building there.' But he said this quietly, always a good sign with him.

'I know it is. But we've got to start somewhere. I want to step up the investigation now. I want to put telephone intercepts on Milraud's shop and we need to identify that woman who works there and get her communications intercepted too. Also all the communications to and from the Fraternity offices need to be on check, and I'm wondering if we shouldn't ask the police to go back to Piggott's place and go in. As you said before, Michael, time is of the essence.'

Binding sat down heavily. There was a pause. Eventually, 'You're right,' he conceded. 'We need to work on the assumption that Dave has been taken by someone. We should waste no more time. We'd better get that investigative team over.'

'No. We do need reinforcement but not an investigative team. I still think that would cause delay and confusion. What I want is to get Peggy Kinsolving from counter espionage over here. If there is anything to find out to connect all this, she'll do it.'

'Well, if that's what you want and if you can persuade Charles Wetherby to release her, then go ahead.'

So Liz now had two phone calls to make and she realised

that she was looking forward to one much more than the other. And she realised with some surprise that her preference was not in the order she would have expected.

First she rang Charles Wetherby in London.

'Hello, Liz. I'm glad you rang. How are you all over there? We're very concerned about Dave. Is there any news? Is there anything I can do to help?'

On any other occasion Liz would have taken the opportunity to tell Charles everything that had happened and ask for his advice. But now something was stopping her. She seemed no longer to feel the old closeness to him, the unspoken understanding that they had had in the past. She didn't want to prolong the conversation, so she just asked if she could borrow Peggy Kinsolving to help with the case. When Charles readily agreed, she rang off.

Why had she done that? It seemed that rather than getting closer, as she had expected they would after Joanne's death, they had got further apart. She knew what it was, though she didn't want to dwell on it. It wasn't just that they were separated by the Irish Sea. It was the thought of Alison, his neighbour, and in particular their 'friendship' as her mother had tactfully called it.

But that wasn't all. She had cut short the conversation with Charles because she wanted to get on with her next call. This was the one she was looking forward to.

'Ah, Liz, how nice to hear from you.' The warm Parisian tones were what she wanted to hear.

'Martin, I need your help. Or at least your advice. I'm trying to find our friend Milraud, but he seems to have disappeared.' She explained how they could find no trace of the arms dealer having left Northern Ireland.

'That is a little puzzling, but perhaps he took another way

back – a private plane even. Or he's taken a holiday somewhere in Ireland. Is this urgent?'

'It is, I'm afraid. One of my colleagues has disappeared. He had an appointment with Milraud at his shop here but he hasn't been seen since.'

'When was this?'

'Yesterday.' She heard his small exclamation of surprise, and she went on, 'I know, it hasn't been very long. But our man isn't one to take off like this. Our observations had confirmed our suspicions about your old colleague. He was here to do business with Seamus Piggott, the American I told you about.'

'I remember. And Milraud's disappearance is connected in some way, no?'

'Yes,' she said, relieved that Seurat understood. 'We have a source who claims that Piggott wants to kill a policeman and an MI5 officer.'

'Could that not be dramatic on your informant's part? You know they always want to have something to sell.'

'Not in this case, I think. From what I've learned about Piggott's background, he's looking for revenge for something that happened in the past. And just before I came to Paris, a senior policeman was shot outside his own house – he survived, but they were definitely trying to kill him.'

'Liz, if it's any consolation, Milraud is not a murderer. Remember, I know the man well. It's not that I view him through – how do you say it? Rosy spectacles?'

'That'll do,' said Liz with a laugh.

'It's rather that I know he's too ambitious to risk spending the rest of his life rotting in prison. For Milraud, his business, legitimate or not, would always come before revenge. In that sense, he's too professional to kill your man.'

'I'm glad to hear that. The problem is, we can't find Piggott either. And he may not have Milraud's scruples.'

'Is there anything I can do to help?'

'I was hoping you might be able to locate Milraud.'

Seurat paused. 'Hmm. As you know, we have our own interest in Milraud, though we've never had enough evidence to devote much time to him. We haven't asked our colleagues in the DCRI to place him under any kind of surveillance. What I can do is speak with Isabelle in DCRI – you met her, yes?'

'Of course.' Mme Florian, the woman in jeans whom she and Bruno had visited in the office near the Eiffel Tower.

'I would ask her as a matter of urgency to discover if Milraud has returned to Toulon. If not, I will also ask her to try and find out if someone there knows where he is.'

'That would be very helpful, Martin.'

'It may not help very much at all. But it's at least a start.'

36

'That's Dave!' Judith exclaimed. They were huddled around a monitor in Michael Binding's office. It was ten in the evening and a pile of pizzas lay in their boxes untouched on a table in the corner.

Dave was easily recognised from his familiar loping stride as he strolled along the shopping centre's main walkway. He didn't seem to be in any hurry. The time on the screen was one-forty-eight, so there were twelve minutes to go before, according to the shop woman, he had arrived at Milraud's establishment. The features were fuzzy and the clothes unfamiliar – Liz didn't think she'd ever seen Dave in a blazer – but there was no mistaking his walk. It was unexpectedly upsetting to see him there, striding confidently along to . . . to what?

The tape was a composite of all the relevant segments located by A4, after a careful search through God only knew how many hundreds of hours of CCTV film. As Dave disappeared from view along the long row of shop fronts, he suddenly reappeared crossing a concrete courtyard full of shoppers. The time on the screen was one-fifty-five. The figure walked quickly across the small square, then reappeared on a broad street lined by what looked like light-coloured brick office buildings. It was less busy here, and Dave was easy to pick out, until he turned left at a corner and disappeared from the screen.

'That's Milraud's street,' said Judith. 'Look, it wasn't quite two o'clock when Dave went down it. That confirms what the woman in the shop said. But none of these cameras show him returning. We've checked others that cover the opposite end of Milraud's street, and there's no sign of him on those either. So where did he go?'

Binding was unusually quiet. He had changed his clothes at some point during the day, and was now back in his quasi-military garb – elbow-patched khaki sweater, corduroys in the curious shade of pink, and desert boots.

Liz asked, 'Do we know how he travelled there?'

Binding gave her a caustic look. 'On foot, obviously. What do you think we've just been watching?'

She looked at Judith, who raised an eyebrow. Binding's mood had darkened; his earlier anxiety was giving way to anger. Liz said calmly, 'I meant, how did he get to the shopping centre? Public transport?'

Judith shook her head. 'We're pretty sure he drove. His car's not at his flat.'

'What's your point, Liz?' asked Binding.

'If he drove, he must have parked somewhere. If we find the car, we'll know he didn't come back.'

Binding's silence seemed assent. Liz said, 'So, since we first see him at the shopping centre, I suggest we check the car park there.'

And twenty minutes later Maureen Hayes and Mike Callaghan located the car, a Peugeot 305 from the car pool, which Dave had been driving for the past two weeks. It was on the upper level of the shopping centre car park, at one end, behind a pillar.

They approached it cautiously, and Callaghan lay down on the hard concrete and peered underneath with a mirror and a torch. When he stood up, dusting his hands, and gave Maureen the nod, she opened the passenger door with the reserve key.

The inside was empty, except for a street map of Belfast lying on the driver's seat, and a half-drunk bottle of water.

By the time they phoned back with news of their discovery the meeting in Binding's office had broken up and Liz was sitting alone in her own office. She asked for the car to be brought back to the A4 garage. As she put down the phone she reflected that it was now overwhelmingly clear that Dave hadn't gone AWOL, not that she had ever believed he had. It was always extremely unlikely that an upset in his personal life would have sent his professional conduct off the rails. Something bad had happened to Dave, and she was trying not to assume the worst.

Ten minutes later she and Judith reconvened with Michael Binding in his office. It was almost midnight now, and Binding stifled a yawn as Liz reported on A4's discovery. Outside the wind had picked up, and the curtains at the office windows were moving slightly in the draught.

'I think he's been taken,' said Binding, and Liz just nodded in agreement. 'It seems the only possible explanation. I'll tell DG in the morning.' He looked accusingly at Liz. 'Then he will want to send a team over.'

'Perhaps,' said Liz, unperturbed. 'In any case, Charles has agreed to send Peggy Kinsolving. She's coming tomorrow.' She added, 'Have we got a press officer here?'

'Of course,' said Binding, as if she'd challenged his competence. 'But why are you talking about press officers? The last thing I want to do is talk to the press.'

'I know that, Michael. The problem is that the press may want to talk with you. Chances are they won't hear anything, but it's not something you can count on. As we broaden the investigation, knowledge of Dave's disappearance will inevitably get to more people – in the police for example. If the media get the faintest suspicion that one of our officers is missing, you can be sure they'll be all over the story. We'll need to be ready for that.'

Binding looked horrified. 'Can't we slap a D-notice on the story?'

Liz shrugged. 'You could try. But I imagine there are still some foreign reporters around. A D-notice won't stop them.'

He said nothing, which she took as agreement – he never openly climbed down.

'What I don't understand,' said Judith, 'is what Milraud would want with Dave. If he saw through his cover story, why didn't he simply refuse to see him again?'

Liz answered. 'I'm afraid it's unlikely to be Milraud who's taken him. When I spoke to my contact in the DGSE in Paris – he's the man who used to be a colleague of Milraud's and knows him well – he said violence isn't Milraud's style. He may have told Piggott about Dave, and we know Piggott's intent on revenge.'

'But why kidnap him?'

Liz and Binding exchanged looks. Liz said softly, 'They may not hold onto him for very long.'

'You mean they'd—?' Judith started to ask, then stopped as she saw the answer to her own question.

Again, Liz could only nod.

37

'Here I was, expecting the grim reaper to come through the door, and in walks the most beautiful girl in the world. Or have I died, and gone to heaven?'

Liz was glad to find Jimmy Fergus back in buoyant form. She hadn't known what to expect; after the shooting it had been touch and go for the first twenty-four hours. He was still hooked up to all manner of machines – an IV feed attached to his arm, wires linking him to monitors. He must have lost a couple of stone, thought Liz; he looked positively gaunt in his thin hospital gown, but at least there was some colour in his cheeks and he was sitting propped up in bed, with the radio playing on his bedside table, and a car magazine on his lap.

She kissed him on the cheek. 'This place looks pretty five star.'

'Appearances can be deceptive. You haven't tried the food.' He made a face.

'I should have brought you a takeaway but perhaps these will help.' She handed him a box of chocolates tied up with a ribbon and sat down in the chair by the window. The sun was glancing into the room, though dark clouds were moving in on a sharp wind.

'So how's business? It would be nice to hear about something other than my potassium levels.' He gave a derisory wave at the rig of wires and monitors around him.

'We've found the van your attackers used. It was burned out in South Armagh, about five miles east of Moy.'

Fergus nodded. 'Provo country. Can't say I'm surprised. There are plenty of people in this world who would like to shoot me – including an ex-wife or two – but only the Republican renegades would actually go and do it nowadays.' He sighed. 'It's depressing when you think that ninety-nine point nine per cent of the population is keen to have peace, and yet we can't stop a few lunatics from jeopardising everything. I just hope everyone can keep their heads, not start blaming each other or using it as an excuse to step up the violence again. Once that starts, there's no stopping it; it's like the Israelis and the Palestinians.'

'So far it's been condemned by both sides equally.'

'Any progress finding the villains?'

'We're getting there,' she said with a confidence she didn't entirely feel. 'There were the remains of a gun in the van – they probably thought it would be unrecognisable after being burned. But it's a .25.'

'Like the slug in my chest. Pretty unusual these days.'

'Exactly. We think we know who one of the guys was – he worked part-time for a laundry service; that's where they got the van. His name's Sean McCarthy, and he's disappeared.'

Jimmy Fergus scratched his cheek thoughtfully. 'That name rings a dim bell but I can't put a face to it.'

'Actually I was hoping that if you felt up to it, you could give us a description of them both.'

'I'll try, but I only got a good look at one of them – that was the driver. He was young, maybe twenty, light short hair, skinny, about six feet tall.'

'That can't be McCarthy – the laundry owner said he was short and dark-haired.'

'Sounds like the guy with the gun. I got a quick look at him and he fits that description, but I couldn't tell you much more than that. He took me by surprise. I was looking at the driver.'

'Hopefully if we find McCarthy we'll find the other guy.'

He looked at Liz. 'But they're just small fry, aren't they? This was well-planned; I don't think two youngsters could have done it all by themselves. Who do you think was behind it?'

'Your colleagues think it's the Real IRA. But McCarthy's never been associated with them. I'm wondering if it may have something to do with our mysterious Mr Piggott.' And she told Fergus what they'd learned about Piggott, and about Milraud and his recent visit. She didn't mention Dave's disappearance, Jimmy was starting to look tired and she didn't want to give him anything more to worry about.

He pointed a finger down at his chest, where the bullet hole lay buried under a blanket of bandage. 'I'm glad this happened before Milraud and Piggott finished their business.'

'What do you mean?'

He managed a wan smile. 'Piggott would have been buying better firepower from Milraud, I bet. Big powerful weapons and accurate too. Compared to them the little pistol that put me here was a pea shooter. And it jammed the first time he pulled the trigger.'

He was silent for a moment, and Liz wondered if he was thinking of his narrow escape. It must have seemed extraordinary, having lived through years when every day brought the promise of death, to get shot in the middle of what was supposed to be an era of peace.

'The funny thing is,' Jimmy Fergus mused, 'those two guys didn't even bother to hide their faces.'

Liz said nothing. 'What is it?' asked Fergus, disconcerted by the look on her face.

'I think they weren't expecting you to be able to provide a description.'

Fergus gave a satisfied grunt. 'In that case, they really were amateurs.'

'Or else you're tough as old boots, Jimmy Fergus. I'd say it was a bit of both.'

38

The winter mistral was blowing strongly at Marseilles airport as Martin Seurat waited with Isabelle for her colleague to bring the car round from the car park. Isabelle was shivering beneath her raincoat. She had left behind her customary scruffy garb of oversized fisherman's sweater and jeans and was dressed smartly in a short skirt and cashmere cardigan.

Seurat had decided at the last minute to join Isabelle on her visit to Toulon, though strictly speaking he should have left it to her – this kind of domestic investigation was not the business of his service. But he had been stirred into action by the intriguing phone call from Liz Carlyle. This was the first firm lead in a long time that might put Milraud away. But if he was honest with himself, he'd also taken the trouble to come down to Provence because he had been so taken by his lunch with the British woman. She'd struck him as straightforward, clever and amusing, but with a sort of modesty too. It was an unusual combination of qualities and he found it, and her, very attractive. He hoped he would see her again.

Martin Seurat had been an intelligence officer a good long time and he had recently had to admit to himself that the adrenalin was beginning to run thin. He'd been wondering if it was time to leave his service and look for some other career that might put the spark back into his life. Not that he had any idea what that might be. But today, standing in a cold wind on a Saturday morning, he realised with some surprise that he felt excited. He was excited at the prospect of catching up with his old colleague, Antoine Milraud. He wondered if he had changed. He'd always sailed close to the wind but it looked as if this time he'd gone right over the line and got himself involved in kidnapping or murder – at present it didn't seem clear what it was – and of a British intelligence officer too. This was so out of character that Seurat was convinced there was more to it than met the eye. And it was the prospect of finding out what that was, as well as working closely with Liz Carlyle, that was stirring him into life again.

For fifty kilometres or so the motorway to Toulon cut along the side of the coastal hills, white outcrops of rock pushing their way through the thick vegetation of pines and eucalyptus. From time to time the Mediterranean came into view, sparkling blue, dotted with white crested waves stirred up by the fierce mistral. Within the hour they were driving into Toulon, past the big iron gates of the Naval Headquarters and the Prefecture Maritime and along the rue de la République to the big car park on the quayside, busy with shoppers, attracted in by the Saturday market.

Leaving their driver with the car, they crossed the rue de la République and strolled through the Place Louis Blanc with its tall blue and grey shuttered eighteenth-century houses, into the market which was still in full swing. The avenue of plane trees that would shelter the market from the sun in summer was without leaves and the canvas canopies covering the piles of vegetables and brown bowls of North African delicacies were blowing in the wind.

As she paused to sample an olive, Isabelle said, 'Do you think it's likely Milraud has come back here?'

'It's possible. Though our British colleague said she thought it unlikely.'

'Ah. The charming Mademoiselle Carlyle?' she said, with the faintest hint of amusement.

'Yes. The officer from MI5 you sent to see me. It's she who wants to know Milraud's whereabouts.'

'Ah,' said Isabelle. 'You explained the MI5 urgency, but I hadn't realised it was the same officer. They're sure Milraud is linked to their missing colleague?'

'She sent a message yesterday saying that it looked that way. Something unexpected must have happened. Milraud has done a lot of bad things in recent years, but he is always careful. It makes no sense for him to get involved in this.'

'There's a woman in charge at his shop – I had a local officer look into it. Her name is Claire Dipeau. We should find her there now, but I doubt she'll tell us anything.'

Seurat shrugged. 'I expect you're right. But we're sure to learn something. It's worth taking the trouble.'

'To show the British we're trying to help?' Isabelle could not suppress her cynicism.

'It's not just that. I'm sure you'd agree we'd all be quite keen to put Milraud away. It may be that MI5 are doing us a favour, rather than the other way around.'

Isabelle picked an almond from a plate on a stall and said thoughtfully, 'I find it surprising that Milraud would choose this town for his base.'

'Why? Not exotic enough?'

'The file says he grew up in Brittany, so it's not as if he had roots here. And yes, not exotic enough. From your description of the man, he sounds more Saint-Tropez than Toulon.'

'It's pleasant enough here,' said Seurat. 'Maybe he finds it a convenient port for his business. Not as heavily policed as Marseilles, close to North Africa. It has its advantages. But I don't expect him to show up here any time soon – not if he's involved in the disappearance of this MI5 man.'

'So let's call on Madame Dipeau before she closes for lunch. If we turn down here we'll come into the top end of the rue d'Alger, where the shop is.'

At the shop, Seurat held open the heavy oak door for Isabelle and followed her into the long dark room. Behind a counter at the far end a white-haired woman in a black jacket and long skirt was polishing a beautifully chased metal scabbard with a cloth.

Madame Dipeau, thought Seurat. She looks very respectable. Clever of him – no one would suspect that a woman of mature years, formidable demeanour and decorous dress would be colluding in anything shady.

The woman looked up and nodded politely, then greeted them in the strong nasal tones of the region. '*Bonjour m'sieurdame. En vacances?*'

'No. We were hoping to see Monsieur Milraud.'

The woman shook her head sadly, as she put the cloth and scabbard down on the counter's glass top. '*Pas possible*. Monsieur is away.'

Seurat said, 'Really? When we spoke on the phone he mentioned a trip to Ireland, but he said he would be back by now.'

She replied quickly, 'He called to say he would be away longer than planned.' Her expression made clear that this was a matter of indifference to her.

'Was he still in Ireland when you spoke to him?'

'I don't know where he was, monsieur. I did not enquire.' Madame Dipeau spoke sharply, making it clear she didn't

211

question her employer about his whereabouts, and that by implication neither should Seurat.

'Possibly Madame Milraud would know where we can find
her husband,' suggested Isabelle. The woman gave an elegant
shrug and did not reply. 'Do you have an address and perhaps
we could call on her?'

'I am not authorised to give out personal information,
madame,' she replied coldly.

'Even if we are old friends of the Milrauds?'

Madame Dipeau raised both hands palms upwards to show
that she remained unable to help.

There was a pause. 'You're right – we're not old friends,' said
Isabelle, speaking brusquely now, fishing in her bag and
producing a warrant card. 'Nor new ones, either. But I suggest
you give us the home address of Monsieur Milraud right away.
Otherwise, in ten minutes I will have the *gendarmerie* here. Not
to mention an inspector of taxes, who will wish to inspect every
item in your inventory, go through all your records, see every
invoice, check every bill that's been paid. I am sure when
Monsieur Milraud eventually returns to find such a thorough
investigation, he will be pleased that he's left his business in
such safe hands. *C'est compris, madame?*'

The woman looked long and hard at Isabelle. She said nothing
but reaching for a pad from behind the counter wrote down
an address and pointedly handed it to Seurat.

'Bandol,' he said with a charming smile, reading the address.
'Antoine has certainly come up in the world. *Merci beaucoup,
madame.*' Isabelle had reached the door but he paused and,
pointing at the scabbard lying on the counter, said, 'That looks
as if it belonged to one of Napoleon's marshals.'

Madame Dipeau was unamused. 'It belonged to Napoleon
himself, monsieur,' she said tartly.

39

As they walked back to the car Isabelle said, 'She'll be on the phone by now to Madame Milraud. What's the next move?'

She didn't need to ask – this was technically her turf; she dealt with the French mainland, not Seurat. Perhaps if it had been Milraud himself they were going to see, she might have asserted that position, taken the initiative. But she seemed to have guessed that Seurat had some sort of an issue with Madame Milraud and decided that if he wanted to handle the interview himself, she wouldn't stand in his way.

So Seurat said, 'If it's okay with you, I'll go on my own. But you're right. That woman in the shop will be phoning around. To both the Milrauds probably – I'll bet she knows where he is. Now that we've put the cat among the pigeons I think we need phone interception on the shop and on the Milraud house. Could you organise that while I go and talk to Annette?'

She nodded. 'I'll take the car back to Marseilles and start putting things in motion. You can take a taxi and we'll meet up again in Marseilles. Here's the address of our office there.'

He slid out of the back seat and walked across to a taxi rank opposite. He was glad she had taken it that way. From what he knew of Annette Milraud, he was quite sure that woman to woman would not have been the right approach.

The taxi turned off the Toulon-Marseilles motorway and began to coast down the winding side-road to Bandol. Bandol. What did he know about Bandol? Seurat asked himself. Some sort of resort where people used to come for golfing holidays, and didn't anymore? Wine! That was it. Quite a well-known wine; pretty pricey too – not a wine he drank himself.

A big rocky outcrop loomed up in front, with a number of large villas set among the trees around its top. You could see the Mediterranean now – and now you couldn't, as the road slithered round another bend and under a viaduct. They climbed steeply and eventually came to a halt at the gates of a big villa facing east towards Toulon. Seurat got out and rang the bell at the tall black security gates. A camera zoomed round to observe him as he gave his name to a disembodied voice. A pause, then the gate opened and the taxi drove in, up a steep drive bordered with carefully pruned conifers and flowering acacias. The two slowly-turning watersprays, the gardener working on a flower bed, the neatness of the scene – everything suggested that Milraud had done very well for himself since leaving the service, and that he was concerned to take care of his property and of himself as well.

No need to press the doorbell. As he got out of the car, the front door opened and a smartly uniformed maid took his card and ushered him into a large, square hall furnished with two sofas and an ebony table. Marble floor; pale grey sofas; mimosa-yellow cushions. Interior design job, reflected Seurat. No human hand had touched this. Expensive as well. Gauzy curtains hanging at the big windows moved gently in the air conditioning, but did not restrict the rolling view over the coastal plain towards Toulon.

Typical of Annette, he thought to himself as he waited. She'll make her entrance after she's given me time to take this in, and not before. He grinned at the thought of the shabby little suburban flat she'd last occupied in Paris. She'd be surprised he'd turned up here but delighted that he'd seen the luxury she now lived in. But softly, softly, he told himself. That was the way to deal with Annette.

The door to the hall opened. She hadn't aged much; she still swept rather than walked. The tan was smooth, professionally correct like the room. She was dressed too young, he thought, looking at her short skirt and low-cut top. With Annette there would always be something not quite right.

As they touched cheeks, she put both her hands lightly on his, as if to suggest a physical intimacy which he was certain she didn't feel. Then she stood back and lifted an eyebrow.

He said, 'It's wonderful to see you. I was hoping to see Antoine as well. Is he away?'

She nodded thoughtfully, as though mentally reviewing the possible reasons for Seurat's arrival.

'Yes, he's away. He's often away. He's very busy. He doesn't always tell me where he is. I don't enquire.'

Seurat could not help admiring the adroit way in which she had taken the bull by the horns and wrong-footed him. Before he could respond, she advanced the conversational contest a further step.

'Is there any particular reason for your asking about him?'

'Well, yes. I need to talk to him.'

'That's obvious enough. I don't expect you came here just to chat me up, Antoine, pleasant though we might both find that. Or did you?'

'Annette – look. He's got himself into a difficult position. I don't want it to get worse for him. It needn't do that – if I could speak to him. You must know either where he is or where he might be. It would help him if you would tell me.'

She smiled, slowly took a cigarette from a silver box on the ebony table, lit it, blew out smoke, tapped her foot on the floor and said, 'I dare say he's amusing himself. There are plenty of places where he could be doing that. When he's finished, he'll let me know when to expect him back.'

Seurat ground his teeth. She knew perfectly well where the bastard was.

'Well then, how long has he been gone? What's he up to at the moment – I mean, business-wise? How long is he usually away?'

'That's rather a lot of questions, Martin – I'm glad we're still on Christian name terms.' She smiled seductively. 'Do you always tell your wife what business you are on? Oh, I'm sorry, I forgot you're divorced now, aren't you? Fond as I am of Antoine, I do actually appreciate his reticence, even his absences for that matter. I don't want to know about his business, so long as it's going well. As far as that goes, I'm perfectly satisfied.'

Checkmate, thought Seurat. We're getting nowhere. What particularly irritated him was the way she moved her head ever so slightly from side to side without moving her eyes, a bit like a snake-charmer with his eyes on a cobra.

'*Eh bien*. You have my card. Please tell him to call me. Tell him I can help him. Tell him I understand his difficulty.'

'Do you? Well, naturally, of course I will tell him that. When the possibility occurs, of course. I'm sorry you should have come so far for so little. Perhaps next time you should telephone in advance. Can I offer you a drink? No?'

He now saw that she had been holding his card in her hand throughout the interview. She gave it a slight flourish, put it face down on the ebony table, and put the cigarette box deliberately on top of it.

'There! All safe now,' she said. 'I'm sure he'll get in touch. Sooner or later.'

Seurat gave up. There was no point in deliberately antagonising her. 'It's a very nice place you have here. Very chic, very comfortable. Rather out of the way though, isn't it? I always thought you were a Parisian to your fingertips.'

'No, no. In fact I come from this part of the world. You never noticed my southern accent?'

He grinned. 'That's the only piece of information you've given me since I got here, Annette!'

For just an instant her eyes darkened, as though some shaft had gone home. Why? The remark had been innocent enough. Curious. He put it away to think about later.

'I'll say *au revoir* then. Do ask Antoine to get in touch.'

'So lovely to see you again. I'm so sorry there's been nothing I could tell you.'

As the front door closed behind him, Seurat swore. Why didn't I hold that taxi? He started on his long walk back down the hill.

40

'We were the first,' Otto Perkins declared, and it took Judith Spratt a moment to understand what he was talking about. 'Concrete barriers, armed police patrolling the terminals, sniffer dogs checking the luggage – we had them all years ago. It took 9/11 for the rest of the world to catch up.' Judith wondered if this was a lead to be proud of, but Otto's enthusiasm made it seem churlish to demur.

The little man was full of irrepressible energy, waving his arms about when he talked, and walking around his tiny office in the Portakabin in the car park so it vibrated with transferred energy. With his prominent upper teeth, which a bushy moustache did nothing to disguise, and his chin sitting at the bottom of his face like a small hard pear, Otto was such a pixie of a man that Judith had to resist the urge to pat him on the top of his head.

Otto had been manager of the Davis Hire car rental agency next to Belfast Airport for eleven years, he told Judith, and before that he'd worked at the adjacent airport as a supervisor in the terminal. Throughout those years he had also been on the books of the RUC Special Branch as an agent, transferring his services to MI5 when they'd taken over the old police force's counter-terrorist duties.

Otto was a useful source; he seemed to know everyone who worked at or around the airport. More specifically, the rental car depot was a convenient location for parking cars safely when MI5 officers travelled. It also served (in the form of Otto) as a conduit for messages, a temporary repository for keys, and a fount of information on his customers when, as now, that was needed.

At last Otto paused to draw breath and Judith managed to get a few words in. 'You had a customer from France last week called Antoine Milraud, who hired a Renault Megane.'

She gave Otto the registration number, and he began to tap at the terminal on his desk.

'Got it!' he crowed suddenly, like a man whose horse had won the race. 'The maroon Megane – I know it well.' He swivelled in his office chair and pointed out of the grimy window towards the car park behind, where two or three dozen cars were neatly parked. 'It's over there at the back.'

'It is?' asked Judith dubiously. Somehow she had expected the car to be missing – just like Milraud. 'When was it returned?'

'Hang on,' said Otto, resuming his manic attack on his keyboard. 'It was the day before yesterday – early in the evening. Just when it was due. No damage to the car and the petrol tank was full.'

'You don't remember who brought it back, do you?'

He looked slightly puzzled. 'I assume it was Mr Milraud himself. But I can't say for certain – I was off duty at the time,' he added, sounding slightly guilty that he wasn't there round the clock.

'Who would have served him when he returned the keys?'

'It might not have been anyone. An awful lot of people use the express service – they write the mileage on an envelope, put the keys in, then put it in the box outside. We never see them. Let me look—' and he quickly flipped through a large file box of recent receipts until he found the right form. 'You're in luck; the keys were handed back in person.'

'Who would have dealt with it?'

Otto looked again at the form. 'It was one of the mechanics in the garage.'

'What garage?'

'Our garage. Over there.' And he pointed to another low building on the edge of the car park. 'We do most of the servicing for the cars ourselves. Right here. And any minor problems – dents, broken wing mirrors, that sort of thing. Believe me, it saves us a packet.' He picked up the phone on his desk. 'Let me give them a ring.' Someone answered right away, and Otto said, 'Danny, you worked the evening for me day before last, didn't you? You know, the evening I was off.' He listened for a moment. 'I thought so. Listen, can you come over for a minute?'

Judith waited while Otto regaled her with tales from his past years at the airport. He was explaining at length some aspect of luggage conveyors when a tall young man in blue overalls pushed open the door and came in. Motor oil was streaked down his cheek and his sandy-coloured hair was flopping in his eyes and over his forehead. His face was unmemorable, except that Judith remembered it, though she didn't know from where.

'This is Danny,' said Otto.

'Hello. Have we met before somewhere?' she asked, trying to place him.

'Don't think so.' He looked at Otto. 'You wanted to see me?'

'That's right, Danny. The maroon Megane. It was rented out last week by a customer who brought it back two nights ago. I was off, and you would have dealt with him. A man named Milraud – he's French.'

220

'Don't remember him. He might have used the express service.'

'Not this guy,' said Otto, and pushed the folder across the counter at the mechanic. 'See, you initialled it right there.'

'Oh yeah,' he said slowly.

'He would have had an accent,' prompted Judith, hoping she was right. 'A funny kind of hair cut – it stands up straight in front. European-looking – he carried a leather sort of little handbag.'

The mechanic gave a snort. 'I don't remember anybody like that. But I don't really look at them. I just take the keys, punch in the mileage, hand them a receipt.'

'You've got CCTV in here,' said Judith, looking up at the camera in the corner of the office. 'Perhaps we could look at the tape for that night.'

There was a short silence. Otto looked embarrassed. ''Fraid it's not working. Went off about a week ago and we're still waiting to get it fixed.'

Judith sighed in disappointment, still trying to think where she had seen the mechanic before.

Danny looked at Otto. 'Is that all?' he asked.

Otto turned to Judith, who shook her head. 'Thanks Danny,' said Otto, and the mechanic left. Otto looked at Judith and shrugged. 'Ryan's a nice enough fellow, though he's not exactly a threat to Einstein.'

But Judith wasn't listening very carefully, for a picture was beginning to take shape in her mind. It was of this same man who'd just been in the office, standing outside a door. Her door, at her flat in Belfast. What had he been doing there? she wondered. Delivering a package? It didn't seem likely. Then Otto's words echoed and she asked sharply, 'Did you say "Ryan"?'

'That's right. Danny Ryan.'

Now she knew where she'd met him – outside her door all

right, one evening when Mrs Ryan had stayed late, and her son had come round to give her a lift home. What a coincidence, she thought. She shifted her attention back to Otto. 'While I'm here, there's something else I wanted to ask you about. One of my colleagues collected a car here a few weeks ago, then had a bad blowout on the A1.'

'I heard about it. Your Mr Purvis paid me a visit.'

'Did my colleague collect the keys to the car from you?'

He shook his head. 'No, I wasn't here.' He seemed embarrassed again, as if afraid Judith was beginning to think he was always taking time off.

'So who took care of her?'

'It was Danny Ryan. He's normally the one who stands in for me. He's the senior of the boys in the garage. I know it was him, because Mr Purvis talked to him. Purvis said the car had been serviced only the week before by the mechanics at your place and he couldn't understand what had happened. Danny told him he hadn't touched it here and it seemed in perfect condition when your colleague took it away. Believe me, Danny would know – he's an excellent mechanic; I'm scared I'll lose him to another garage one of these days.'

Judith found Liz poring over reports.

'Well, I've found Milraud's rental car. What I don't know is whether he returned it, or someone else did.'

Liz grimaced. 'Since he didn't fly from the airport, chances are it was someone else.'

'It's the weirdest thing. Otto Perkins, the manager at the car hire place up there, wasn't working when the car was returned. One of the staff in the garage handled it. His name's Danny Ryan.'

'So?' asked Liz absently, her mind on something else.

222

'He's Mrs Ryan's son.'

Liz looked at her with surprise. 'Our Mrs Ryan?' When Judith nodded, she asked, 'Are you sure?'

'Absolutely. I thought he looked familiar, then I remembered where I'd seen him before. He picked his mother up from the flat one evening, not long after she started working for me. Isn't that a coincidence?'

'I'll say,' said Liz, looking down grimly at the reports on her desk. A4 had been unable to locate Dermot O'Reilly; suddenly it seemed as if the world and his dog had gone missing. She was still only half paying attention when Judith said, 'By the way, you've met Danny Ryan too. It was he who gave you the keys of that car you picked up at the airport the day you arrived.'

Judith had all of Liz's attention now. 'The car that had the blowout?'

'That's right,' said Judith. They looked at each other and Judith suddenly sat down.

'Did you speak to this Danny Ryan?'

'Not really. I saw him. Otto called him into the office to confirm that he'd been on duty when Milraud's car came back. He wasn't much help; he said it had been too busy for him to remember any individual customer. Now that I think about it though, that seems pretty unlikely. There aren't that many evening flights from the airport and there are several other car hire firms there to share the custom. The CCTV camera in the office is broken too, so there's no photographic record of who came and went.'

'I don't like this,' said Liz slowly. 'What does Danny Ryan look like?'

'Young, light hair, quite tall, lanky – his mother would probably say he needed feeding up. What are you thinking, Liz?'

'I'm thinking he fits the description Jimmy Fergus gave me

of the gunman's accomplice.' Liz was biting at the side of one of her fingers. Judith knew that habit of Liz's. It meant that her mind was racing; she was slotting information and events into position like a computer. Though she knew Liz was not prone to jumping to conclusions, Judith nonetheless felt she should inject a note of caution.

'I tell you what, Liz. Why don't I give Otto Perkins a ring and ask him if Danny Ryan was working on the day Jimmy Fergus got shot?'

And three minutes later Judith Spratt put the phone down and looked wide-eyed at Liz. 'Otto looked up his duty roster. Apparently Danny Ryan had the day off when Fergus was shot.'

'I don't like this at all,' said Liz.

'That's the good news.' Judith paused. 'Danny Ryan went home ill just after I left their office this morning. Otto was mystified. He said Ryan's never been off ill before, and he looked perfectly well earlier in the day.'

'We'd better find him fast.'

'We know he lives with his mother. I've got her address in my book. Do you really think he's involved in all this?'

'I don't know. But there are too many coincidences to be just chance. Danny Ryan's been involved with Milraud's car; my car; he fits Jimmy's description; he was off work at the right time and the moment you ask him a question, he goes off sick.'

'So do we have him pulled in?'

'Not yet – there's nothing firm enough for a charge. But we need to talk to him.'

'Then I think I should go to his house. He should be alone because his mother will be at my place cleaning up before she goes to get Daisy from school.'

Judith suddenly went very pale. 'Liz,' she said and her voice was shaking. 'If Danny Ryan's involved in this – what about his mother? Do you think she knows anything about it? She's looking after Daisy . . .' Judith's voice was rising as she spoke. 'She'll be collecting her from school in an hour.'

Liz put a calming hand on Judith's arm as she thought for a moment. 'Listen,' she said. 'You'd better go to the school and be there when she collects Daisy. Just tell her that you had a meeting nearby and then decided to take the rest of the afternoon off and spend it with Daisy. Try to act normal, and don't let her think there's anything more to it than that. Meanwhile, I'll go round to the house to see if Danny Ryan's there. But this time I'm taking the police with me.'

41

'I must tell you, Miss Carlyle, that we were surprised to hear that you and Mrs Spratt have got Annie Ryan working for you. She's from an old IRA family. Her husband was Tommy Ryan – served five years for a plot to kill a Special Branch officer. Tommy was the intelligence officer as they called them. He was the one who did the background research for the hit men.' Detective Inspector Kearne spoke matter of factly but his anger was close to the surface.

'My God,' said Liz. 'I didn't know that. I took her on from Judith. I think she got her from an agency. I can't imagine she wouldn't have had her checked out but I'll certainly find out. Where's Tommy Ryan now? She's never mentioned a husband.'

'He was shot dead by the army twenty years ago trying to ambush a patrol.'

The car pulled up outside a small red brick house, one of a long terrace with the front doors up one stone step from the pavement. As soon as Liz knocked, the door of the next-door house opened. Their arrival in the street had clearly been observed by the grey-haired woman who now stood at her open door, hands on hips. Her neatly ironed apron, the sparkling net curtains at her window and the polished door step all spoke of someone who spent much of her time at home.

'There's no one in. Never is at this time of day. She picks a kiddy up from school and the lad'll be at work. I saw him going off this morning – usual time. There hasn't been an accident, has there? Can I give her a message?' she asked eagerly.

'No thank you, madam. It's just a routine enquiry,' replied Kearne.

'I'll tell her you called.'

I bet you will, thought Liz as she climbed back into the car.

'What now?' asked the inspector.

'Just a minute.' Liz got out her mobile phone. 'I'll see if I can find out where Mrs Ryan might be.'

Judith answered immediately. 'Yes. I've got Daisy. We're in the tea shop. I don't think Mrs Ryan suspected anything. She said she'd go back to the flat and tidy up. I didn't tell her not to as I didn't want to alert her to anything.'

'OK. Stay out for the moment and I'll ring you when I've talked to her.'

At her house, Liz let them in with her key and knocked on Judith's door. They waited tensely, but no one answered. Kearne looked at her questioningly; she was listening to something. Then, motioning him to follow, she climbed the single flight of stairs to her own flat. Through the half-open front door came the sound of a vacuum cleaner. Liz paused; pushing by her, Kearne went in first.

Mrs Ryan was in the sitting room with her back to them, vacuuming the carpet. Liz called out, but her voice was lost in the din. Looking around, she saw where the plug was pushed into the socket and switched it off. The vacuum gave a strangled moan, then went silent. Mrs Ryan looked round and

jumped when she saw Liz and Kearne standing in the doorway.

Putting a hand on her breast, she said, 'Oh, you've frightened me, miss. I wasn't expecting anyone.'

'I wasn't expecting you either,' said Liz. 'I thought you'd be
at Judith's today with Daisy.'

'I should've been. But Mrs Spratt picked Daisy up herself. I
knew you'd been away so I thought your place could stand a
bit of sprucing up. I hope you don't mind, miss,' she added.

'That's very thoughtful, Mrs Ryan. Thank you. It's lucky you're
here because I wanted to speak to you. This is Detective Inspector
Kearne.' Beside her, Kearne nodded.

'Why don't we all sit down?' said Liz, motioning Kearne to
take one of the chairs and gesturing at the sofa for Mrs Ryan.
She crossed the room to close the front door and as she passed
the open doorway into her small study she saw that the stack
of files and papers on her desk still lay where she'd left them,
but the top file was open – and Liz knew she had left it closed.
She'd never brought secret documents home – so Mrs Ryan's
snooping, if that was what it was, would have been rewarded
with nothing more interesting than her electricity bill.

Back in the sitting room Kearne and Mrs Ryan were sitting
awkwardly across from each other, neither speaking. Liz pulled
up a chair next to Kearne, and smiled reassuringly at Mrs Ryan.
But the woman avoided her gaze. She never looks me in the
eye, Liz thought, alert now in the light of her new information
about Mrs Ryan's background. And that's why I've never looked
very closely at her.

She inspected the woman carefully and realised that Mrs Ryan
was younger than she'd believed. It was as if she wore the trap-
pings of old age – the grey tousled hair, the slight stoop, the
thin-framed glasses, the dowdy clothes – as a cover.

'Is there something wrong, miss?' asked Mrs Ryan quietly.

'Inspector Kearne and I have a few questions to ask you.'

'Questions?' asked Mrs Ryan. 'What about? Is there something wrong with my work?'

'Not at all. It's about your son Danny.'

'Has something happened to him? Is he all right?' Her concern was real.

'I don't know, Mrs Ryan. I was hoping you could tell us. We wanted to talk to Danny but we can't find him. We thought you might be able to help.'

'Isn't he at work at the garage?'

'He left there earlier. He said he was going home ill. But he's not at home.'

'How do you know?' For the first time she looked straight at Liz, her voice rising in agitation. 'Have you been round there causing a fuss? What's Danny supposed to have done?' she demanded, looking at the policeman.

'That's something we're wanting to talk to him about. Where do you think we could find your son?' Keane asked sharply.

'If he's not at home, then I haven't the faintest idea. He's old enough to look after himself.'

'I must warn you, Mrs Ryan, that we have reason to believe that your son may have been involved in a serious offence. If you fail to provide information, you may be charged with obstructing the police and it will be worse for him.'

'Worse?' Suddenly Mrs Ryan's voice was rising. She stared at Liz, her eyes filled with hatred. 'How could it be worse? You murdered my husband. Are you saying you're planning to murder my boy now?'

Liz said, 'Calm down, Mrs Ryan. This has got nothing to do with your husband. Listen, this entire country's having to learn how to live with its past and move on. You should be helping

Danny accept that, not harking back to the past.'

Mrs Ryan sat straight up in her chair, colour rising in her cheeks. 'Don't you lecture me about the past – or the future. This is our country and you've got no right here. Your lot haven't given up a thing, have you? Peace agreement my back-side,' she said bitterly, all pretence of gentility gone now. 'You bastards are still here, aren't you? You think you've won, don't you? But just wait and you'll see what we think of your peace process.'

Her voice was shrill, and Liz raised a hand in a calming gesture. But Mrs Ryan was having none of it. There was no deference now, just loathing, a hatred cast so deep it chilled Liz. 'Don't you shush me!' the woman shouted. 'Oh, it's all sweetness and light on the surface – you and your friend, with her spoiled little brat. 'Thank you so much, Mrs Ryan,' and 'Have a good day, Mrs Ryan.' You'd think this was bloody Africa and me a native working for a pair of colonial women.'

She took off her glasses with one hand, and when she leaned forward and glared at Liz her eyes were a raging blue. 'Women who couldn't keep a man, though at least Mrs Spratt's got a child. Look at you: you haven't even got a husband, much less a family. How dare you lecture me? You haven't got a clue what it's like raising a child on your own, without a penny to spare, and the man you loved gone because a soldier decided it was his turn to die. How am I supposed to move on from that, *Miss* Carlyle?'

Inspector Kearne had heard enough. 'That'll do, Annie. I think you'd better come with me down to the station. I should warn you—'

'Suit yourself,' she broke in. 'You can do what you like to me. You'll never catch my son. He's a clever boy.'

'We'll see about that,' said the inspector, putting his hand on her arm and manoeuvring her towards the door. When they'd gone, Liz sat down heavily on the sofa. The sudden transformation of Mrs Ryan from deferential cleaning lady to hate-filled harridan had left her thoroughly shaken.

42

'Peggy, I can't tell you how glad I am to see you.' Liz was looking affectionately at her younger colleague's earnest face. Peggy Kinsolving had arrived the previous evening and was now installed at a small table in the corner of Judith's office.

Judith wasn't expected in that day; she was having to look after Daisy. Judith had been mortified by her failure to check out Mrs Ryan with the police. Her only explanation was that she had been so focused on getting things sorted out quickly for Daisy, so that she could start work without delay, that when the references from the agency had all been fine, she had simply forgotten to do a separate police check. But yesterday she had had a call from Inspector Kearne's wife, Bridget. Bridget was a qualified childminder and – something that had seemed to Judith a gift from the gods – she was looking for a job. They were to meet that afternoon.

Peggy had been in the office since seven-thirty and had already mastered the main facts of the case. Her table was strewn with papers and Liz could see that she had drawn up a list of questions. The two women had worked closely together for the last few years, both in counter terrorism and in counter espionage, ever since Peggy had transferred from MI6 after working with

Liz on the case of an IRA mole in the intelligence services. They were perfect foils for each other: Liz the driving, quick-thinking, inspirational case officer, who to Peggy's admiring eye always seemed to know what to do. Peggy, with her clever, enquiring mind; the scholarly lover of detail who took nothing at face value, and who, having recently acquired a boyfriend, had begun also to acquire the self-confidence of knowing she was attractive.

When Liz had finished bringing Peggy up to date with the previous day's events she said again, 'It's such a relief to have you here, Peggy. Not that Judith's not great. But this business with Mrs Ryan has really knocked her for six. And to tell you the truth, I'm beginning to wonder if Michael Binding's having some kind of a breakdown. He's never been the easiest person to work with, but he's behaving really strangely. You never know what sort of a mood he'll be in. He swings from seeming almost eerily calm one minute to getting in a rage in the next. Then yesterday when he heard about Mrs Ryan, he was crying. I just don't think he can take the strain.'

'Why don't you ring up Charles and tell him what's going on? He sent you his best, and I'm sure he'd be happy to help – he'd want to know if it's that bad with Binding. And he'd tell DG, without making a big fuss.'

Liz flushed. She had avoided asking Peggy about Charles, though part of her had wanted to. But the truth was that she didn't want to think about him. She had to admit to herself that she'd been very hurt by her mother's implication that Charles and Alison were going around as a couple. Since Joanne's funeral Charles had said hardly a word to her, let alone told her that his affections were now engaged elsewhere. Liz had decided that she would move on, knowing that for now she had nowhere to move on to. Never mind. She certainly wasn't going to run to Charles for help in the present circumstances.

'Oh there you are, Liz,' said Binding, poking his head round the door and nodding in Peggy's direction to acknowledge her arrival. 'Any news? It's been three days now and you've turned up precisely nothing.'

Liz and Peggy both stared at him, startled by the outburst. He looked flustered, sweating slightly, his tie loosened and hanging crookedly from his unbuttoned collar. He went on, 'I'm not happy about this at all; you don't seem to be getting anywhere. I've got to brief DG and the minister this afternoon. Is there anything for me to tell them, other than that you and Judith have been employing a known IRA sympathiser in your households?' His voice rose almost to a shout as he finished speaking.

Liz resisted the urge to shout back at him and said soothingly, as if speaking to a child, 'A few things are beginning to fall into place now, Michael. Why don't we go into my office where we can all sit down and I'll tell you what I make of what we now know?'

'I don't have time for a lot of chat, Liz,' said Binding, but she ushered him firmly along the corridor to her office and sat him down. Peggy followed them in, and Binding gradually fell silent as Liz began to set out the case.

'Firstly, we know from Brown Fox that Seamus Piggott's intention was to kill policemen and an MI5 officer, and the FBI have given us the background on why he wants to do that. It can't be coincidence that there's been movement on both fronts – Jimmy Fergus got shot and Dave's . . .' she paused, trying to find words that encompassed both their worst fears and their uncertainty '. . . Dave's been taken.'

'Secondly, we know from Brown Fox and A4 surveillance that Milraud is involved with Piggott, probably supplying weapons. We know from CCTV and the woman in the shop that Dave

234

made it to see Milraud, though from the absence of any CCTV coverage of him leaving – and the fact that his car was still in the shopping centre car park – I think we can assume that Dave disappeared *from* the shop. Because of that, I'd say we can assume Milraud was involved with his disappearance, and I don't think it's too much to argue that Piggott was as well. Now we can't find Piggott or Milraud – or Dave,' she added. 'We don't know whether Piggott and Milraud are together but it's a fair assumption that one of them has Dave.'

'What do the French say?'

'They're looking for Milraud. But they don't see him as a kidnapper.'

Binding snorted while Liz went on.

'Then there's Jimmy Fergus – at least we've got a lead there. A man named Sean McCarthy has been linked to the van that Fergus's attackers were driving, and possibly to the gun that was used to shoot Fergus. The problem is, we don't have anything to tie McCarthy to Piggott, and he hasn't been found yet either.'

When Binding sighed, Liz held her hand up. 'I haven't finished. McCarthy had a sidekick. The man who drove the van. Jimmy Fergus's description of him resembles Danny Ryan, the son of Mrs Ryan, Daisy Spratt's minder and our cleaning lady, whom you've heard about. He's disappeared.'

'And what has Mrs Ryan said about it all?'

'Nothing. She's not talking. And the police haven't enough on her to hold her. So she's back home.'

Liz went on. 'Danny Ryan works at the Davis Hire agency at the airport. He was in charge the night Milraud's car was returned, and apparently he signed it off. Finally, it was he who handed me the keys of the car I drove when I first arrived. The one that had the blowout. It'd been in their car park for several hours before I collected it.'

'Oh God, Liz, are you still going on about that? They might have killed Dave by now, and you're still obsessed with a flat tyre.'

This was the last straw; Liz found it impossible to restrain herself any longer. 'How *dare* you?' she said angrily, rising from her desk, her voice loud and clear. 'My close friend and colleague has disappeared, and you have the nerve to imply I'm being paranoid? Do you actually think I care more about a flat tyre as you call it than what has happened to Dave?' She looked at him incredulously. Peggy shifted in her seat but said nothing.

Binding stood up and just for a moment Liz thought he was going to explode. She tensed, but then, to her relief, his fists slowly unclenched, and his whole frame seemed to relax. He sat down again and slumped in his chair. 'I'm sorry,' he said, barely audibly. 'I didn't mean to suggest –'

'Forget it,' said Liz dismissively. 'I have already.'

Binding nodded – not graciously, but it was still a nod. 'What should we do next?'

Liz sat thinking for a moment, gnawing gently at the side of one of her fingers. 'It seems to me that everything points to Piggott. Think about it: Dave's informant Brown Fox – O'Reilly – worked for Piggott; Milraud was doing business with Piggott; and I'd bet my bottom dollar that when we track down Danny Ryan we find there's a connection there as well.'

'But you can't find Piggott. Or any of these other people.'

'A4 has Piggott's flat in the city under twenty-four-hour surveillance. And the police have been to his house in County Down.'

'Where is that?' asked Peggy.

'It's about thirty miles south of here. On the coast.'

'On the coast?' repeated Peggy.

'That's right. Why?'

'Well,' said Peggy hesitantly. 'It's just that if all these people have gone to ground, maybe they're not still here. And they haven't got a natural place to hide, have they? I mean, an old IRA hand like this Brown Fox guy must have all sorts of old 'comrades' – here or in the Republic – who would put him up almost indefinitely. But not Piggott, and certainly not Milraud. I wonder if they've left Ireland altogether.'

'We've checked all the obvious possibilities,' Binding said. 'Airports, trains to the Republic.'

Peggy was nodding vigorously. 'Yes. But what if they've gone out by sea? In a boat. Has Piggott got a boat? That would have been the easiest way out.'

'I should have thought of that,' said Liz. 'I think we need to have another look at the County Down house.'

'I was just about to suggest that,' said Binding importantly. The *entente cordiale* had been too good to last. But if they'd gone by sea, thought Liz, what had they done with Dave Armstrong? She could only pray they had taken him with them. The alternative was too awful to imagine.

43

The rain was streaming down the jacket of the policeman who opened the National Trust gate and waved their car through. The gatehouse seemed to have become a temporary police post. If there had been visitors staying there they must have been sent packing. Further up the drive two patrol cars were parked and as their car swung round to park on the gravel apron in front of Piggott's house, a sergeant came out to greet them.

'We're inside, sir,' he said to Binding, as they moved quickly, heads down against the driving rain, to the front door. 'There's no one here except the housekeeper.'

'Have you got a warrant?'

'Yes. We're going room by room now, but so far nothing unusual has shown up. I've got two men searching the grounds as well. The housekeeper claims she hasn't seen Piggott for over a week. She's rather an old lady, sir.'

Liz was surprised by how almost unnaturally clean the inside of the house was. On the ground floor a large sitting room ran the full length of the front of the building, its tall, oblong windows giving a dramatic vista of the shore. The sea was rough, filling the bay with white-crested waves, which came crashing onto the beach of the little cove.

Across the hall was a dining room with a large oak table and matching chairs and behind it a small room with a modern desk in one corner. Its drawers had been forced open but they seemed to have contained nothing more exciting than a telephone directory. If this were Piggott's study, he certainly didn't use it.

Upstairs, more policemen were combing the three bedrooms. All were pristine, decorated in the antiseptic style of a chain hotel, and so devoid of anything personal that it was impossible to make out in which of them Piggott slept.

When they came downstairs they found the sergeant in the kitchen, where the elderly housekeeper was sitting at the table drinking a mug of tea, seemingly oblivious to the comings and goings of the policemen.

Binding, showing his frustration, asked, 'Anything?' But the sergeant shook his head.

'Is there a cellar?' asked Liz.

'Yes. There is. But there's nothing down there. Do you want to see? 'He led her down a flight of stairs by the back door into a small, empty room, with a rough cement floor and cold brick walls.

'Not even a rack for wine,' said Binding, who'd followed them down.

Liz was looking round at the walls. 'There's something weird about this room,' she said suddenly.

'What?' asked Binding.

'When do you think this house was built?'

Binding shrugged. 'Not that long ago. I'd have thought the land was part of the estate, then got sold to someone who put a house on it. I don't know – maybe thirty, forty years ago. Why?'

'Well, an old house would have a cellar – a wine cellar, cold rooms for storage, that sort of thing. But if you built a cellar in a house this age, surely you'd make it a decent size, wouldn't you? Why go to the trouble of digging it out just to make a tiny little room like this. What's the point of it?'

'You're right, Liz,' chipped in Peggy, who had joined them in the little room. 'You'd make it a basement, like the Americans have. Rooms you could use.'

'Meaning what?' asked Binding.

'Meaning we've been looking for even one room that showed signs of Piggott using it, and there haven't been any. So maybe there's another room. Hidden. One that we haven't found yet.'

Binding's lips tightened, but he said nothing.

'What do you think that's for?' asked Peggy, pointing to a metal box on a bracket halfway up one of the brick walls.

The sergeant poked at it, trying to open it. 'It's locked. There's no sign of a key anywhere here. Perhaps the housekeeper has it. I'll go and ask her.'

'Don't bother with her,' Binding ordered. 'Break it open.' And five minutes later, with the aid of a crowbar from the boot of one of the patrol cars, the small metal door was off its hinges.

Inside was a switch, like the switch in a fuse box. It was up. The policeman looked questioningly at Binding, who nodded. 'Here goes then,' said the policeman, and pulled down the switch.

Immediately a low grinding noise came from behind them, and the entire far wall started moving on tracks, opening to reveal a room on the other side.

Liz moved forward slowly, taking in the comfortable furnishings. On the desk lay a neat stack of files; she picked up the top one, then showed its label to Peggy who was standing beside her. *Fraternal Holdings* Q4. This must be Piggott's office.

The sergeant was pointing to something in the corner of the room. 'Yes, what is it?'

'It's a folding bed, miss.'

Binding said, 'Surely Piggott didn't sleep here.'

'I suppose he might have done. Or possibly,' Liz said grimly, 'it's where they kept Dave.'

Just then a young constable came running down from the kitchen, his shoes clacking loudly on the stairs. 'Sarge,' he said, panting breathlessly, 'they've found something in the grounds. Can you come?'

'What is it?' asked Binding.

The constable hesitated, and looked to his sergeant for guidance. 'Go on lad,' said the sergeant. 'Spit it out.'

The constable nodded. 'It's graves, sir. Two of them. They said you'd want to know right away.'

Liz counted seventeen people, all of them male, including two pathologists and a deputy superintendent of police. Three hours had elapsed since the youthful policeman had run down the stairs to the cellar, time that seemed endless to Liz as she waited for what she felt was certain to be bad news.

The wind had dropped and the rain had turned to a steady drizzle as she and Binding and Peggy stood huddled together under one of the tall oaks. Someone had produced coffee in plastic cups and they warmed their hands as they waited for news in the fading light. Not fifty feet from them two white tents had been erected over the graves – temporary morgues. Inside them the grizzly work of disinterment proceeded. There had already been a leak to the press – they'd heard that several reporters had arrived, but were being held at the police post in the National Trust gatehouse.

At last a policeman beckoned and Liz went forward. Binding touched her arm, but she shook her head – she'd do the identifying, since she was more likely than he to recognise the second body. They would all be able to identify one of them, she thought grimly.

She stooped down to enter the tent and was momentarily blinded by the dazzling light of the halogen lamp hanging from the top pole. A curious, sickly, chemical smell hung in the air. The pathologist looked eerie in his white suit and surgical gloves and beside him a constable in uniform stood looking. A sheet covered the body on the ground.

'Ready?' asked the pathologist.

Liz nodded, taking a deep breath, trying to prepare herself for the worst. The constable pulled back the sheet and she looked down.

She allowed herself to breathe out. It wasn't Dave. A young man with dark hair lay on his back, looking startlingly peaceful. He could have been asleep, were it not for the black hole in his temple. The bottom of one of his trouser legs was darkly stained, as if it had been soaked in ink.

'Do you recognise this man?' asked the constable.

'No,' said Liz quietly, and saw out of the corner of her eye that Michael Binding had come into the tent. 'But I think I know who it is. Tell me how tall he is. I can't judge, looking down at him like this.'

'Between five six and five seven,' said the pathologist.

Liz turned to Binding, who was still blinking as his eyes adjusted to the harsh light of the overhead lamp. 'It's almost certainly Sean McCarthy. He was the gunman who shot Jimmy Fergus. Jimmy hit him in the leg when he fired back at him. He described him as short and dark-haired.'

Binding nodded, looking stunned. Liz took another deep breath. 'Right. Now let me see the other one.'

They followed the pathologist and the constable in a sombre procession, outside through the drizzle and into the adjacent tent. Again, a sheet covered a disinterred corpse lying on the ground. And the same sickly smell hung around.

Liz felt sick and as she stepped forward she gritted her teeth to prevent her gorge rising. Why had Dave been so stupid? And why hadn't she rung from Paris, or London? Anything to avoid this. She waited as the police officer reached down to pull back the sheet, bracing herself for how the familiar features would look. She only hoped it had been quick for Dave at the end.

'No!' she shouted as the sheet went back. For the face that stared up at her with dead blank eyes was not Dave's. Someone else lay on the ground. A much older man than Dave. But the face was familiar.

'What is it, Liz?' Binding demanded, seeing her astonishment.

'This is Dermot O'Reilly.' Her voice trembled with a mixture of relief and horror. 'It's Dave's informant, Brown Fox.'

44

Nausea. Whenever it seemed to subside, it would quickly come back. Dave couldn't think about anything else, as fresh spasms gripped him.

He felt the floor beneath him rocking gently, and heard a faint smacking sound – water slapping against wood. He must be on a boat, below deck, in some kind of hold. The throbbing background noise was the engine; the rocking, which was making him feel so sick, was the boat's movement through choppy waters.

Dave had no idea where he was, but he knew that he had been out of it for a long time. He wanted to flex his arms, but as he tried to lift one he found it held fast to his side. He was lying on a low camp bed and he saw that he had been tied up – very neatly, like a chicken painstakingly trussed before cooking.

So he was a prisoner. But whose? He tried to remember how he had got here. Gradually coming to, he found images were flickering in a bewildering sequence through his head. A small room, with a desk and chairs. Across the desk a man, speaking with a strong accent – a foreigner, who had been trying to sell Dave something, hadn't he? He remembered the voice behind him, guttural, foreign, and a bulky man with a gun in his hand.

Then another room, some sort of library this time, and the cold unfeeling eyes of the man who'd injected him in the arm. What was his name?

Suddenly the hold door swung open and Dave was half-blinded by an incoming rush of light. He blinked and made out a figure looming in the doorway. A familiar man with a dark face – did he know his name either? – who was holding a tray, which he put carefully on the floor. Reaching down, he suddenly grabbed Dave with both hands and flipped him over like a fish, so that he flopped off the bed and lay face down on the floor.

He could feel the man fiddling with the rope that bound his hands. 'Where are we?' Dave managed to ask. The man ignored him. When he'd untied the knots he hauled Dave roughly up onto his knees and put the tray down with his free hand in front of Dave.

'Eat,' he said tersely.

Dave looked down at the plate, where a watery stew lay on a small pile of mash. It looked revolting, and his nausea surged again. He clenched his jaw, but there was nothing he could do to stop himself as he vomited straight onto the plate.

The foreign man stepped back in disgust, then quickly left the room. Dave moaned and retched again, propping himself on his hands and trying to still the spasms in his stomach. I need to get out of here, he told himself dimly, realising that his legs were still tied. He reached down and touched the knots of the ropes at each knee, then tried to pick at them with his fingernails.

The foreigner returned. He held a syringe in one hand and a pistol in the other. He pointed the gun at Dave and motioned him to leave the knots alone. Then the man leaned down, ignoring the spattered plate on the floor, and plunged the syringe straight into Dave's arm before he had time to object.

'Where are we?' Dave asked again, this time more feebly. He felt fatigue settling on him like snow, and struggled to keep awake. It was no good; he barely noticed as his head fell back against the wall, and realised he could no longer keep his eyes open.

'*Suenos dulces*,' the man said.

45

Peggy put the phone down at the end of yet another call. She lifted her head for a moment to look out of the window and realised that it was morning. A brilliant red sun like a perfectly round tomato was just appearing over one of the barracks buildings, making the frost-covered tiles sparkle. She had been working all night.

The discovery of the bodies buried at Piggott's County Down house had energised everyone. Until then, no one had admitted that they thought Dave was dead, but Peggy knew that she wasn't the only one who had been secretly thinking it. Now, perhaps illogically, when dead bodies had been discovered and Dave's was not one of them, they had all begun to think that he was alive.

The forensic teams were still hard at work in the County Down house and its grounds, and it would be some time before their efforts produced anything for the investigators to work on. But one thing had been discovered straight away that had kept her at work all night. When Dermot O'Reilly's body had been disinterred, in his trouser pocket they'd found his mobile phone. In their haste to get rid of the body and go, his murderers must have overlooked it. The pathologist had said that O'Reilly had been dead no more than twenty-four hours and that he had been buried very soon after death. So as Peggy had trawled through the phone's memory of calls made and received, she had concentrated on the period shortly before his death.

It was the final call that the phone had received that interested her most. And, after a night spent in conversation with a variety of contacts in different agencies, she now knew that the call the phone had received at five p.m. the afternoon of Reilly's death had been made from a mobile phone that was at that time somewhere in County Down. Dermot's phone had been in Belfast when the call was answered.

It seemed to Peggy fair to assume that the call had been connected to Dermot's visit to Piggott's farmhouse. It could well have been the call summoning him to his death. As she contemplated her night's work, she had the satisfaction that though she didn't know who had made that call or even whose phone it was – it was a throw-away phone, bought recently at a shop in Belfast with no service contract – if that phone came on the air again, she would be immediately notified. She'd circulated the details to all foreign liaison intelligence agencies and at last, it seemed to Peggy's tired mind, there was a chance of getting somewhere in the search for the people who had taken Dave.

She stared again at the list of numbers on the sheet in front of her, wondering if there was anything more she could do. Most were landline numbers in Belfast, some mobile calls traced through the local transmitters. One number had immediately stuck out – a twenty-minute call three days ago to a landline with an area code in one of the southern suburbs of Dublin. Peggy had been onto the Garda in the Republic, and they'd moved quickly, but it turned out that the number belonged to the sister of Dermot O'Reilly's wife. Two hours wasted on a false alarm.

As she sat at her table, her eyes drooping now, Judith Spratt came into the office.

'Morning, Judith. I wasn't expecting you. Who's looking after Daisy?' asked Peggy.

'Bridget Kearne's taking her to school. Daisy's taken a real shine to her. She's now saying she never liked Mrs Ryan; she said she was scary. Children *are* strange. She always seemed very fond of her to me.'

'What have you told her about why Mrs Ryan's leaving?'

'I just said she had to stay at home because her son was ill. It's funny how you tell lies to kids without a second thought.'

'Well, that seems reasonable enough. You could hardly tell her that Mrs Ryan hated us all. Or that her son had tried to kill Liz.'

'No. That's true,' said Judith. 'By the way, you probably haven't heard, but A4 now accept that Liz's car was tampered with. Apparently the nuts holding the wheel bearing had been over-tightened; if you do that the bearing can collapse and the tyre shreds. Suddenly you're veering all over the road. It's the kind of mistake an amateur can easily make, but not an experienced mechanic. So they're certain it was done on purpose.' Judith shook her head. 'It's difficult to imagine how someone as young as Danny Ryan could feel that level of hatred for someone he'd never met. Anyway the police have got him now – he was caught speeding just outside Newry yesterday. He was going eighty-five in a forty-mile-an-hour zone.'

'Good. Maybe they'll get something out of him,' said Peggy. 'Though if his mother's anything to go by, he'll keep his mouth firmly shut. A nasty piece of work – that goes for both of them.'

'I know. It doesn't do to forget how much hatred there is still around in this place. But tell me about last night. I've only heard snippets from Liz – I saw her when she got back to her flat and gave her a whisky. She seemed shattered.'

'We all were. Especially when the bodies were found. I think everybody was certain one of them would be Dave. It was worse for Liz than any of us. She was really brave, Judith. She had to look at the bodies to see if she could identify them; I know she was expecting to be staring down at Dave's face.' Peggy shuddered and the shudder turned into a yawn.

'Peggy, you've been here all night, haven't you? Go and get some breakfast. The canteen's open. I'm going to start working on this boat theory.'

'Boat?' said Phil Robinson. He was up in Antrim, cleaning up the National Trust hides on the coast ready for the bird count that would begin in April. He sounded confused at first by Judith's question. She had explained again that she was talking about the National Trust property in County Down and the neighbouring house. Had he seen a boat moored at the jetty there?

'Ah,' he said with sudden comprehension. 'Yes indeed, I have seen a boat there sometimes. One of those rigid inflatables. It's the dinghy from a big motor cruiser. I've seen the big boat anchored just offshore where the sea's deeper. It's hard to forget it. It's one of those glitzy sort of things you see in the Caribbean or the Greek islands; there aren't many of those on this side of the Irish Sea.'

'It's the motor cruiser I'm interested in. Can you describe it?'

Robinson thought for a minute. 'Well, I'm not an expert, but I'd say it was a good thirty metres long, maybe longer. White with chrome railings all around, and a big open space on the rear deck. You could see it had several cabins below. Then there was a small upper deck, with a glass window all round it. I suppose that's where it's steered from. There was a sort of winch mechanism at the back that they used to haul up the dinghy. I watched them doing it one day. Very smooth operation it was.'

'Was there anything else about it you remember?'

'Yes, now that you mention it. It had a kind of squashed bow – it was wide, like a hammerhead shark. It gave the boat a powerful look.'

Judith had saved the obvious question for last. 'I don't suppose you noticed its name by any chance.'

Robinson laughed. 'I thought you'd never ask. I do, because it sounded so peculiar. *Mattapan*, with a Roman numeral III next to it – so I guess you'd say 'Mattapan the Third'. Not an emperor I've ever heard of.'

No, thought Judith, thinking of Liz's account of her meeting with Daryl Sulkey of the FBI. It was the Mattapan *Three*, the trio of Boston-Irish gun runners sent to prison, of whom only Piggott's brother had failed to come out again.

Peggy was back now from breakfast, looking much brighter.

'Let's suppose they've gone off in *Mattapan III* and taken Dave with them. Where might they be going?' asked Judith.

'America?' suggested Peggy hesitantly. 'That's the logical place for Piggott to go.'

'Surely even a boat like Phil Robinson described couldn't sail all the way to America at this time of the year, could it?'

'Probably not,' Peggy admitted. 'What about France? Milraud's base is at Toulon, near Marseilles. They might be going there. Let's do a bit of phoning round and see if anyone has had sight of *Mattapan III* in the last twenty-four hours. How far do you reckon they could have got by now?'

Several hours later they had come up with nothing. It seemed incredible that a boat of that size could disappear on the high seas in these days of heightened terrorism alerts. But none of ·the obvious port authorities had any record of *Mattapan III* putting in for the night or for fuelling. When Liz put her head round the door enquiringly in the middle of the afternoon she was greeted with shakes of the head.

'It can't have disappeared, unless it's sunk,' said Peggy gloomily. The lack of sleep was beginning to catch up with her. 'Do you think we should ask the RAF to put up a Nimrod?'

'No. We can't do that,' Liz responded. 'Binding is still insisting we keep the enquiry low key and DG agrees with him. So in a way we're working with one arm tied behind our backs. The fear is that if Dave's disappearance leaks out or Piggott and Milraud detect us close behind them, they may just kill Dave.'

'If they haven't already,' said Peggy, now close to tears.

'Peggy, go home and go to bed,' ordered Liz. 'You can't do any more here for the moment. Remember that O'Reilly told Dave that Piggott was into all sorts of drugs – and the vice trade. If he's been using this cruiser in that business, he may have dodgy contacts in ports all over the place who are prepared to cover for the boat's movements. And since Milraud is an arms dealer I bet he knows how to move stuff by sea without being detected. We'll have to hope the police get something useful out of Danny Ryan or the French come up with some development on their side. They've got Milraud's wife under close surveillance, so perhaps we'll get a breakthrough from that.'

46

On the sixth day they cast anchor in mid-afternoon just off the coast near Marseilles. It had been a steady enough voyage, though they had lost half a day by putting in at a small harbour on the Portuguese coast to avoid a late winter storm that had moved in from the Azores. *Mattapan III* was well known there and Piggott had certain arrangements with the harbourmaster which ensured discreet service. Both Piggott and Milraud had contacts in a number of Mediterranean ports who regularly helped them hide their movements from the attention of the authorities. They did not grudge the expense; it was the only way to be successful in their business.

A similar storm had delayed them briefly off Cadiz, where they had ridden it out at sea, fearful of straying close to shore and smashing up on the rocks. As they passed the Balearic Islands Milraud had decided to take a risk and ring his wife. The rule they had was no communication when he was away on business, unless he initiated it. He had not spoken to her since he left France. '*C'est moi*,' he'd announced when Annette answered the phone. 'Have you missed me, *ma cherie*?'

Usually she replied in kind to his endearments, so he'd been surprised by the urgency in her voice. 'Listen, Antoine. What's been going on? There's been a visitor here.'

'Yes?' He was impressed but not surprised that the British had moved so quickly. '*Un anglais?*'

'*Au contraire.* A Frenchman. Someone you used to know very well in Paris. Your closest colleague—'

'Enough!' he said sharply, cutting her off. If the British had already roped in Seurat to help in the search, things were serious. Seurat was good and he was thorough. He would certainly have all angles covered and that meant that the phone line at the Bandol house was being intercepted. 'Tell me later. Is all well otherwise?'

'A bit lonely *toute seule*, and worried. Your colleague seems very determined.'

I bet he is, thought Milraud.

Two days after the call, as the sun began to go down, Milraud started up the engine of a small but powerful motor yacht moored in an unremarkable boatyard in the Marseilles docks. He steered the boat gently out to come alongside the larger and more splendid craft, lying at anchor off the harbour. On the offshore side, a swarthy man helped a pale-skinned, ill-looking figure to transfer from the larger to the smaller boat, which then in turn dropped an anchor. The large cruiser sailed slowly and carefully into the boatyard and slotted itself with some difficulty into the vacant mooring. Then two men in a dinghy sailed out to the smaller boat; the dinghy was hauled on board and in the gloom of the evening the smaller boat sailed on south-eastwards, hugging the shoreline until it passed Toulon.

Twenty minutes later Milraud could make out the shape of the island, then the hazy glow of light from the houses in its one hamlet on the north side, facing the mainland. He sat in the pilot's seat with Piggott next to him. As they moved sharply south to the side of the island furthest from the mainland, the lights receded into the night-time black. Here on the south side the island was uninhabited, its shoreline composed of rocky crags rising sheer from the sea and bare of vegetation apart from the odd Corsican pine, clinging on by roots that had miraculously found a hold. As they neared the south-eastern tip of the island, Milraud turned on the boat's powerful spotlight and saw what he was looking for – a small cove, the only possible landing place, sheltered on each side by rocks. *Oustau de Dieu* the locals called it. He knew that near the shore a boom lay across the mouth of the cove – a wooden beam, the length of a telegraph pole, designed to keep craft from landing. But he knew the trick of moving it because this was not the first time he'd landed here.

'Voila,' said Milraud, pointing to the dark shadow of the small cove, and as he slowed the boat down to idling speed, Piggott clambered back to the stern where Gonzales was beginning to lower the inflatable dinghy.

Two hours later Milraud sat on the rickety porch of an old farmhouse perched a hundred feet above the cove, on top of the rock that rose straight up from the sandy beach below. The house, the only one on this side of the island, was reached from the cove by a twisting path through the trees. It had taken Piggott and Gonzales twenty minutes to climb, half-carrying their barely conscious prisoner, while Milraud took his motor cruiser round to the other side of the island and moored it in the small marina where it was well known enough not to attract particular attention. He then walked back across the island, along familiar paths, guided by a torch.

The house had woods on either side, but on its inland-facing north end a small meadow fronted onto a now-wild vineyard that had been untended since the death of its owner. That was Annette's father, who had also owned the house and woods; before him the property had belonged to his family for almost two hundred years. Yet, despite the long family ownership of the place, Annette claimed never to have liked it. She had spent all her holidays there as a child and Milraud suspected that it was only after her years in Paris that this rustic hideaway had lost its charm. After her father's death, when she had inherited, Milraud had persuaded her to hang on to it and though Annette herself never visited nowadays, the property had served a useful purpose. He had probably spent less than ten hours in the house during the last five years, allowing it to fall even further into disrepair, but its outbuildings, which included a stout brick shed hidden in the woods, had proved an excellent site for storing items that would never be displayed in his antique shops. His boat, kept normally in the Marseilles boatyard, though modest in appearance, was deceptively fast and roomy. It could comfortably hold a dozen crates of assorted weapons, and sat so lightly in the water that it could come in close enough to shore for his North African employees to load and unload his cargoes, wading waist deep, carrying crates on their heads.

Milraud was gently swirling the contents of a small balloon glass. It was cold out here, but it was even colder in the house and the Calvados was pleasantly warming. There was a wood-burning stove in the sitting room, but he'd insisted it should not be used – smoke from the chimney might be visible on the other side of the island. He took another sip as he considered his next moves. The MI5 man was safely confined to the cellar; no chance of his breaking out of there. Above him, in a small, draughty bedroom, Gonzales sat playing patience in his shirt-sleeves, with a holstered 9 mm pistol under one arm. Piggott was in the sitting room, with his laptop open, doing God knows what.

So Milraud had come out here on the southern side of the house, overlooking the cove, where they had tied the dinghy up under some bushes at the edge of the small beach. Peering out over the top of the rock cliff, he could just make out the black well of the Mediterranean, which stretched directly south all the way to the North African shoreline of Algeria. As he finished his drink he pondered the situation. Ever since Gonzales had pulled a gun on Willis in the Belfast shop, he had been managing a fast unravelling crisis, acting by instinct. Now that they had arrived at the house, for the first time he had a chance to look calmly at what had happened and think what to do next.

Maybe if Willis had admitted straight away to being an MI5 officer the situation could have been saved. Milraud could have apologised for Gonzales' behaviour, put it down to a mistake, claimed perhaps that they'd thought he was a crook trying to get his hands on illegal weapons and let him go. But Willis had denied it, putting on a professional, almost convincing performance. Milraud had been in the same profession once and he recognised the drill. Willis had done well in an impossible situation.

Piggott had wanted to kill Willis without more ado and Gonzales was just waiting to pull the trigger. But Milraud knew that if they had killed him there and then, the sky would have fallen in on all of them. And if Piggott had allowed Gonzales to kill Willis, why wouldn't they have killed him too? He didn't think for a moment that his long working relationship with Piggott would have saved him if he'd been in the way. Milraud had needed to get control of a situation that was rapidly running away from him and the only way that he could think of at the time was to do what he'd done: persuade Piggott that a better plan to damage British intelligence and to save themselves at the same time was to transfer Willis to another group as a hostage. The publicity that would then result, he had persuaded Piggott, would ruin the reputation of MI5 for good.

Piggott had bought the plan and agreed to come here to the island house which Milraud had described as a safe base where they could hide out while he arranged the onward transfer of Willis. And that's what Piggott was expecting him to do now. He felt fairly sure he could do it too. He had mentally drawn up a list: the FARC – the Colombian rebels with their long-standing links to the IRA; the Basque separatist movement ETA, weakened now but not to be underestimated and in need of a coup; an Al Qaeda cell who would be natural customers though he had little faith in their internal security; the emissary from Hezbollah he had done business with once before.

But this would take time to arrange and even from his short conversation with Annette it was quite clear that there was little time left. The British, helped by his former colleagues, were on their tail. There was no time for the complexities of a hostage transfer, though he had no intention of telling Piggott that. Particularly because he was convinced now that Piggott was unhinged. He had started ranting in an excited fashion that was untypical of the steely character Milraud had known for years. 'We've struck a blow against the Brits they won't forget,' he'd crowed as he stood at the helm of *Mattapan III*, and in his exuberance he'd revved the throttle up so high it crossed the red danger line on the cockpit dial. 'The prime minister himself will know what we've done.' And now, having just arrived, he was already talking about leaving the island, blithely mentioning a possible run to North Africa to buy drugs, before returning with the shipment to Northern Ireland – where he seemed to forget that the province's entire security forces were looking for him.

No. Milraud made up his mind. There was only one way out for him and that meant acting fast. He'd need Annette's help. For all her Paris-acquired chic, she was still a girl with a steely rustic core – she'd always helped him, pulled him clear when doubt threatened to paralyse him, always kept his eyes firmly fixed on what to do next. Probably she was already under surveillance, but the encrypted email he'd send her in the morning would warn her of this, and tell her that they needed to meet, but only if she could be confident she wasn't being followed. There were ferries from the mainland to this island all day long, but it wasn't worth the risk unless she knew she was alone. She should make a trial run, he'd told her, just as far as Toulon to flush them out, see if they were onto her already, and more important, see if she could shake them off. Well, at least they could communicate now, to make a plan, even if they couldn't meet. It would take Seurat and the Brits some time to get into his email.

47

Martin Seurat put down the phone. The poor girl. She sounds distressed, he thought, looking out of the window of his office at the thin sprinkling of late snow that lay like powdered sugar on the old parade ground. Not surprising. She seems to have a mass murderer loose in Belfast, bodies buried in the countryside and her colleague still missing. Unfortunately he had nothing new to tell her. There had still been no sign of *Mattapan III* in French waters and Isabelle had so far turned up nothing useful from the checks in Bandol and Toulon. Milraud and Piggott, if they were together, seemed to have disappeared, along with Liz Carlyle's colleague. He couldn't understand what had got into Milraud.

Liz Carlyle had wanted to know if Milraud had a boat. There was nothing on his files about a boat, though given where Milraud lived and the business he was in, he must have one.

Seurat was just about to pick up the phone to the DCRI to pass on the enquiry to Isabelle when his phone rang again.

It was Isabelle. 'I have some news for your Liz Carlyle. Milraud has been in touch with his wife. The conversation was most uninformative and it's clear they know we are listening. The call came from Majorca, so yesterday he was in the Mediterranean region. You can tell her we're happy to share the information with the Spanish if she wants to involve them.'

'Many thanks, Isabelle. I'll pass that on. Just before you phoned, she rang to ask whether Milraud owned a boat. I have no record here of such a thing. But could Milraud have been at sea when he made that call?'

'Possibly. But I have something else for your Liz. Tell me, how well do you know the wines of Provence?'

'What?' he said, puzzled. 'What's that to do with Liz?'

'Seriously, Martin, have you ever come across a wine called Chateau Fermette?'

A small farmhouse chateau – the name a joke, he supposed. He sighed. 'No, Isabelle, I haven't. Are you doing a crossword puzzle?'

'Martin, you sound cross. Don't be. The wine I'm referring to was made on the Ile de Porquerolles. It lies just off the coast in the south. The nearest town of any size is Toulon. The vintner was named Jacques Massignac.'

'So?'

'He had a daughter, something of a beauty according to people who knew her years ago. She inherited the vineyard but she moved to Paris, and had no interest in making wine. Chateau Fermette is no more.'

'I'm beginning to get your drift. You are talking about Annette Milraud, aren't you? She told me she had southern roots.'

'I am. Monsieur Massignac's daughter is Annette. When he died she was his heir and as well as the vineyard she inherited the '*fermette*' for which its wine was named. It seems she was going to sell it after her father's death, but according to the tax people she didn't – just last month they had a cheque for this year's taxes.'

Now they were getting somewhere. 'Isabelle, tell me everything you know about the Ile de Porquerolles and this *fermette*.'

After listening to what Isabelle had to say, Martin Seurat felt confident that he had something useful to tell Liz Carlyle.

Lightning, ear-shattering thunder, cascading rain – no film version of a storm could have been more dramatic. The clouds that had been hanging over the hills for hours had finally come east, and stayed put. Having watched half an hour of these pyrotechnics through her office window, Liz was wondering if the storm would ever pass.

The phone rang and she reached for it mechanically, her eyes still on the display outside. 'Liz Carlyle.'

'Liz, it's Martin Seurat again. I think I may have some news for you.'

Liz listened raptly as Seurat recounted Isabelle's discovery that a farmhouse and vineyard on the Ile de Porquerolles belonged to Annette Milraud, a legacy from her late father.

'Where is this exactly?'

'Just off the south coast, and only a few kilometres by sea from the harbour in Toulon.'

'An island you say?'

'It's one of a small group. Not very large – it's about seven kilometres wide, perhaps three across. Said to be very pretty, and quite unspoiled. It's mainly a holiday resort in summer. Most of the island now belongs to the state, I believe. There is an old fort there; it's now a museum.'

'Does anyone live there?'

'Very few people live there all the year round. There is one village, also called Porquerolles, on the north side of the island, near the fort, with a small harbour. Other than that there are a few hotels and restaurants open in the summer. There's a passenger ferry to it from a tiny place called Gien. Outside the village there are virtually no houses.'

'Is Milraud's in the village?'

'No. Annette's *fermette* is on the other side of the island, facing out to the Mediterranean and North Africa. There are no beaches there, just high rocky cliffs. From the map I would say it's very isolated. Isabelle's people have made discreet enquiries and found that the house isn't used now. It and the vineyard have fallen into disrepair. '

'It sounds ideal if you wanted to hide something. Or someone,' she added.

'Exactly. Let's talk about where we go from here.'

Liz paused to think. She was torn between wanting to send armed police to the island right away, and the realisation that any mistake might alert Piggott and Milraud, and end up with Dave being killed.

Seurat seemed to read her thoughts. 'It's a tricky one, *n'est-ce-pas*? I was going to propose that my people have a look around, but very carefully – I will supervise the operation. I'll go down to Toulon tonight and we'll look around in the morning. But if we do establish that someone is there, then I think we should move in quickly. The longer we wait . . .' He left the sentence unfinished.

'Of course,' said Liz, already making arrangements in her mind. 'In which case I'll want to be there. Can you let me know as soon as you have any more information? If it's positive I'll come down to Toulon tomorrow afternoon. Unless you have any objection,' she added as a formality.

'Of course not. I was expecting you to want to come and I'll be delighted to have your company. I'll ring you tomorrow, and don't worry: our people are very good. *À bientôt*.'

48

Pit pat, pit pat, pit pat. If the noise didn't stop he'd go mad. The ceiling was too high for him to reach the pipe running along the beam in one corner, with its tiny leak causing this infuriating continuous drip of water onto the concrete floor. Why was he so obsessed with the noise when he had so much else to worry about?

You've got to concentrate, Dave told himself. Stop thinking about that bloody drip. Everyone will be looking for you by now. You've got to help them find you. He was trying to beat his tired, confused brain into action.

It had been pitch dark when they'd put him in here, and now he could see sunlight through the slit of a window high up in the wall. It must be afternoon, so he'd been here at least eighteen hours. By standing on tiptoe he could just look out and see trees and undergrowth. By the look of it he must have been brought south, Spain possibly or somewhere along the Mediterranean coast – France perhaps, given that he'd been in Milraud's shop when all this started. Near the sea in any case; he could smell it when he put his face to the little window, and hear waves breaking on a shore.

He'd been on a boat for days, though he couldn't remember

much about the journey. He must have been drugged – and then he remembered being injected. He also vaguely remembered two occasions when they'd transferred him from one boat to another. The last one had been small – probably just a dinghy; he'd heard the outboard motor start. He'd had a bag or something over his head – and he'd been pushed and dragged up some kind of steep path. His wrists were tied and he'd fallen several times.

Then the foreign man had forced him into this place. He was Spanish – Dave was sure of that, since he had a dim memory of the man saying 'sweet dreams' sarcastically in Spanish. *Suenos dulces* – that was it. It must have been on the boat, but Dave couldn't remember for sure.

Thank God the Spaniard had taken the bag off his head and untied his wrists. He'd also shoved a mattress and a blanket in before he locked and bolted the great heavy oak door.

Dave figured he was in some sort of old wine cellar, possibly a place where wine had been made. A faint aroma still hung in the air. There was a wall of empty bottle racks and two huge oak barrels which sounded hollow when he tapped them.

Who were they? Why were they holding him and what did they want with him? Think back, he said to himself. What happened? He could remember sitting in Milraud's shop. They'd been looking at a derringer and he was just about to proposition Milraud when the Spaniard burst into the room waving a gun. Milraud must have alerted him. But why? For a moment he thought of Judith Spratt, sitting in her office, saying that he should have back-up and wait for Liz to return before he went to see Milraud again. She'd been right, but it was no good thinking about that now. If he ever saw her again he'd apologise.

They'd taken him off to the house in the National Trust place – he'd recognised the sound of the gate squeaking and banging – and they'd questioned him in a sort of library. He remembered Milraud standing in the corner, saying nothing while Piggott asked questions. He'd kept his cover – he was sure of that – but then it all went hazy. He couldn't remember anything clearly until he was on a boat. Then just a lot of what seemed like muddled dreams. There'd been several people on the boat; he'd heard voices but couldn't recognise them and he'd only ever seen the Spaniard.

None of it made sense. But now, as he thought about it, he realised how very little he actually knew about Piggott and Milraud. Not much more than Brown Fox had told him. If this was some renegade Republican conspiracy aimed at British intelligence, surely they'd have kept him in Northern Ireland. That way, he could have been ransomed or simply killed and his body dumped in a country lay-by as a clear indication that the struggle continued.

Why bring him on this long journey? It can't be Republicans, he thought. Why was a Spaniard involved? He remembered Jimmy Fergus had said something about Piggott bringing in a hit man from the Costa del Sol. Was he in the hands of ETA? Did they take hostages? Why were they operating in Northern Ireland? Did Milraud work for ETA? And if so, what did he want with Dave?

He had no answers. But he kept asking himself the same questions to avoid sinking into despair. He felt ill. His wrists ached from being tied up so long; his back had been banged against something when he'd been deposited like a sack of potatoes into the little outboard-driven boat that brought him to the island. His knees were bruised from falling up the path to this place and his head ached with a dull, throbbing pain that made him feel dizzy.

There was the sound of a key in the lock; the bolts were drawn back and the door swung open. The Spaniard stood in the doorway holding his 9 mm. 'Up,' he ordered. What now? Dave wondered as he walked slowly up the cellar stairs, his jailer behind him.

At the top a stone-flagged kitchen led into a yard. At a signal from the Spaniard, Dave pushed open a screen door and walked outside, squinting in the bright sunlight. The Spaniard followed. He waved his pistol at the dusty yard. 'Walk,' he said, and Dave began to walk stiffly round the yard, his feet crunching on the dead pine needles that lay thickly on the ground.

As he walked he looked furtively around him, trying to get a better sense of where he was. His cellar was part of a farmhouse, a long stone building, badly run down, with a crumbling roof of red pantiles and a wooden porch with missing rails and steps that looked rotten. Around the yard were outbuildings, one an open barn with an ancient 2CV inside. Its rusty number plate was French. So I'm in France, thought Dave, triumphant at making a discovery. As he turned for yet another circuit of the yard, he looked again at the house and saw, through a window, Milraud, gesticulating and talking to someone else whom Dave could not see. Then he disappeared from view and a second figure came up to the window, talking on a mobile phone. It was Piggott.

Dave felt cold fear. What had Brown Fox said about Piggott? He wanted to kill a policeman and a British intelligence officer. Well, perhaps it was he who'd had a go at Jimmy Fergus, and now he'd got Dave.

'*Bastante*,' the Spaniard shouted, and reluctantly, Dave trudged over to the kitchen door and paused, warming himself in the sun. The Spaniard grew impatient. 'Inside,' he said irritably, gesturing with his pistol.

Dave opened the screen door and stepped into the kitchen. To his left a baize-covered door was slightly ajar. He could hear Piggott's voice; the door must lead to the room where he'd seen him.

The Spaniard was having trouble closing the screen. Dave quickly edged left and glancing behind him and seeing his jailer still occupied, he pushed the baize-covered door with a flat hand and it swung open.

'What the hell—' said Piggott.

'*Gonzales!*' Milraud shouted.

Suddenly a rough hand grabbed Dave's shoulder and spun him around. Gonzales stuck the barrel of his 9 mm right under Dave's nose, pushing it against his upper lip. He was furious and for a moment Dave thought he would pull the trigger. Then Gonzales seemed to regain his self-control. He stepped back through the doorway into the corridor and motioned Dave to come out.

Behind him Dave heard a voice say coldly, 'Get him back down there.'

A second later he felt the world had collapsed on the back of his head.

When he woke up it was dusk.

He winced as he touched a bump the size of an egg on the back of his head. His fingers came away sticky, and he looked at them a moment before realising the dark gummy stuff was blood. He was desperately thirsty but when he tried to stand up one side of his lower chest erupted in pain. He collapsed back onto the floor until the agony subsided. With his hand he gently touched the affected side, and through an excruciating prodding process of trial and error concluded that he had at least two broken ribs. How had that happened? All he could remember was Piggott shouting, then the world had gone black. He must have been hit hard on the back of his head and pushed down the stairs onto the hard floor.

Dave managed to get up on his knees and crawl over to the tap in the corner. When he turned it on, water splashed on the floor around him, quickly soaking his trousers. He cupped his hands and let the running tap fill them again and again while he drank. He tried to recall what had happened before he'd been hit. He could remember walking outside round and round the yard, and seeing Seamus Piggott, the man who wanted to kill an intelligence officer.

This would be a good place to do it, thought Dave gloomily, as he surveyed his prison. They could put a bullet in his head without fear of being heard, then bury his body deep in the woods – or weigh it down and throw it in the sea. But they hadn't done it yet, so there must be another plan. But what? Did they plan to ransom him? He almost grinned at the thought of Michael Binding negotiating for his release – he'd probably try to knock the price down – but then suddenly depression settled on him like fog and he crawled back to the mattress and lay down.

Then he heard something outside, quite far away. *Thumpa thumpa thumpa.* He strained to hear it, and this time the noise was louder. *Thumpa thumpa thumpa.*

It was a helicopter, probably military, by the sound of its bass rumble. He opened his eyes and waited. Again, *Thumpa thumpa thumpa.* Was it coming closer? 'I'm here boys,' he found himself saying aloud, half prayer, half appeal.

He listened for the deep throb, but this time it seemed no closer. He held his breath and waited again, but now the noise was definitely receding. A moment later and he couldn't be sure if it was the helicopter he heard, or the beating of his heart.

Then silence. *Pit pat, pit pat, pit pat.*

49

She loved window shopping, so Mireille Vitrin was perfectly happy strolling along the rue d'Alger, looking in the shop windows, admiring the clothes and scrutinising the antiques. And because she was enjoying herself, she looked quite unremarkable. But Mireille wasn't going to buy anything; her window shopping was cover. She was waiting for the little device in her hand to vibrate, signalling that the target was on the move ten miles away.

'She's coming out.' The gardener, cutting the grass verge at the top of the hill in Bandol, spoke into a tiny microphone fastened to his collar. He wasn't the usual gardener and anyone who'd watched him closely might have wondered how he got the job. But he wasn't staying. As soon as the white Lexus convertible passed him, he put his mower on the back of his truck and drove away. In Toulon, Mireille's hand vibrated.

Down the hill in Bandol two women sat in a dusty-looking Renault consulting a map. As the Lexus passed, they seemed to make up their minds on the route and drove on, slotting in behind it. The woman at the wheel of the Lexus, wearing a bright Hermès silk scarf wrapped round her head, was Annette Milraud.

'On our way,' the passenger in the Renault announced, as they followed the Lexus in the direction of Toulon. At the bottom of the hill the traffic lights turned amber just as the Lexus approached, but Annette speeded up and flashed through as they changed to red. The Renault stopped and waited, watching as the Lexus purred off onto the motorway. But a Volvo was already on the motorway, driving cautiously in the slow lane but speeding up as Annette went by. When the Lexus left at the exit for Toulon, the Volvo stayed on the motorway, leaving the job to another team already waiting outside the Musée de la Marine.

Under their watchful eye, Annette drove into the centre of town and parked on the quayside. She crossed the rue de la République and turned down the rue d'Alger. As she approached her husband's shop, she may have noticed the woman with strawberry-blonde hair just coming out of the pharmacy opposite, because she didn't stop and go into the shop, but continued along the street at a fast clip. Behind her the blonde woman, apparently muttering to herself, passed the target on to colleagues at the end of the street.

Walking briskly, Annette turned into the street where the market was in full swing and went into a cafe. She sat down at a table in the corner and ordered a *café crème*. She was smartly dressed, still wearing the Hermès scarf, and she carried a fashionably large designer handbag, like a small Gladstone bag. A man in a beret came in and sat two tables away, holding a sketch pad. He looked at Annette appreciatively, but she ignored him and concentrated on her mobile phone. When her coffee arrived she paid the waiter, left the change on the saucer, and taking her handbag got up and retired to the ladies' toilet.

Several minutes later, when she hadn't reappeared, the man in the beret lifted his hand to his mouth and Mireille Vitrin, who had circled around from the Milraud shop, came into the cafe and went directly to the ladies' room.

Inside, she found one of the cubicles occupied, and quietly went into the next one. When she heard the door of the neighbouring cubicle open she waited several seconds, then opened her own door and emerged in time to glimpse a woman leaving – she wore blue jeans, trainers and a T-shirt, with her hair tied back in a pony tail. She was carrying Annette's large handbag. Mireille turned around and went into the vacated cubicle. Nothing. She radioed Annette's new description to all colleagues as she went swiftly to the door of the cafe and looked out to see the woman in trainers striding swiftly back to the quayside and into the range of two more colleagues.

About noon a small dinghy, no more than two inflated rubber pontoons, came meandering along the rocky south coast of the island. It was sailed by a solitary fisherman. But the outboard motor was 110 horsepower and Henri Comptoire of the surveillance division of the DGSE felt confident he could out-race any threat that came his way.

Henri had spent the morning inspecting the satellite photographs of the island from the Ministry of Defence records – photographs taken about ten years ago. He had been comparing them with photographs taken just hours earlier, at daybreak, by the small helicopter that was normally used to chauffeur visiting dignitaries but which also provided low-key reconnaissance.

The shots had been captured by a camera mounted on the helicopter's forward strut and the images were crystal clear. Both sets of photographs showed an isolated farmhouse, perched near the rock cliff that rose dramatically from the sea. It sat with woods on either side fronting onto what in the older photographs was clearly a vineyard but now looked more like a meadow, though you could just discern the rows of overgrown grapevines. In the satellite pictures a person could be seen in the yard, along with what looked like a tractor. The new pictures showed no signs that the house was occupied – no smoke from the chimney, no washing on the line, no cars in the yard. In both, the little cove looked deserted. But the older pictures showed what seemed to be a line of buoys moored across it, just out to sea. They were not there in the recent photographs.

Comptoire had also been talking to the customs officer whose long grey patrol boat was moored in the little harbour in the village. Porquerolles was part of his beat though he didn't visit much in the winter, he'd explained. Comptoire had told him that he was doing a recce for a possible Naval Special Forces training exercise. They were looking for somewhere new for trainees to practise rapid assault from the sea. He was intending to look at the south side of the island, he'd said. The officer told him, 'If you're looking for something difficult you'll find plenty to choose from round there. Mostly the rocks come down to the sea. There's only one landing place, a tiny cove called *Osteau de Dieu* and we've got a boom across that to prevent tourists landing. It can be moved, but you've got to know the trick.'

So where was the boom? wondered Comptoire, as he puttered through the still waters, calm beneath the high noon sun. It hadn't been there in the helicopter photographs this morning and it wasn't there now. As he approached he glanced only casually towards the shore.

Then the outboard motor suddenly spluttered, coughed and died. While Comptoire tried to restart it, his dinghy began to float on the tide closer and closer to the cove's sandy beach. As he pulled at the starter cord, he also managed to survey the beach. There was no one there, and no sign of a boat, but what he saw confirmed what the helicopter photographs had shown. The little beach was very disturbed. You could see where a boat had been pulled up and there were footprints in the sand and up towards the muddy path that led away into the undergrowth. People had landed on the beach; the only question remaining was whether they were still there. It was someone else's job to try and discover that.

Starting the engine at last, he sailed out to deeper water, before turning west, speeding up and returning to Toulon.

'*Charmant*,' said the old woman to her husband, and it was true that the couple disembarking from the ferry this afternoon and setting off across the Ile de Porqucrolles on foot looked madly in love.

The man, Alain, wore a knapsack from which protruded a baguette. Françoise, his companion, had a pair of binoculars on a strap around her neck – the island was not famous for its bird life, but there was a large population of waders on the south side, which justified both the binoculars and the two-mile walk.

The couple were heading for the walking trail that crossed the island and led to a promontory on its rocky southern shore. They took their time, holding hands, and every now and then stopping to exchange a kiss. But once they'd passed the first bend in the trail and could no longer be seen from the village they picked up pace, walking briskly with their eyes alert, no longer holding hands. They were not lovers, but they had worked together many times before. Alain was cautious, thorough; Françoise was wily and inventive; the combination seemed to suit their kind of work.

Now they stayed on the tree-lined path, passing a small hotel and some deserted holiday homes. Suddenly, as if on cue, they moved off the path and into the woods. Here they walked quickly but carefully through pines and acacia trees, stopping often to check their bearings as they neared the island's rugged south coast. There were no tourists here, no signs of habitation; at one point Alain stopped to consult his compass, then slightly adjusted the angle of their advance.

When they heard the sound of waves ahead of them they split up, and taking the binoculars Alain moved towards the seaside cliffs in search of the narrow path that went down to the beach. Françoise stayed on the higher ground looking for a way to approach the *fermette* they couldn't see but knew was there.

Locating the path down to the beach at last, Alain decided to avoid it and instead to work his way down the steep bank through the lush vegetation. At one point he thought he heard someone on the trail, which was less than twenty metres away, and he ducked down behind the shrubs. Tourists? There were said to be a million visitors a year to Ile de Porquerolles but very few at this time of the year and anyway this was well away from their usual haunts.

He waited until he was sure no one was nearby, then continued his descent. The cove was exceptional on this side of the island, with its strip of white sand. Alain could see no one on the beach, although his colleague Comptoire was certain someone had been there and it was true the sand looked disturbed. Any boat that had landed here would have to be small – small enough to be lugged out of sight.

Alain was still above the beach, and from behind three euca-lyptus saplings he used his binoculars to scan the bushes that started where the sand of the beach stopped. For ten minutes he moved them inch by inch over the dense undergrowth, but saw nothing unusual. Eventually, when his eyes were tired with the effort, he let the binoculars hang from the strap around his neck, wondering whether he was missing something. It was then that a reflection of the sun, now straight ahead of him, briefly blinded him. He blinked and realised the flash was coming from the bushes directly below him – the one place he had not examined with the binoculars. Peering down, he moved his head slowly back and forth, until again a dazzling flash hit his eyes.

There it was. The boat had been tucked deep underneath a large myrtle bush, but a steel corner of its outboard engine was exposed – just enough to catch a glint of sun.

Got you, thought Alain.

Twenty minutes later he was back in the woods above the cliffs, a quarter of a mile now from the sea, at the place where he had arranged to meet Françoise. He waited impatiently, and then suddenly, soundlessly, she was standing next to him.

'Christ, you startled me,' he said.

'Good. If you'd heard me coming they might have heard me as well.'

'*They*? You've found people?'

She nodded. 'I discovered the farmhouse. Very run down; I was sure no one could be living in it. But then two men came out; one of them was walking in the yard. He didn't look too good. I'll radio in when we get a bit further away and tell them we've found them.'

Alain hesitated. Always cautious, he did not share Françoise's certainty. He said, 'We shouldn't jump to conclusions. I found a boat – a little dinghy, well hidden. But that could just be to keep it from getting stolen. And the two people you saw might be perfectly innocent visitors to the farmhouse.'

'Trust you,' said Françoise with a deprecating laugh.

Alain looked at her, slightly offended. 'What's so amusing?'

'You and your caution. The man I saw walking in front of the house was being *guarded* by the other fellow.'

'How could you tell?' Alain demanded.

'Because the man on the porch was covering his prisoner with a gun. I don't think that's how innocent visitors usually behave.'

50

As she emerged from the baggage hall at Marseilles airport, she saw a young man in naval uniform holding a sign reading 'Carlile'. She introduced herself, '*Bonjour. Je suis* Liz Carlyle.'

'Good afternoon, mademoiselle,' he responded, shaking her hand. 'Follow me.' He led her to a smart black car parked in a reserved space just outside the terminal.

Having apparently exhausted their knowledge of each other's language, they drove towards Toulon in silence. Liz gazed out at the Provençal landscape and the glimpses of the Mediterranean glittering in the midday sun, wishing that her first visit to this part of France could have been in happier circumstances.

Martin Seurat had telephoned late the previous afternoon to report the results of the surveillance on Porquerolles – the signs of a landing at the small cove, the dinghy concealed in the bushes, and finally the sighting of occupants at the *fermette*, with an armed man guarding a prisoner. He was, he'd said, sending a photograph taken by one of the surveillance team. He waited to see if she could identify her colleague. Shortly afterwards Liz was looking at a hazy photograph on her screen – a man apparently walking in a dusty yard as another man, holding a gun, stood watching him from the porch of a ramshackle house. It was the Spaniard, Gonzales, and Dave Armstrong – she recognised him even with his back to the camera.

Liz had taken the last flight from Belfast to Paris, frustrated that she couldn't be instantly whisked straight to Toulon. Martin Seurat had told her that no rescue attempt could be mounted before the following night, but she still wanted to get there and not hang about wasting time in Paris. Strangely, she felt even more worried about Dave now that she knew where he was, than she had when she knew nothing.

Her anxiety increased when, just before she went to bed in the airport hotel, an excited Peggy had rung. She'd heard from a colleague of Isabelle Florian in the DCRI. The mobile phone number that she'd circulated around the world, the phone which had called Dermot O'Reilly (Brown Fox as they'd labelled him) shortly before he was killed, had come on the air again that afternoon. The French had noted it making a call to a number in Algiers, but more importantly, the call had been routed through a mast near Toulon. It must be Piggott, thought Liz. So he's on the island too.

As the car turned through tall iron gates on the coast at Toulon, she dragged her mind back to the present, feeling suddenly tense at the thought of what was to come. She was surprised when a sentry saluted smartly as they passed; not sure how to respond, she acknowledged the courtesy with a wave. She had no idea how good the French were at operations of this kind; she could only hope that they knew what they were doing.

They drew up in front of a long, elegant, pink building and Martin Seurat stepped out and opened the car door.

'Welcome to Naval Headquarters, Liz. Come inside and I'll

show you your cabin. This place is run like a ship, but you'll soon get used to it.'

Seurat looked reassuringly calm and in his navy-blue polo neck sweater, ready for anything. Liz felt her anxieties begin to slide away; now she had someone else to share both the worry and the responsibility.

'It's not the Ritz,' said Seurat, opening a door, 'but I hope you'll be comfortable. Not that you are likely to get much sleep, I'm afraid. We're planning to go in at three-thirty tomorrow morning.'

Liz looked in at the room. It was spare and functional: a narrow bed, a bedside table, a cupboard and a small desk along the wall. It looked like a college room except that it was painted, fittingly for this environment, battleship grey. She was pleased to see that it had its own small bathroom.

'I'll meet you downstairs in fifteen minutes and brief you about what we're planning,' said Seurat, closing the door behind him.

Liz looked out of the window. She could see an enormous aircraft carrier moored in the dockyard; in the harbour itself two submarines and an assortment of grey battleships rocked gently as the tide came slowly in.

She changed into trousers and a sweater and went downstairs to find Seurat waiting for her in a comfortable lounge. 'Good,' he said smiling. 'Let's go and have a cup of coffee. We've got half an hour before we go into the briefing meeting. The teams are all here. Crack commandos from our *'berets verts'*, the Commandos Marine. They are good, Liz. If anyone can rescue your colleague alive, they will do it. Don't worry.'

Liz smiled at him. 'It was an immense relief to know that Dave is alive, and we're very grateful for all you've done,' she said. 'I just hope we can get him out of there unhurt. But you know, I'm mystified about why he's been brought here. What is Milraud up to? He must be the reason they've come here, but I can't see why he'd travel all this way just to kill Dave – he could have had that done back in Northern Ireland. You know the man. What do you think he wants?'

Seurat shrugged. 'Antoine will have no interest in harming your colleague. Quite the opposite – he will be desperate not to get involved in a murder. I can only think he got mixed up in this by mistake; if I'm right, he will be trying to find a way out for himself. Your colleague Miss Kinsolving,' he hesitated over the pronunciation, 'has let us know that she thinks that the American Seamus Piggott is also on the island, and that the armed guard our surveillance saw must be working for him.'

'Yes. She picked up a trace of Piggott's mobile phone from down here – it came through the Toulon transmitter.' She shook her head with worry. 'Milraud may not be the murdering type, but this man Piggott won't hesitate to kill Dave. He's been willing to kill before, and we know he'd like to murder a British intelligence officer. This guard of his is a Spanish hit man Piggott hired to come to work for him in Northern Ireland.'

'Well, as they haven't killed your colleague yet, Milraud may be stopping them,' replied Seurat calmly.

'But if he thinks we're closing in . . .' Liz said anxiously.

Seurat gave a long, regretful sigh. 'Milraud will certainly know by now that we are nearby. It was probably a mistake going to see Annette, but I thought I might get something out of her,' he said quietly, almost to himself. 'Instead, it's only alerted her husband that we're after him.'

Liz looked at him, impressed that he could so easily admit he might have made a mistake. 'He'd have known that in any case,' she said. 'And you did get something out of her. You learned that she had old family connections in this part of France.'

Seurat smiled. 'It's kind of you to say that, but I think we both know you're being too generous.'

Looking at his watch, Seurat announced the time had come, and led Liz to an office upstairs where he introduced her to the base commander, a burly bearded figure called Hébert. Commandant Hébert held Liz's hand and bowed in a disconcertingly formal way, then made a short speech of welcome in French, most of which Liz could understand. She replied briefly in English, and the formalities over, the three of them walked along a corridor to a conference room.

Here a group of about twenty men dressed in white T-shirts and navy-blue trousers were lounging on chairs talking. They stood up as Liz, Milraud and the commandant came into the room and sat down at a table facing their audience. Forty eyes were focused on Liz, with expressions ranging from lasciviousness to amusement.

Hébert clapped his hands and they sat down. Liz looked coolly back at the men whose job it was to free Dave Armstrong. They were unremarkable, except for one thing – they were all lean, fit, wiry, and agile-looking. In any kind of fight, the smart money would be on them.

The commandant spoke. His French rolled out in slow, sonorous sentences, and he reminded Liz of newsreel footage she'd seen of General de Gaulle addressing the nation at the end of the war. It was a dangerous task the men would embark on, Hébert announced, but he knew they would do their utmost to accomplish it on behalf of France and our good allies the British – here he introduced Liz as 'our colleague from the English MI5,' and every eye in the room turned to scrutinise her again. Their task, he continued, had the full authority of the minister, and the government at the highest level was aware of their mission. He knew they would conduct themselves as the professionals they had always shown themselves to be, and for which they were known – he turned in Liz's direction – throughout the world.

This all seemed so impossibly French that Liz's heart began to sink; she was relieved when he concluded his remarks and left the room, leaving the practicalities to Seurat. The commandos listened intently now. On the screen behind Seurat a map of the Ile de Porquerolles appeared.

'You all know the purpose of this operation and you've had the chance to study the aerial photographs and the plan of the inside of the *fermette*. You should remember that the plan is several years old, but we don't think any significant alterations have been made to the building in recent years.'

Seurat went on, showing photographs of the island and outlining the plan for the operation. Liz understood just enough of what he was saying not to need an interpreter. 'You will be in three teams of six,' Seurat said. 'The first will land on the north side of the island at the harbour where the ferry arrives from the La Tour Fondue terminal on the mainland.' He took a pointer and indicated the place on the map behind him. 'The second team will stay out at sea, off the south coast of the island, facing the cliffs here,' he said, moving the pointer down the map. 'You will be ready to intercept anyone trying to escape from the south.'

Seurat paused, then looked at one of the commandos sitting in the front row, a man with startlingly blue eyes in a deeply tanned face. 'The third team will lead the assault on the farmhouse, landing on the island's south side, in the small cove where we believe the targets also landed. It is the single accessible place on that side. Commando Laval, you will be responsible for taking the farmhouse, and freeing the hostage.'

Laval nodded sombrely, and Seurat said, 'As you know, we now believe that apart from the hostage there are three people in the house.' Four photographs came up on the screen behind him. 'One is a former colleague of mine.' He pointed to a photograph of Milraud. 'Our English visitor, Mademoiselle Carlyle, can tell you what she knows about the other two hostage takers – and of course the hostage himself. She will speak in English, but I'll translate.'

Liz stood up, sensing some amusement on the part of her audience, presumably unused to having a woman address them right before a dangerous mission. She began with a short description of the situation in Northern Ireland, pointing to the picture of Piggott. 'This man is American, of Irish descent. He was born James Purnell, but changed his name to Seamus Piggott when he moved to Northern Ireland. He is a former physicist and expert in missile technology, but in Ireland he has been running an organisation that deals in drugs, extortion, prostitution.' She gestured at the image of the bespectacled man. 'Don't be fooled by his appearance. This man is highly intelligent and very dangerous. He will not hesitate to kill.'

The commandos were listening intently as Liz went on to describe Gonzales, the Spanish hit man, who she explained was probably responsible for the deaths of two members of Piggott's organisation – the two bodies discovered on Piggott's property in Northern Ireland.

She paused, glancing at the alert faces watching her. 'It might be useful if I tell you how my colleague became a hostage.' As she spoke and Seurat translated, describing the circumstances behind Dave's capture at Milraud's shop, she felt a certain scepticism, even hostility growing in the audience. Commando Laval raised a hand.

'Yes?' said Liz, but he addressed his question to Seurat.

'From what I understand, this Englishman Dave must have behaved very recklessly in putting himself into this situation. How can we be assured that he is a genuine hostage? Could he not be a willing captive, perhaps cooperating with this Piggott and Milraud for some unknown reason? And we might find ourselves fighting all four of them?'

There was a murmur of assent in the room. Seurat looked at Liz. She had understood the question and was astonished at the suggestion. How could anyone think that of Dave Armstrong? Dave, who'd been her friend for years, whom she knew to be as honest as the day is long.

But of course these men didn't know Dave, and after all, they were about to put their lives at risk to rescue him. It was true, too, that Dave had behaved recklessly.

'Let me tell you about Dave Armstrong,' she said. And as she talked, she tried to give a picture of the Dave she knew so well – recounting his enthusiasm for the job, his honesty and bravery, the key roles he'd played in operations when they had worked together in counter terrorism. Gradually, she sensed the mood of her audience changing.

'It is the case,' she said finally, 'that on this occasion Dave Armstrong acted impetuously, even recklessly. He made the wrong decision. There were reasons, perhaps, for his misjudgement: an affair of the heart had gone wrong, which had upset him terribly. It was wrong – and uncharacteristic – for this most professional of men to let personal reasons interfere with his professional conduct. But I want you to know nonetheless that he is a brave and good man, and whatever he did was with the motive of serving his country and preventing harm to others. I assure you, you need not fear that he will be cooperating with his captors.'

She sat down, and to her surprise a small ripple of applause came from the commandos. '*Merci*, mademoiselle,' said Laval. 'That is both well said, and most reassuring.'

Another commando from the group around Laval raised his hand. He said to Seurat, 'It can be chaotic in the confusion of an assault. If it turns out that there are more people in the house than we expect, will you be on hand to help identification?'

'Yes,' said Seurat. 'Though only Milraud is known personally to me.'

Liz spoke up. 'I can identify these targets, and of course the hostage, too.'

'You are landing as well?' asked the commando with unfeigned astonishment.

'Naturally,' said Liz simply. 'But don't worry – I won't get in the way.'

The briefing concluded, Liz and Seurat withdrew, leaving the three teams to discuss the final details. As they went downstairs to the lounge Seurat said, 'I have to say they were a little sceptical at first. But what you said about Dave changed all that. And they are most impressed that you're coming with us. They had assumed you'd stay here or wait offshore in the frigate.'

'I am sorry to shatter their preconceptions,' she said a little tartly.

Seurat looked embarrassed, and she immediately regretted her sharpness. He said, 'I'm afraid this type of Frenchman is rather . . . traditional . . . Is that the word?'

'Yes, though unreconstructed would also do. But don't worry,' Liz said, and she was smiling now, 'we have plenty of them on our side of La Manche as well.'

51

They were running out of food. There was nothing fresh left – no vegetables, no bread or milk, just a few tins. Milraud reckoned they could hold out for another day and then they'd have to get supplies from somewhere. The only source of food on the island lay on the shelves of the Casino mini-market in Porquerolles village three kilometres away.

That was where he had intended to get provisions, when he'd planned all this before they'd set off from County Down. *Planned*, he thought ironically. That was the trouble: nothing had been properly planned; it had all just been a panic reaction.

He supposed it might still be safe to send Gonzales over to the village, but it was a risk, and in more ways than one – Gonzales, with his strong Spanish accent and his tendency to pull a gun at the slightest provocation was hardly unnoticeable. There was also always the chance that, stupid Spaniard though he seemed, Gonzales might simply get on the ferry with a one-way ticket, and never come back. That is, if he managed to get away. Milraud guessed that Gonzales's description would have been as widely circulated in France as his own – and Piggott's.

As he thought of Seurat's visit to Annette he became increasingly certain that time was running out. He was beginning to feel like an animal in a forest as a fire closed in from all sides. He had an intuitive sense that his former colleagues were circling ever closer, getting ready to move in for the kill.

Food was not the only problem. James – Milraud simply couldn't get used to the new name 'Seamus' – was growing increasingly volatile. He seemed a man very near the end of his rope. The night before he had lost his temper when his laptop computer had frozen, and he'd hurled it across the room. God knows if it was still working. Piggott was showing more and more signs of impatience; the man couldn't seem to sit still, and three or four times a day he walked down the cliff-side path to check that the dinghy, buried beneath bushes, was still there.

More worrying still, he was ignoring Milraud's advice not to use his mobile phone. Every few hours he enquired if there was any reply from the contacts Milraud said he had emailed with the offer to sell Dave. If something didn't happen soon, Milraud feared he would snap, and that could mean very bad news for Willis in the cellar. And possibly for Milraud himself.

There was no sign of a response from the contacts because Milraud had not actually sent any emails. His original idea instead had been to convince James that Annette was to be the intermediary with the purchasers. Then somehow she would get Willis off the island and Milraud would find a way of following her, leaving James and the Spaniard to fend for themselves. He and Annette would then lie low until the situation calmed down.

That had been his plan, but for it to work he needed Annette's calm brain to work out the details. And for that he needed to see her. But this was out of the question now, as the email he had received from Annette this morning made clear: *I think it best to postpone my visit for a while. Too crowded, even at this time of year.* She was under surveillance and had been unable to shake it off.

Which meant there was now only one way out.

It took Milraud ten minutes to compose the email. He sat on a cane chair at the old pine table in the sitting room, keeping several windows open on his screen as he typed – ready to switch over at a click of his mouse if anyone came in and tried to look over his shoulder. But Gonzales was in his bedroom, smoking cigarettes and listening to tapes of Spanish pop music, while Piggott was pacing the porch outside. Each time his steps stopped, Milraud waited nervously. Finally he finished, and hit the Send button.

Greetings Martin

I have in my possession something of value to you and your colleagues across the channel. I can deliver this package and those responsible for taking it, and I will do so and help to bring the perpetrators to justice on one condition.
I need assurance that I have official immunity from prosecution from both the French and British authorities.
I have kept the package unharmed but may not be able to do so much longer.
I await your response. Time is running out.

Antoine

52

'The wind's getting up,' said Liz. She was watching the yachts in the marina through the window of the restaurant where they were having an early supper. 'It won't stop us going, will it?' she enquired anxiously.

'It's the mistral. It comes and goes at this time of the year. But don't worry,' said Martin Seurat with a smile. 'It would take a hurricane force ten to stop Laval and his colleagues. It may mean they'll change the plan and load the rigid inflatables onto a frigate rather than sailing them out from the base. But that'll be a lot more comfortable, I can tell you. Have you ever been in one of those inflatables? They're not pleasant, especially if the sea is rough.'

'When will they decide?'

'Some time in the next few hours. The weather is very uncertain on this coast at this time of the year. The wind may drop again.'

'I thought down here in the south of France it was always warm and sunny. Shows how much I know.'

There was silence as they drank their coffee. Then Liz said, 'The waiting is always the worst part. I feel far more nervous in the run-up to an operation than when it's actually under way. And this one isn't even in our hands – there's nothing for us to do but wait.'

'You're right. Wait, and hope that it will all go well. But I think we have every reason to expect that it will.'

She smiled at him. 'You are an optimist, Martin. I just hope you're right.'

'In our line of work you have to be optimistic. You expect to succeed, or you'd never do anything. It's what drives us on. Don't you agree?'

'That's true. But there's always in the back of your mind the thought that things might go wrong – and the consequences if they did.' She thought of Dave and the consequences for him if things didn't work out in the next few hours.

'That's what this job is all about: the excitement, and the fear. But there's also the satisfaction when things do go right. Whatever happens, at least it's never boring. That's a great help when other things aren't going so well.'

Liz looked at him, sensing that he wanted to say more. 'Is there something in your life that hasn't gone well?' she asked gently.

He gave a small shrug. 'Recently there was.' He sighed, then seemed to decide he wanted to tell her about it. 'One Friday, last year, my wife suddenly announced that she was going to Alsace for the weekend. I was surprised because she hadn't mentioned it before. I was even more surprised when the weekend ended and she hadn't come back.' He gave Liz a wry look. 'She never did come back. She had neglected to tell me that she was still in love with her first boyfriend.'

'That's awful. I'm so sorry.'

Seurat shrugged. 'I was sorry too at first. Very sorry. But it's history now. We've been divorced for six months. And that's where the job came in. However bad I felt at the time, I always felt better the moment I got to work.'

Liz said nothing, but she knew what he meant. When her personal life had seemed especially bleak (there'd been Mark the married *Guardian* journalist, Piet the Dutch banker who'd dropped her, and always, the tantalisingly unavailable Charles Wetherby), she had always found one consolation. The job. As a cure for heartache it was unbeatable.

'Anyway,' Seurat said, 'that's enough of that. If you've finished, I'll get the bill. I propose we walk back to the base through the town and I'll show you Milraud's shop. It'll be shut by now so no chance of meeting the so-discreet Madame Dipeau. She's given nothing away since Isabelle and I called in there. No phone calls except strictly business ones, and she hasn't been out in the evenings at all.'

Half an hour later they were back at the gates of the naval base. Liz was hoping to catch a few hours' sleep before the three-thirty a.m. rendezvous. But she had not been in her room for more than ten minutes when the telephone on the desk rang. It was Seurat. 'Liz. I'm sorry to disturb you but there's something I need to show you.'

Her stomach lurched. Was it some bad news about Dave? At the bottom of the stairs Seurat was standing, clutching a sheet of paper and his face had lost its usual calm expression. As soon as she was within earshot he said, 'I've had an email from Antoine.' He handed her the paper, and as she read it, he said, 'He says he can hand over your colleague.'

Liz read the email carefully, making sure she completely understood the French. She looked at Seurat, mystified. 'I don't get it. This can't be what he's been planning all along or he would have been in touch before. What do you think's going on, Martin?'

'There must have been a different plan that hasn't worked out. I think he knows we're getting close; Annette's been sending him emails and she'll have told him the noose is tightening. Milraud's trying to leave Piggott and his Spanish hit man to face the music, while he cuts a deal to save his own skin. That's typical of him.'

Liz thought for a moment. 'You know Milraud – I don't. But I don't see how he can deliver on this offer.' She waved the printout with one hand. 'I can't believe Piggott would ever let it happen. He's too astute for that, and suspicious to the point of paranoia. And don't forget, Gonzales works for Piggott, not Milraud – I think if Piggott knew about this email he wouldn't hesitate to order Gonzales to kill him.'

'I would think Antoine's getting desperate. He's caught between a rock and a – how do you say it?'

Liz just smiled, for she was thinking hard. Seurat waited, then he said, 'How would you like to proceed? It is after all your colleague who's at risk.'

She said, 'I need to consult my head office. But I also need your view – do you think Milraud can deliver what he's promising?'

Seurat thought for a moment. 'I think he wants to, in part to redeem himself. But whether he can depends on the situation on the island, and that we don't know.'

'Exactly,' said Liz.

'One thing I do know is that Antoine can look after himself. I would be surprised if even this Piggott could easily get the better of him. But that doesn't help us with your problem – in the end, Milraud will look after his own interests, and your colleague will come second, whatever he's promised us.'

Which would leave Dave at the mercy of the psychopath Piggott and his hit man Gonzales. No thanks, thought Liz. 'I'm going to recommend we go ahead as planned. Can I use the communications on the base?'

Twenty minutes later, Binding's reply proved noncommittal. He would need to consult Thames House. But Liz had copied her message to DG's office and five minutes after this an answer came back. *DG agrees with your recommendation. Please go ahead as planned and good luck.*

53

Dave was shivering. The more he moved around to try to keep warm, the colder he got. When he was first locked in the cellar, it hadn't seemed particularly cold. But now it felt chilly and dank. His ribs hurt a lot and his head was still throbbing. He must be running a temperature. If someone didn't rescue him soon, it would turn to pneumonia and he'd die in this miserable place, without ever knowing where he was or why he was here.

That was if the Spaniard didn't kill him first. There was real hatred in the man's voice now. If Dave gave him the slightest excuse he'd put a bullet in him. Each time Gonzales unlocked the door to shove in a tray of food, he looked at him with real venom. Food, thought Dave – you could hardly call it that. He was getting less and less of it, too, hardly enough to keep a bird alive, and more and more disgusting. They must be running out, which was another reason why something had to happen soon.

There had been no further sound of helicopters since the one he'd heard the day before, but this must be a good sign. If the French were onto this bunch, they'd want to be sure not to alert them. He told himself that Liz and the team would be scouring the earth for him, helped by every foreign service they were in touch with. Sooner or later they'd find out where he was, and help would be on its way. It must be just a matter of time.

Meanwhile, he had to stay alive until they came, and be ready to help them if he could. For he had no doubt that Piggott and the Spaniard would do everything to resist the rescuers – including shooting him. It would be the worst kind of luck, Dave thought bitterly, if on the very point of liberation he were to be murdered.

Well, he wasn't going to wait around to see that happen, and if only to keep his spirits high he decided to act. Which meant finding some sort of weapon – any sort, however primitive – which would increase his chances if the shooting started. The problem was, the cellar had been stripped clean: there was his mattress, a bucket that functioned as a disgusting toilet, two large empty wine barrels, propped on their sides on stands, and a wall of empty wine racks. That was it – except for another rack, really just a long slab of pine on the wall, with hooks that must once have been used for hanging tools. But the tools were long gone, and when Dave tried to extricate one of the hooks – a feeble weapon, but better than nothing – he found they were all immovably lodged deep in the plank.

Don't give up, he told himself. Moving slowly, and wincing each time he took more than a tiny shallow breath, Dave systematically explored the rest of the cellar. The thin shaft of light from the slit window didn't reach into the corners, so he had to stick his hand in and feel around, sending spiders scuttling.

After ten minutes he was exhausted and ready to give up; he'd found nothing at all. He leaned against one of the two empty barrels for support, and suddenly whatever was propping it up gave way. The barrel rolled off its stand, crashing onto the floor, and Dave fell down, landing on his damaged ribs.

The pain was colossal, and he lay on the floor winded and in agony. After a time, the agony retreated into pain and he dragged himself up onto his knees and looked at the damaged barrel. It had split apart, its ribs fanning out like an opening flower. Could he use one of the wooden ribs as a weapon? No, they were too big to conceal. What about the circular metal bands? Again they were far too big, and anyway, he had nothing to cut them with.

But as he looked at the pile of wood lying on the cellar floor, Dave saw something small and metallic glinting among the wooden staves. Ignoring the pain, he crawled over and reached out to where he'd seen the glint, only to be rewarded with a sharp prick on his finger. He'd cut himself, but he didn't care. He gingerly felt around again for whatever it was. Got it! He looked at the object in his hand. It was some kind of blade.

Lifting it up to the light, he saw that he was holding a small knife, no more than four inches long, with a worm-eaten wooden handle and a thin rusty blade with a wickedly sharp point – blood was dripping from his finger now. The blade was sliver-thin and wobbled precariously in the ancient handle. But if it had been made of the finest steel, Dave could not have admired it more. It felt wonderful in his hand and he held it lovingly. It was a weapon. He could only use it once and he'd choose his moment carefully.

54

Liz was wide awake when the alarm on her phone went off. It was three a.m. She'd dozed rather than slept for three hours, troubled by muddled dreams of Dave, Piggott, Milraud's shop, and boats rocking in the wind.

She'd only just got into bed after helping Martin compose a stalling reply to Milraud, when the communications officer had rung her room. There was a message for her from Belfast. So she'd had to get dressed again. The message was from Peggy – Liz could picture her in the office, refusing to go home while there was anything to be done to help Dave.

Peggy reported that Malone, the local thug who'd worked for Piggott in Belfast, had cracked during questioning. He'd told the police everything he knew about Piggott's activities, including the murders of Dermot O'Reilly and Sean McCarthy, and about the plan to kill Jimmy Fergus. Peggy wanted Liz to know that warrants had been issued for the arrest of both Piggott and Gonzales on murder charges; extradition requests would be filed the minute they were captured. Let's hope they're needed, Liz had thought, since she was sceptical those two would ever be taken alive.

She dressed in warm clothes and went downstairs to the

rendezvous point in the lounge. Martin was there looking threatening in a black battledress and trousers, with light black waterproof boots. In his hand he held a black balaclava and helmet.

'Put these on over your clothes,' he said, pointing to another set of black garments laid out on a chair. 'They're the smallest size there is, so I hope they won't be too big.'

'Where are the commandos?'

'They're down at the harbour, loading the inflatables onto the frigate. The wind's died down a bit but it's still blowing, so they've decided not to go out in them.'

'Thank God for that,' she said as she pulled on the suit.

The frigate was a long, lean, evil-looking vessel with a stern that was open like a car ferry. Liz and Martin were welcomed on board by one of the crew and taken up to the bridge to meet the captain. As she looked out through the narrow window in front of her, Liz could see that the sweep of the bow was broken by a large gun.

'This ship looks capable of blowing the island out of the water,' she remarked to Martin.

'It is. And behind us there are surface-to-air missiles. So if Piggott launches an air attack,' he said with a grin, 'we can deal with that too.'

On the dot of four o'clock the frigate slipped out, sailing quietly past Toulon harbour, where a slumbering flotilla of sailing boats and motor cruisers filled the lines of jetties. As they moved out into the open sea, picking up speed, the wind began buffeting the ship and spray splashed against the window in front of them. Two lights on the bow cast dual beams across the waves as the frigate swung in a long arc eastwards towards the Ile de Porquerolles. Liz thought for a moment that she saw the first hints of dawn breaking in light-grey streaks against the horizon, but her eyes were deceiving her – it was still deep night and the sky was black as coal.

As they approached the island, Martin put his hand on Liz's shoulder. 'Laval asked me to make sure you understood the rules for this operation. When we land on the island, he's in charge. You and I are merely here as advisors. I have communications but you haven't, so you must stick very closely to me to avoid getting out of touch. If there's trouble we'll follow Laval's orders.'

Liz nodded. This was not the first military operation she'd been on. '*Compris*,' she said.

The frigate slowed to a stop and with a gentle splash the first inflatable, with six commandos on board, emerged from the stern and, riding the waves lightly, its outboard motor muted, headed off towards the ferry terminal on the island's north side.

'Time to go,' said Martin and they climbed down companion ladders to the ship's belly. The twelve remaining commandos were a frightening sight, dressed as they were entirely in black, their faces streaked with black pitch, balaclavas on, night vision goggles on top of their heads, with their guns and equipment hanging at their sides.

Ten minutes later the frigate stopped again, this time on the Mediterranean side of the island, half a mile out and half a mile down the coast from the farmhouse. The second team climbed into their boat and peeled off rapidly to take their position well back from the cove, covering that exit route.

'Here we go,' said Martin, smiling at Liz, and her stomach gave such a lurch that she thought for a moment she would be sick. Laval shook hands and they wished each other *bonne chance*. A few seconds later it was Liz's turn to climb out of the open stern into the rocking rubber boat.

'Let me help,' said Seurat.

'I'm fine,' but she was grateful nonetheless when he kept a steady hand on her arm as she lowered herself into the boat, where a commando was waiting to help her sit down on the side of the middle pontoon.

'Hang on tight,' said Seurat, joining her on the pontoon, and a moment later Laval sat down in the stern, the outboard whirred and they were off.

Liz's eyes took a while to adjust to the dark – at first she could see nothing but the white spray of the waves as the boat bumped over them. Then she made out the looming overhanging cliffs of the shoreline to her right, and began to get her bearings – they were working their way west to the cove. She was amazed how little noise they made – some device was muffling the sound of the outboard motor, though it wasn't restricting its power, for they were moving fast.

Suddenly Laval closed down the throttle, the throaty noise of the engine became a purr, and the boat slowed abruptly. The commando in the bow stood up and as the engine cut out he jumped over the side, holding a rope attached to a hook on the prow. Seconds later, the bottom of the dinghy jarred against the beach, and the boat stopped.

Following Seurat, Liz jumped out into the shallows and waded up onto the little beach. It was pitch dark. Taking her cue from the others, she pulled on her night vision goggles, and a strange eerie monochrome world appeared.

Three commandos stood guard on the beach, facing the path they'd seen on the map of the island, while two others went rapidly off to one side of the beach. A minute later this pair returned; they'd found the boat Seurat's surveillance officers had discovered.

Laval said, 'Pierre, you stay here and guard the boat.'

The commando named Pierre disconsolately kicked the sand, then headed off to his post. Laval said something, and the other commandos laughed.

'He seems very disappointed,' Liz said to Seurat.

He chuckled. 'Yes, this is his first mission so he wants to make his mark. Laval said once he had more operations under his belt he'd be less keen. That's why they were laughing.'

Now Laval turned to the other commandos, and pointing to the path just visible on the edge of the beach, announced, '*Allons-y.*'

The path climbed sharply and was wet. Liz was not used to the night vision goggles and found it difficult to gauge her footsteps. She slipped twice; each time Seurat was there to help her up. At last they reached the clifftop, where she was able to catch her breath as Laval conferred with the other commandos. Then, from further along the cliff, a noise. The commandos moved swiftly and silently into the cover of the wood and Liz, led by Seurat, joined them in the trees.

They crouched in silence, the commandos with their weapons at the ready. Suddenly a shriek broke the silence – then again, even higher-pitched, squeal-like.

Laval whispered somewhere to their left, and Seurat said in Liz's ear, 'A fox. And now it's got a rabbit.'

They regrouped on the path, which ran through the wood in the direction of the farmhouse. Laval was about to speak when there was another noise, just yards up the path. This is no fox, thought Liz, as they all moved back into the trees. Footsteps. Someone was approaching.

55

'I am sure we'll hear from FARC tomorrow,' Milraud had said before he went up to his bedroom, but from Piggott's absent nod he could see the man wasn't listening. It was then he'd realised that Piggott didn't care about selling Willis any more. He'd decided to do something else.

Milraud lay now on his bed in the dark with his clothes on, listening carefully. He was filtering out the noises of the wind and the wildlife outside – the owl hooting and the bats squeaking – from the sound he was expecting to hear at any moment. It was four-thirty. He was tired, very tired, but he'd managed to grab a cat nap in the early evening precisely so he wouldn't fall asleep now, when he most needed to be alert.

He had received an email from Seurat. It said that he needed more time to consult the British before replying to Milraud's offer. Perhaps that was true; equally, though, it might be an effort to buy time while he and his men hunted them down. He had replied tersely, *Time is running out*, and hoped Seurat would understand the urgency.

For Piggott's behaviour had if anything become more unbalanced – he had begun talking to himself, and pacing continuously. He had started complaining of being 'cooped up', and he'd even threatened to take the ferry for a visit to the mainland.

This had forced Milraud's hand – he'd had to tell Piggott then about Seurat's visit to Annette, and explain that there was surveillance on the mainland. Piggott had taken this news badly, and had started making even more forays out to 'check the boat', which still lay hidden down by the beach. On one of these jaunts, Milraud had taken the opportunity to search through the American's belongings, and he was glad that he had. In the small hold-all beside Piggott's bed he'd found a Smith & Wesson .38.

He felt it first, rather than heard it – a faint reverberation, a slight shuddering of the floor. If it was an earthquake, it was very mild. But then he heard the soft burring noise. What was it? A helicopter some distance away, or something else?

As he listened, he heard a creak from the landing. A door was being quietly opened. Silently, he swung his legs off the bed and sat up, straining to hear. Another creak, then the distinct sound of a padded footfall.

Getting up, he went to the door, which he had left open a crack. Peering out, he could just distinguish a figure moving slowly, cautiously. Slim, tall – it was Piggott. He's leaving, he thought.

'James,' he said calmly, opening his door.

Piggott didn't seem startled. 'Did you hear that?' he asked. 'It sounded like a chopper.' He was moving towards the porch. Was he carrying something? In the half-light, Milraud couldn't tell.

'Where are you going?' asked Milraud.

'To check the dinghy,' said Piggott over his shoulder. He opened the screen door and stepped onto the porch. 'That's our only ticket out of here, and I'm not letting anybody take it.' And the screen door banged shut behind him.

Milraud waited, counting to ten, then went back into his room and picked up a heavy torch. He walked across the landing into Piggott's room. In the torch beam he saw the bed, unslept in, and looked around for the hold-all that held the .38. It wasn't there – Piggott must have taken it with him.

That confirmed what he suspected – Piggott wasn't checking the boat; Piggott was going to *take* the boat, to get away. Which would be disastrous – left with a homicidal Spaniard and a hostage, Milraud calculated that he'd either be shot by the Spaniard when he discovered Piggott had fled, or shot by Seurat's men when they arrived to rescue Willis. If he somehow managed to survive, he'd be in prison for ever after kidnapping a British intelligence officer. None of these options appealed. Should he get out himself – hide and catch the first ferry to the mainland in the morning? No good. He'd be picked up before he'd gone far, and the Spaniard would kill Willis if he found he'd been left on his own. Then the charge Milraud would face would be accessory to murder, as well as kidnapping.

The only thing to do was to follow Piggott and persuade him not to leave. That would buy enough time to alert Seurat that he must move in fast.

But how was he going to do that? Milraud had no idea. Strangely for an arms dealer, he never carried a gun. He had a deep-seated personal aversion to them, and he'd never owned one. Even in his former incarnation as an intelligence officer, he had always refused to carry a weapon. He was quite ready to be guarded by armed men (like his chauffeur), and very happy to sell anybody the means to kill. But when it came to using one himself, he wouldn't. But now for the first time in his life, he wished he had a gun. With Piggott, bullets spoke louder than words.

But there was nothing for it. He had to go after Piggott and stop him leaving. Opening the screen door, cautiously switching on his torch and shading the beam with his hand, he moved gingerly outside, towards the path that led down to the beach.

56

They would be here soon – very soon. He didn't stop to wonder who 'they' were – French or British or even the FBI. Any one of them would be intent on arresting him.

That wasn't going to happen. As soon as Piggott reached the woods he stopped and unzipped his holdall. The .38 lay on top of a folded towel and he took it out and stuffed it into the waistband of his trousers. Then he threw the holdall into the bushes that lined the sides of the path.

It wasn't going to help him escape – for that he needed only his wits about him. And the gun.

He moved quickly, ignoring the brambles that scraped his arms and face as he tried to stick to the path. He hadn't dared bring a torch, since that would draw the people closing in on him.

He should never have trusted Milraud and never have let him bring him here. Not to an island, so easy to seal off. The only way out was by boat, and that was why he had insisted on checking that the dinghy was still there so many times each day. Once he got to it now, he'd be free and clear.

Next stop Algeria, he thought. Ahmed there had replied to his email at once, saying Piggott could pick up a consignment of hashish. He could also pick up a larger boat, and he figured a good five days hard sailing would see him back in County Down, no one the wiser about where he'd been or what had happened.

He supposed it would have been best to silence Milraud before he'd left, or at the very least leave orders with Gonzales to kill both him and the prisoner. Still, Milraud was the one left holding the can, not Piggott. As he began to descend the trail to the beach, he was cheered by thoughts of returning to Northern Ireland and finishing his business there.

He'd need some help of course, and he wasn't going to use Ryan again, that was for sure. He needed someone more experienced. Malone had killed before, if the gossip of the IRA veterans was to be believed, so Piggott was certain he'd be willing to kill again. If other volunteers proved scarce, he could always call on old associates in Boston to come over and join in the campaign. Soon MI5 would rue the day they'd taken over intelligence duties in the province.

Suddenly Piggott heard footsteps along the trail, coming up from below. He moved quickly, silently on the balls of his feet, into the thick brush where he crouched down. He waited tensely, hand on his pistol, and listened as several people – at least four, maybe five – climbed up the path. Then they were above him, and he silently rejoined the path and continued his descent.

Take it slowly, he told himself, as he drew to within a stone's throw of the cove. To his right the dinghy lay covered in brush, but he knew better than to go straight to it. These people after him were doubtless fools, but even fools took precautions, and Piggott expected a sentry to stand guard over the boat. *Hah*, he thought with a scornful laugh to himself – as if some soldier was going to keep him from getting away.

He left the path again, a good twenty feet above the beach,

and edged inch by inch, circling the dinghy. He stared hard at the shadows on the beach cast by the overhanging trees and pulled the gun out from his waistband.

57

The footsteps were getting closer. Liz crouched behind the trunk of a eucalyptus tree, waiting for the commandos' challenge.

'*Halte!*' Laval shouted. '*Qui va la?*'

There was silence for a moment, then from the trail a voice called out, 'Antoine Milraud.' He seemed to hesitate. 'I am not armed.'

'Are you alone?' Laval called out.

'*Oui.*'

Seurat interjected, 'You had better be telling the truth, *mon ami*, because it will cost you your life if you're not. Where are the others?'

'In the house. Except for James – the American. Piggott as he calls himself. I was following him when you stopped me just now. He has gone to check the boat.'

'The boat hidden by the beach?'

'Yes. That's the one. And he's armed.'

Laval spoke urgently into his radio, warning the young commando in the cove. He turned to the commandos around him. 'Fabrice. Jean. Go back and help him.' Two men slipped away through the trees.

Then Laval, Seurat and the two remaining commandos

emerged onto the path, while Liz stayed behind in the shadow of the woods. She could see Milraud's face now, illuminated by the commandos' lights, as they surrounded him.

'Where is the hostage?' demanded Laval.

'He's locked in the cellar. I will show you. But be careful: the man guarding him is not likely to hand him over without a fight.'

'Is that the Spaniard, Gonzales?' asked Liz, emerging from behind her tree to stand beside Seurat.

'So. The English are here too,' said Milraud, looking at the slender black-clad figure in surprise. 'You are well informed, mademoiselle.'

'Is anyone else here?' asked Laval.

'No one,' said Milraud, shaking his head. 'Just three of us and Willis. That's all.' He looked at Seurat. 'That's the truth. You know I wouldn't lie to you about that.'

'I don't know what you'd do any more, Antoine.'

'It's been a long time, but some things don't change. I would never have harmed this man. And I offered you my help in my email. Don't forget that.'

Seurat said dryly, 'Well, we managed to get here without your help.'

Suddenly there was the sound of a gunshot, a solitary *crack* breaking the pre-dawn silence. It came from the beach.

Seconds later Laval's radio crackled. 'Pierre here – I've been hit,' the voice said in a high-pitched tone of pain. 'I didn't hear the bastard coming. He's winged me in my shooting arm and he's got the dinghy. I can see him.'

The radio crackled again. 'Fabrice here. We were just seconds too late. We're with Pierre now. The target is in the boat, twenty metres from the shore. We're leaving him to Team Bravo.'

'We have him in our sights,' came back immediately from the team waiting offshore.

Led by Laval, the group on the path moved quickly through the trees, taking only a minute or two to cover the short distance to the cliff edge. A hundred feet or so below, the sea shone grey as the early-morning light just began to touch the water. As they looked down, they could see a small dinghy moving out into the cove, the puttering of its outboard motor just audible from where they stood.

'That's him,' said Milraud, and Laval radioed confirmation to Team Bravo. He issued an order: 'Attempt to detain. Otherwise destroy.'

They watched as Piggott picked up speed, heading straight towards the south. Next stop Algeria, thought Liz.

But then she saw the commando craft appear at the mouth of the cove. Even loaded down with its team of commandos, it was going much faster than Piggott. As it drew closer, on a line to cut off his escape, Piggott changed course sharply to the east.

Suddenly a long arc of red dots jumped out of the commando boat, syncopated tiny flares, fluorescent against the dark-grey sea. They disappeared just ahead of the bow of Piggott's little dinghy. Tracer bullets, thought Liz. Watching in silence, she heard the sharp crack of a weapon. Piggott was returning fire. He must be crazy.

The commandos fired another line of red bullets, this time even closer to the target. And again Piggott fired back, accurately enough to cause the commando dinghy to veer. There was a momentary lull, then the commando boat fired again, and these were not warning shots.

Suddenly flames appeared at the back of the small dinghy. Piggott jumped up from his seat in the stern, his clothes on fire. As the illuminated figure moved to leap overboard, the dinghy wobbled perilously. But before he could jump, the outboard motor burst into flames, and a split second later exploded with a bang that reverberated round the cliffs. The sky above the dinghy lit up like a rosy-pink firework, and the shockwave reached the watchers on the cliff.

'*Mon dieu*,' exclaimed Seurat. Liz looked in vain for signs of the dinghy. But it had completely disappeared, blown to bits by the force of the explosion.

58

They stood for a moment in silence. Then Laval said, 'We must get to the house fast. That must have been heard from there.'

Milraud pointed to a track. 'This way is quickest.'

They moved along as fast as they dared; it was still quite dark in the woods, and the track was overgrown with tangled shrubs and tree branches that hung low. Laval led the way with one of the commandos, while Liz, Milraud and Seurat proceeded in a line behind them. The second commando brought up the rear.

Suddenly Laval stopped and held up his hand in warning. He had reached the edge of the trees. In front of him was an open courtyard and, looming in the background, a long stone building with a veranda up wooden steps to one side. The farmhouse.

Laval gathered the group round him. 'If the Spaniard is still asleep where will he be?' This was addressed to Milraud.

'That leads into the kitchen,' the Frenchman said, pointing at a door covered by a fly screen. 'There are two doors out of it. The green baize one leads into a sitting room; the other one opens into a corridor running the length of the house. Gonzales sleeps in the first room off the corridor.

'The stairs between the kitchen and his room lead down to the cellar where Willis is locked up. There's another door to the house at the front. It opens into the other end of the corridor. If you go in that way, Gonzales's room is the fourth off the corridor on the left-hand side.'

Laval nodded and turned to one of the commandos who was short and stocky but looked very strong. 'Gilles. You cover the front of the house. Once you get there, wait till you hear my order then move inside and throw the stun grenades into the Spaniard's room. If he comes out your way, don't let him escape. *Compris?*'

Gilles nodded, his jaw clenched.

He turned to the second commando. 'We'll go in through the kitchen door. We will try to flush out the Spaniard before we release the hostage. Seurat, you go in up those steps and watch our backs and keep Milraud with you. We may need him to talk to Gonzales. *Madamoiselle*, you keep under cover out here in the trees.'

Next, Laval radioed the team on the other side of the island and told them to stay in place in case Gonzales escaped and made his way over towards the ferry. That done, he said, 'Let's get going. It's starting to get light.'

As she positioned herself behind the broad trunk of a pine tree on the edge of the courtyard, Liz felt her heart beating painfully against her ribs. This was the moment when Dave would either be saved or killed. It seemed to her that Laval had split up his forces far too much. Pitifully few of them were actually here to do the job they had come to do: rescuing Dave. He's left the courtyard unguarded, she thought, her spine crawling at the thought that Gonzales might already be out of the building and in the woods, perhaps creeping up on her, unarmed and unprotected as she was.

She watched as Martin Seurat and Milraud crept up the rickety wooden steps and disappeared into the farmhouse. Then she

316

turned to look at Laval and the commando moving stealthily round the edge of the courtyard, towards the kitchen door, keeping low, holding their weapons ready. They had reached an open-doored barn containing an old car, when suddenly the screen door of the kitchen was kicked open from inside and Dave appeared, staggering as though he was being pushed. Right behind him, clutching Dave's shirt in one hand and holding a 9 mm automatic against the back of Dave's head was Gonzales. He was using his hostage as a human shield.

Laval stopped moving at once and slowly stood up from his crouch, raising his gun. The other commando had disappeared. Laval hesitated. He couldn't fire for fear of hitting Dave. There was a momentary stand-off. Then suddenly Gonzales pushed Dave to the side, still holding onto him with one hand, and fired at Laval. Then he quickly pulled Dave back in front of him.

Laval fell, dropping his weapon and rolling over on the packed earth until he lay sideways, one arm twitching in obvious agony. Gonzales took a step towards him, as Dave suddenly twisted in his grasp and raised his hand. As Gonzales lifted a protective arm and tried to bring his gun round, Dave's hand flashed down and he plunged something into his captor's chest.

'Ahhhh!' the Spaniard shouted, flinching in pain and letting go of Dave.

Dave ran for the edge of the yard. He was perhaps twenty feet away from where Liz was standing when Gonzales lifted his gun and fired. Dave went down at once, clutching his side. Simultaneously the commando stood up from behind the car and fired at the Spaniard. He hit him in the leg and the Spaniard fell heavily but held onto his gun.

Lying where he'd fallen, he lifted his hand and pointed his gun at Dave, still alive but groaning and helpless on the ground. He's going to finish him off, thought Liz. She had to do something. Stepping out from behind the tree she ran forward to Dave, shouting at the Spaniard at the top of her lungs. 'Stop! Stop or I'll shoot.'

Gonzales' head jerked up, and he raised his gun to fire at this new target. Liz watched with a growing sense of horror as the black gun pointed directly at her. She tensed, waiting for the shot, but though she heard the flat crack of a gun, she felt nothing. Had Gonzales missed?

She dived flat onto the ground before he could fire again – surely he couldn't miss twice at such short range – but then she saw that Gonzales had dropped his gun; his head had flopped to the ground and she watched with macabre fascination as blood poured from it, staining the ground like spilt juice. The commando and Seurat had fired together and this time neither had missed.

Liz staggered to her feet as Martin Seurat rushed down the wooden steps and across the yard, kicking away the Spaniard's gun as he passed, though there was not the remotest chance he'd ever use it again. 'Liz!' he shouted, 'Are you all right?' He put his arms round her as her legs gave way and she almost fell again.

'I'm so sorry,' she said. 'I did a very silly thing, rushing out like that. But I thought he would kill Dave.'

'No, no. You were very brave.'

But she wasn't listening. She was kneeling beside Dave. He was alive but barely conscious, breathing shallowly. The bullet had hit him low on one side of his stomach, and blood was spreading like water through a sponge, gradually turning the blue of his shirt ominously black.

'He's going to die if we don't get him to hospital,' whispered Liz as she helped Seurat gently open up Dave's shirt. Blood continued to flow from the bullet hole in his lower stomach, as Seurat folded the cotton fabric back against the wound to staunch it.

The commando who had fired at Gonzales had been talking on the radio and was now kneeling beside Laval next to the garage. His colleague Gilles came running from the front of the farmhouse with his gun at the ready. 'It's all over,' Seurat called out to him, and he lowered his gun, though his eyes warily scanned the woods around the yard.

Then almost directly overhead Liz heard the *phut-phut-phut* of a helicopter, and felt the lightest of breezes stirring her hair. Soon the breeze was a stiff wind, then a gale, and within moments she watched as the underbelly of the helicopter hovered above the middle of the yard, sending up dust in a fine spray.

As soon as the chopper settled on the yard and the blades began to slow, the side door slid open and an armed man in military fatigues jumped out, followed by two men in whites. Stretchers and medical equipment were unloaded and within thirty seconds the doctor had taken over caring for Dave from Liz and Seurat. Before long Dave was strapped to the stretcher, drugged now with a morphine injection, a drip in his arm, and loaded into the helicopter. The doctor quickly turned his attention to Laval, who had been hit high in the collarbone. He too was strapped to a stretcher and loaded on board.

Liz, Martin Seurat and the two commandos stood in the courtyard looking up as the helicopter lifted away. As the noise died down, Gilles came over and spoke to Seurat. '*L'autre, monsieur?*' was all Liz could hear above the deafening whirr of the chopper.

'*L'autre?*' asked Seurat, frowning with incomprehension.

'*Oui, oui. L'autre. Le troisième. Où est-il?*' said the commando insistently.

'He means Milraud,' said Liz, suddenly conscious of what the commando was saying. 'Where is he?'

Seurat froze, a look of anguish on his face. 'He's gone. He slipped away while I was focused on what was happening in the courtyard.'

'Oh no,' said Liz. 'Just when you thought you'd got him.'

'He can't have got very far,' said Seurat. 'Radio to the team at the ferry and alert them,' he ordered Gilles. 'I'll call for air surveillance. He knows the island well but it's pretty small, and if he can't get off it I'm sure we'll soon track him down.'

59

But they didn't. All day helicopters hovered over the island of Porquerolles and the surrounding sea. Some had heat-seeking equipment that flushed out a couple of cyclists, a walker, and two lovers furious to be disturbed from above. But no Milraud.

Gendarmerie had been recruited from as far as Marseilles to search the mainland ferry port and the nearby town of Hyères. The CRS had sent a platoon to go through the empty houses and hotels on the island, and the navy had been patrolling a two-mile sea perimeter around the island. But the results for all these seekers, on land and at sea, was so far the same: no Milraud.

As Liz sat in the naval base canteen in Toulon the next afternoon, watching through the window the daily life of the base going on outside, she gave a silent prayer of thanks for the hundredth time that Dave had survived. Although Martin Seurat was furious that Milraud seemed to have escaped, Milraud had not been her priority.

She'd been to see Dave that morning in the base hospital. He was drowsy with morphine but he'd given Liz a weak smile as she came in. 'I'll be fine again sooner than you know,' he'd declared, and Liz had refrained from sharing with him what

321

the doctor had told her the day before – a half-inch higher, and the bullet fired by Gonzales would have killed him. A close call then, but Dave would be well enough to be flown back to hospital in London the next morning. As it was, he had a deep gunshot wound, two broken ribs, and a persisting concussion to show for his involuntary stay in the Ile de Porquerolles. Liz wondered if he'd be sent back to Belfast after recuperating, and hoped so. Life there would not be the same without him.

'I suppose I'll be in trouble when I get back,' Dave had said ruefully. 'Judith warned me not to go back to Milraud's shop and she was right. I can't think what I was doing.'

'Don't worry, Dave. Everyone will just be delighted you're alive.'

'Do we actually know what Piggott and Milraud were trying to achieve?'

She'd given him a look of mock-sternness, like a ward sister with a recalcitrant patient. 'There will be lots of time for that. Right now, you just concentrate on getting better.'

'Okay, okay. But I can't do that till I know what it was all about. Why did they bring me all the way down here if they were going to end up shooting me? Did they have a plan?'

'Hard to say. Our French colleague Martin Seurat thinks they panicked and made it up as they went along. His guys found two laptops in the farmhouse. They'd been sending emails to somebody. They may tell us what the plan was, but it will take a bit of time to unscramble it all. And that's all I'm telling you now. Go back to sleep; I'll see you in the UK.'

Now as she watched some workmen erecting a grandstand on the parade ground, her mind still on the dramatic events of the day before, she felt a hand on her shoulder and a voice asked quietly, 'Where are we now?' Martin Seurat sat down at the table opposite her.

'I was just thinking about our mysterious Monsieur Milraud. How did he get away and where has he gone?'

'There's some news about that. We've been conducting a house-to-house search on the island – and it appears that a summer cottage on the outskirts of the village has been broken into. Nothing's been taken, but some food from the freezer was heated up in the kitchen. We've also just heard from the harbour master that a resident in the village reported his skiff's been stolen from a small jetty near the harbour.'

'When was this?'

'The owner can see the skiff from his house, but he was off the island yesterday. When he got back this morning, it wasn't there. We think Milraud may have taken it some time yesterday, before the cordon round the island was in place. They're looking for it now along the mainland coast.'

'Where would Milraud head for?'

'He could go anywhere, especially since I think he had help once he reached the mainland. I've just come back from his house in Bandol – Annette Milraud has disappeared as well. We had surveillance outside the house but she fooled them. We found her maid tied up in the kitchen.'

'The maid?'

'She'd been there since last night – *mon dieu*, was she cross! Especially as she was in her underwear.'

'What?' asked Liz, laughing.

'Annette made her take her clothes off, then she put them on herself, before driving away in the maid's car. Our surveillance thought she was the maid going home and didn't stop her. They are very embarrassed – I'm not surprised. They should have been onto a trick like that.' He frowned and shrugged. 'But it's too late now. She's gone.'

'Presumably the car will be stopped soon.'

'It's been found already. Parked in Cannes. We think they must have a safe house there. Knowing Milraud, he'll have a set of false documents too.'

'So where do you think they'll go?'

'Somewhere far away – like South America. Or perhaps one of the former Soviet Union states. But Milraud will pop up again – give him time. Annette will grow dissatisfied with life in a backwater, and the lure of the arms trade will have Antoine back in circulation. He'll need the money too. I would say my hopes of catching him have been deferred, not destroyed.'

Seurat brushed his chin thoughtfully with one hand. 'You know, it's a very strange feeling, sitting here talking like this – I mean, after so much *événement* only yesterday. It seems slightly unreal.'

Liz nodded. 'I know. I feel the same.'

'I was considering taking a few days off. If only to readjust oneself to the obvious fact that life goes on.'

Liz laughed. 'That sounds like a good idea. What are you thinking of doing?'

Seurat paused, then said lightly, 'There's a little hotel I know. Not far from here, up in the hills – a beautiful setting, though the hotel itself is nothing fancy. Still, it has excellent food, and the walks are simply wonderful. At this time of year, you're beginning to see the first signs of spring. It starts early in the south.'

He turned and looked at her, and Liz realised it was not his intention to stay at the hotel alone. Her heart began to beat a little faster but she waited until his meaning was absolutely clear. Not that she had many doubts.

Then Liz's mobile phone rang.

It was a London number, which seemed familiar. The name

came up on the screen: *Charles*. How funny that she hadn't immediately remembered a number that she used to know so well.

'Liz, it's Charles. Are you all right?'

'I'm fine, thanks. And so is Dave – or at least he's going to
be.'

'So I gather. Michael Binding's over here and he's been keeping
us informed. You've all had quite a time of it, I gather.'

'Quite exciting,' she said dryly. 'Unfortunately there's one
loose end – Milraud the arms dealer seems to have got away.'

'I wouldn't worry much about that. Piggott was by far the
greater threat, and you've taken care of him – and his organisation. As well as his Spanish hit man. A job well done by any
standard.'

That was true, and she wished she could take more satisfaction from it. The cost had been high – and Dave was very lucky
to have survived with his life. She knew that if she'd been more
on the ball and had reported straight away from Paris instead
of lunching with her mother and Edward, and forgetting to
switch her phone back on, she could have stopped Dave from
rushing in. They would in time have managed to put Piggott
away.

He would never have given up peacefully, though. He'd have
fought to the end, and more people might have been hurt, even
killed, in trying to arrest him.

'But that's not the reason I'm calling,' Wetherby was saying,
jolting Liz out of these post-mortem thoughts.

'Oh,' she said cautiously, wondering what was up.

'DG wants you to call in at Thames House before you go back
to Belfast. He wants a full report on everything that's happened.'

'OK,' she said, slightly puzzled. She'd expected to report back
to Binding in Belfast.

Liz glanced at Seurat, and found his dark eyes watching her

intently, appraisingly. She found herself starting to blush like a schoolgirl. How ridiculous, she thought furiously, which only made her blush more. 'Am I needed immediately?' she managed to say.

'Are there things you have to do there?' Wetherby paused. He sounded nervous, thought Liz. What about?

'Because it would be very nice to see you over the weekend,' he said suddenly. 'I was thinking we could have lunch. Or dinner. You could come out to the house perhaps.'

Liz didn't know what to say. What has happened to the ever-helpful Alison? she wanted to ask. Another part of her was simply astonished. Pleased? Yes, of course: how could she not be, when for years she had hoped for just what she was getting now – a signal that he cared for her and was at last willing to show it.

But she didn't feel as excited as she should have done. And that surprised her. She felt oddly detached. How strange, since here she was, hearing what she had wanted to hear for so long. Yet now it almost seemed unreal. Or, if not that, at least something removed from the present, something that belonged to the past. To the days before Gonzales had pointed a gun at her and she had known with certainty that she was about to die.

Was that what was making her feel so ambivalent, as Charles waited on the line for her reply? Perhaps, though, it was also a strong sense that she had to get on with life now, that there was no point in retreating yet again into the patchwork of code that had characterised her relationship with Charles for so long.

She looked up at Martin and smiled, then said to Charles, not unkindly, but in a voice that was entirely certain, 'Actually Charles, I was thinking of staying on here for a few days. Spring is just about to start in the south.'